A Suitable Heir

Elsie King

Published by Indie Scriptorium SPC, 2023.

A Suitable Heir

A Suitable Heir first printed in 2023.

A copy of this book is in the National Library of Australia

IBSN: 9780645868111

Cover design © Kate Smallwood 2023

https://www.deviouscat.com.au

Blue roses – original art work © L. C. Wong 2023

Publisher: Indie Scriptorium – Self Publishing Collective

https://indiescriptorium.com

Contact Elsie King - https://www.elsiekingauthorartist.com

Table of Contents

In Loving Memory of Isla

Acknowledgements

Writing history requires considerable research and I would like to acknowledge the definitive guide to all things of the Regency era, "Georgette Heyer's Regency World by Jennifer Kloesters (Arrow Books 2005)

All my characters are fictional but Birchover, Rowter's' Rocks, Lyndon, Lynmouth and Ash are actual places that can be explored to this day. I love to add some reality to my stories by including places I know or would like to visit.

Thank you to Henni Parry for being a wonderful friend and my enthusiastic first reader. Also, my gratitude to Carole, Jane, Emma, Anna, Michelle and Eileen, my beta readers who contributed so much to improving the multiple drafts of this novel. Thanks also to James Green, President of Marion Art Group who kindly lent his name for Eleonore's art teacher and mentor.

A big thanks to Lee-Anne Kling and Mary McDee from Indie Scriptorium who provide inspiration, information, support and fun as we plough through the intricacies of the self-publishing process. Accolades to the Create/Write group who challenge and support group members to become the best possible writers they can be. Also, thanks to Woodcroft Writers who incubate new writers and inspire them to achieve their dreams.

Creating this novel was a long process and made so much easier by the excellent professional editing provided by Nicola Marcus and the artistic flare of Kate Smallwood who designed the cover. A big thank you to Marie and Alison who mopped up all the typos and extraneous commers.

And last but not least, to my husband Peter, who leaves me in peace for hours when I'm writing and cooked, cleaned and drove me around when I was sick. A hero indeed.

Chapter One

May 13th 1818

"Eleanor, Eleanor Finch. What are you still doing up here? You should have changed and be ready for dinner by now. Your mama is beside herself."

Eleanor stood back from the canvas that had taken all of her attention for most of the afternoon, and giggled. It was tempting to throw a towel over the portrait, but it was a wonderful likeness and she always enjoyed Bertha's acerbic critiques of her work. Footsteps thumped up the stairs, signalling her governess' displeasure. She lifted a small dab of red from her palette and struck down at the corner of her mama's mouth, making her expression even more sour than justified.

"Goodness, Eleanor," Bertha snapped, then stopped as she saw the portrait of Mrs Winifred Finch. She gasped, uttered an unintelligible grunt, and then laughed. "Oh Eleanor, that's terrible."

"Do you like it?"

Bertha stood immobile and silent as she examined the painting. She moved to get a better light on the work, then stepped forward and looked at the detail. "Humph, you've captured her face and posture perfectly, and her colouring, and the dress is finely wrought, but, Eleanor Finch, it's a cruel likeness. Are you still so angry with your poor mother?"

"Yes, of course I am. I should be in London, enjoying balls and musical evenings. I should be going to the theatre and visiting galleries. Mr Turner has a new exhibition at the Royal Gallery and I wanted to see it, Bertha, I really did, but I'm stuck here. It's not fair."

The governess put her hand on Eleanor's shoulder and gave a small shake. "Eleanor, I know you're disappointed, but you're making much of a slight inconvenience. Your mother has tried, but she cannot travel with her lumbago, and Gillian wasn't to know she'd be expecting again. You're only seventeen and I'm sure one of your sisters will accommodate your coming out next year. And perhaps your mother's health will have improved by then, and she'll be able to go to London too."

Eleanor glanced back at the portrait; her shoulders slumped. "I can only pray she will, Bertha, but sometimes I think she'd prefer me as a spinster. I'm the youngest and she's needing a companion and carer now that Papa's passed away. She doesn't seem to fret about my chances of a suitable match, not like she did for Isabel, Lily, or Gillian. It will mean I'm trapped here, and I'll go mad if I can't escape."

Bertha shook her head and her lips stiffened into a straight line. "Eleanor, don't act like a coddled child. Now, your mother has guests and you smell of turpentine and have black paint on your cheek and hands. You need to hurry to be ready for dinner. These are just silly fears which we'll talk about later, but for now you can act the pleasant young lady, even if you are in a temper about your poor mother's ill health."

"It's only the Andersons coming over. They wouldn't notice if I turned up with purple spots on my face." Eleanor picked up her brushes and dumped them into a jar of foul-smelling turps. They'd need a proper cleaning in the morning, but she knew better than to tarry when Bertha was being the strict governess. As Eleanor removed her paint-splattered overdress, she glanced again at the spiteful portrait of her mama. She'd alter it tomorrow, make the expression more benign and the posture straighter. She did love her mama, most of the time.

The attic stairs were dark and steep. Eleanor was a little afraid of the dark, but Bertha clumping ahead made the descent somewhat easier. Bertha's voice echoed backwards in the small, bare-walled space. "Mr. and Mrs. Anderson are bringing visitors. Your mother said you should wear your new pink evening gown, and she wants Jane to do your hair. But you need a bath, Eleanor; you smell something fierce of turpentine."

The pink dress. A favourite new gown, never worn and meant for her coming out in London. It was palest pink with hints of lavender. Eleanor had picked out the silk herself and loved it. It was lower cut than any of her other dresses and the little capped sleeves showed off her shoulders and arms. It was beautiful and flattering, designed to gain the attention of young men in search of a wife. A frisson of excitement disrupted her ill humour.

"Visitors. Who are they? Mama never said we had company!"

"If you didn't busy yourself in the attic all day you would have known." Bertha had reached the landing of the manor house and opened the door of the servant's stairs. The hall beyond was wide and panelled in dark wood. A richly patterned runner of green leaves and roses covered the gleaming floorboards. The last of the day's light streamed through the large, mullioned windows, lighting up the portraits of ancestors and the small tables holding blue-and-white China vases filled with displays of white garden flowers. The air smelt of roses and jasmine. Like the rest of the house, the hall reflected the good taste and unique style of Mrs Winifred Finch, who, thanks to her late husband, had the wherewithal to devote to her passion for interior decoration.

"But who are they?" Eleanor persisted.

"Lady Heyer, a cousin of Mrs Anderson, I believe, and her son, Viscount Heyer," Bertha replied succinctly.

Eleanor tried to recall her mother's interminable lists of local aristocratic families. It was her mama's fondest desire to marry her daughters well, and her preparations had included having her daughters memorise all the titled families in the county. It had only worked for Isabel. She had won the attention of Baron Radcliff, a rather dull, ugly gentleman who had provided Isabel with a title, much to Mama's satisfaction.

"They can't be local," Eleanor concluded. "I've never heard of them."

Bertha paused at Eleanor's bedroom door and turned. "If you kept your mother company, instead of spending all your time painting, I'm sure she would've appraised you as to the particulars of Mrs Anderson's relatives. I'm not privy to such information and I won't speculate. I suggest you hurry with your ablutions and discuss this with your mother before the guests arrive."

"Yes, Bertha. Sorry, Bertha." Eleanor gave a small curtsey and grinned at her peeved governess. Bertha knew full well that Jane, her mother's maid, would impart all she needed to know. Bertha might not condone gossip from the servant's hall, but Jane had no such qualms.

"Ring for me when you're dressed." Bertha barely contained her own smile. "I'll need to ensure you're presentable," — and this time she did smile — "and that Jane has missed none of the black paint or important information."

Eleanor watched as Bertha marched noisily down the hall, her footsteps loud, her posture rigid and her head held high. But Bertha, while her only real friend and confidante, was getting old. Her hips were wide, she puffed loudly climbing stairs, and complained about her aching knees. She also had a tendency to doze if reading a novel in the late afternoon.

It was difficult being the last of seven children. As a baby, all Eleanor's older siblings had cosseted and played with her. Even her eldest brother, Godfrey, who had already turned eighteen at the time of her birth, had played hide and seek with her and tossed her in the air to make her giggle. The house had been full of laughter and arguments, scolding and fun. Then gradually her sisters, Isabel, Lily, and finally Gillian, had gone to London, married and moved away and had babies, lots of babies, so they rarely visited anymore. Godfrey, Henry and Bevan had married a little later than the girls, but they had left early to study, travel, or just be rich young men enjoying London and visiting their peers at country estates. But even they were all married now and had busy lives and families of their own. Gillian, the second youngest, had departed five years ago. Now, already blessed with two children in three years, she was expecting again. Brampton Manor had become a silent, empty shell. Her papa had died, and her mama had gone into decline, and Eleanor feared that she'd never escape the manor's creeping decay.

Eleanor gave herself a small shake. Yes, she was disappointed, but Bertha was right. Next year, one of her sisters could sponsor her for the Season. She would escape, she would, next year. But tonight, they had visitors, and that was an unusual diversion, and she'd look pretty and grown up in her new pink gown. She opened her bedroom door to be met with the aroma of lilies and the sight of a steaming tub set before the fire. Jane hovered by the bath holding a jug.

"Ah, there you are Miss Eleanor, and goodness look at the state of you." Jane sniffed as Eleanor approached. "And the smell of you. That hair will need washing, so we'd best be quick or it won't be dry enough to curl."

Jane was a small, brisk Welsh woman who had tended her mother's dressing and toilette for the past ten years. She consistently presented in a sensible black dress and tiny polished half boots. She had lovely skin and hair that was immaculately drawn into the tightest chignon Eleanor had ever seen. Eleanor often wondered if the severely pulled bun contributed to Jane's flawless, wrinkle-free complexion.

Two hours later, Eleanor looked in the mirror and gasped. Jane had turned her into a young lady she barely recognised. Her brown hair was still damp underneath, but the curls and tendrils were dry and shone in the candlelight as they softly framed her face and bounced deliciously on her neck. The pink gown fitted to perfection. It enhanced her pale skin and was just low enough to capture the shadow between her small breasts. It flattered her small waist yet covered her rather wide hips. Wide hips were a family trait, so her mama said, and contributed to the well-known fact that the Finch women were uncommonly good at breeding. Eleanor inhaled deeply to capture the applied scent of Lily of the Valley, a favourite perfume of Jane's.

"There, Miss, you look a treat, even if I say so myself. You will impress the Viscount and his mother. Shall I ring for Miss Smith now?"

Eleanor smiled at her reflection and nodded. As well as working wonders with her appearance, Jane had also imparted important information about their titled visitors. And Jane had the information "on good authority", having heard the report from "Mrs Penn, the housekeeper herself." Mrs Penn rarely condoned gossip in the servant's hall and it was therefore unusual that she'd visited the neighbouring estate specifically to clarify information from Mrs Watson, the Anderson's housekeeper.

"It was all Polly's fault, Miss," Jane disclosed with her singsong voice. "She's the new laundry maid, and she's only young. Well, she got the news about the Anderson's visitors from her sister, who's the scullery maid over at Paladin Court. Well, Polly being Polly, and not the brightest bunny in the burrow, had it all wrong." Jane giggled deliciously. "Polly made out the visitors were very grand, close to royalty as she would have it. Mrs Penn wasn't averse to putting the record straight. She gave young Polly a clip 'round the ear for her impertinence, then took a stroll over to visit Mrs Watson and got the true account."

Jane passed on the "true account" with alacrity to Eleanor as she scrubbed away paint and washed out the smell of turps. Viscount Heyer was a man "in his prime", according to Mrs Penn. He had a large estate in Devon and another somewhere in Scotland, as well as a manor in Surrey, where his mother resided.

He also had a grand townhouse in Mayfair. The Viscount was a widower and still in mourning for his good lady wife who'd died in childbirth a year ago. The Viscount and his mother were returning to London for the Season after spending the winter grieving and shooting deer in Scotland. Mrs Penn had not furnished herself with information about the Viscount's age or appearance, much to the disappointment of all in the servant's hall. Though Polly said she'd heard 'he was fabulously rich and handsome'. No-one believed this was the case, given Polly's propensity to exaggeration. Polly also implied that the Viscount had no offspring and was looking for a wife. A more acceptable premise, as this was the usual way of the gentry.

Lady Caroline Heyer was, in fact, The Dowager Viscountess Heyer and had been a widow for many years. Mrs Watson said she had married young and had three boys, the eldest two being twins and a third son five years younger. She was a cousin of Mrs Anderson on her mother's side, and the two corresponded several times a year, but Lady Heyer hadn't visited Derbyshire before. They usually only met in person at weddings, christenings, and funerals.

As Lady Heyer was of an age where travel was onerous, she had written to Mrs Anderson, expressing a wish to break the journey from Scotland by enjoying the pleasure of her cousin's hospitality in Derbyshire for an entire week. Mrs Anderson had been delighted, while Mr Anderson had expressed a desire to show the Viscount the pleasures of the district, allow him to shoot his pheasants, and introduce their titled guests to their friends and neighbours.

It wasn't much information, but Eleanor gleaned enough to extrapolate that Viscount Heyer was a rich widower who was on his way to enjoy a London season and to start his search for a suitable bride after the customary year of grieving. She thought it likely he was well past his prime, fat, ugly and seeking a brood mare to ensure his line continued unabated. But, no matter how ugly and disagreeable he might prove to be, he and his mother were visitors, and that was an uncommon occurrence at Brampton Manor.

If nothing else, it'll allow me some practice with the boring conversation topics Mama believes are acceptable, Eleanor thought. And it would be exciting to converse with someone other than Mama, the Andersons, and Bertha.

A knock on the door indicated Bertha had arrived to escort Eleanor to her mother in the parlour. "Will I do?" Eleanor curtseyed prettily to Bertha as she turned from the mirror.

Bertha was not a person to gush or give away unnecessary compliments. She walked closer, sniffed, and then twirled her fingers, suggesting her charge should make a pirouette for inspection. Bertha nodded, then gave a rare laugh. "Yes, of course you'll do. But appearance gives only a fleeting impression, Eleanor. If you wish to be considered an attractive young lady, it'll require much more."

"I know, I know. I must listen attentively, think before I speak, and always respond with thoughtfulness and kindness." It was a mantra Eleanor had learned from her mama and her sisters most of her life.

Bertha's amusement dissolved. "Eleanor Finch, that's excellent advice, but you'll also need to be yourself, child. Your mother may want a compliant daughter, but I'd prefer that you reveal you have some intelligence, are well educated, and have ideas and opinions that deserve consideration by others. Is that understood?"

Eleanor nodded and suppressed her amusement. Her mother's ideas about a correct education for girls were certainly very different from the schooling she'd received from Miss Bertha Smith. Her governess was a devotee of the late Mary Wollstonecraft, the philosopher and author of two radical texts about the rights of daughters to education and women to equality. Eleanor had instinctively learned to keep the breadth and range of her scholastic accomplishments from her mama. In her view, Mama didn't need to know she spoke both Latin and French, read William Goodwin as well as Jane Austen, or that she was a regular correspondent with Sir Thomas Lawrence, the recently knighted artist famous for his portraits of royalty. Sometimes Eleanor walked a fine line between what her mama considered acceptable behaviour and that demanded by her governess.

"Yes, of course, Bertha. I'll be myself, and try not to give Mama hysterics."

A nod of acknowledgement was all that was needed. At the bottom of the stairs Eleanor straightened her spine, gave Bertha's hand a last squeeze, took a breath, and walked with what she hoped was grace and dignity to meet her mother's guests.

It was encouraging to see several of the maids, including Jane, peering out from behind the door leading to the kitchens and obviously making much of her inclusion in the entertainment of titled guests. A year ago, Eleanor would've been enthralled to be a spectator rather than a participant. She gave a discreet wave and was cheered to see pride in Jane's face. John, the footman, opened the parlour door with panache, but spoilt the grandeur of the occasion by giving a straight-faced wink as she murmured her thanks.

The parlour was Eleanor's favourite room in the entirety of Brampton Manor. It was light and airy, and had large windows offering a delightful view out to the terrace, which could be accessed by French doors. Tubs of roses, jasmine, and all manner of dwarf trees in pots, including lemons and oranges, filled the outdoor space. The parlour itself was well appointed and of pleasing proportions, with walls painted in soft gold with a white trim. There was a display of comfortable sofas and chairs in all shades of gold, cream, and pale green. The centrepiece of the parlour was the fireplace surrounded by white marble, which was intricately carved with oak leaves and birds. It was a masterpiece and designed to draw a visitor's attention to the large bevelled mirror that reflected the light from silver candelabras around the room. The room was a consummate combination of textures, colours, and design, and it reflected Winifred Finch's passion for elegant décor. It was a room that revealed her mama's artistic talent, as well as her refined taste.

"Ah, there you are, Eleanor. About time." Mrs Winifred Finch was standing, actually standing, beside the fire, albeit leaning heavily on her cane. She looked magnificent. Her gown was dark blue, a shade lighter than indigo, her gloves were silver, and her neck swathed in lace and pearls. Mama's hair was mostly grey and her face lined more by pain than age, but when not slumped in despair, she could still be a commanding presence.

Eleanor dropped a low curtsey and approached with arms open. "Mama, you look wonderful." She gave her mother a rare hug and received a warm smile in response.

"So do you, my darling girl, so do you!"

Eleanor felt a flutter of guilt. She would definitely change her portrait of her mother tomorrow.

"Now, Eleanor, I'm sure Jane has brought you up to date regarding our visitors. Make sure you address them as Lord Heyer and Lady Heyer when you do your curtsey and my lord and my lady after that. You can, of course, use ma'am and sir too, but only if the conversation is informal. I also want you to acknowledge the Viscount's loss of his dear wife. He's still in mourning, so it's appropriate. A quietly spoken 'My condolences, My Lord' when introduced will be sufficient, with a curtsey and downcast eyes, of course. And if the subject comes up again, please leave it to the adults to respond. It is a delicate matter."

Eleanor nodded. "Yes, Mama." She hadn't thought of the consequences of meeting, and entertaining, a visitor recently bereaved. Correct behaviour in all situations was the mark of a well-brought-up young woman, and her mother was an expert on correct behaviour.

"Good." Winifred Finch sniffed. "I'm sure you'll do well, child. Now, straighten up. I believe I heard the carriage. We'll receive our guests in here. I don't think I can walk as far as the hall, and I'll need to be seated as soon as possible. If you see me wobble, you may need to bring a chair over, but I hope it won't come to that."

Mrs Winifred Finch was made of stern stuff indeed. She managed to stand as her guests arrived, and while a curtsey was impossible, she managed a bow of her head when introduced to Lady Heyer and the Viscount by Mr Anderson.

Eleanor kept her eyes downcast as instructed, managed her message of condolence without a flaw, and curtseyed low with every introduction. She also watched her mother for signs of fatigue, but it impressed her that her mother hid her pain with skilled ease and stayed robustly on her feet. Fleeting impressions of rich dark dresses, well-fitted gloves, dainty slippers, tightly fitting breeches, and shined evening shoes were all Eleanor could glimpse with downcast eyes. One of the male guests smelt of nutmeg, the other of moth balls, which made her giggle. It wasn't until her mother sat safely in her usual tub chair that Eleanor could raise her eyes and consider the visitors with her full attention.

Lady Heyer immediately drew the eye with her magnificent plum-coloured gown, up-swept dark-brown hair enhanced with violet feathers and pearl pins. She looked to be several years younger than Mama and had the bearing of a duchess with her straight back and proud expression. There was little grace or flexibility in this woman. Eleanor thought she'd be a formidable lady to cross. She yearned to grab a sketchbook and capture the stoic intractability of their guest.

Viscount Heyer was neither old nor fat, but less impressive than his mother. He was short, with a lean build and dark-brown hair, which he wore long with a fringe. He had eyes of a burnt umber hue. His skin was smooth, except around the eyes where tell-tale creases revealed his age, and his grief. His voice was low and revealed a slight accent, possibly Scottish, or it could have been from Devon. It gave him some character, which his appearance failed to do. His clothes were well made, but unassuming. Eleanor got the feeling he had little interest in creating an impression. He did smile at her when she glanced his way. He had a kind smile that was somewhat sad, but she knew better than to study her mama's guests as an artist, and returned the smile briefly before lowering her gaze to her lap.

Mr Anderson took over the conversation by discussing the Brampton Estate. He explained to the Viscount, in detail, the acreage, number of tenants, and the past year's produce of the estate as if it were his own. He'd been her papa's friend, and they'd been constantly in each other's company for as long as Eleanor could remember. She knew her neighbour was as bereft as her own family at the unexpected demise of her papa. And Mr Anderson, bless him, had taken over much of Papa's management of the estate, keeping a close eye on the steward and finances, looking out for the interests of the family. He was a sweet, garrulous older gentleman with a round, crinkled face rather like an apple after it emerges from winter storage. Eleanor loved his smile, and that he always gave her a hug when they met in the park or garden. He'd hugged her tonight, and it had felt wonderful, even if the aroma of moth balls was overwhelming.

Mrs Anderson was as round and cheerful as her husband. She had grey hair which was frequently escaping from her pins. She favoured dresses of pale blues and pinks with lots of flounces and ribbons that, on her short stature, made her appear childlike. Eleanor loved Mrs Anderson's snicker, and how she'd roll her eyes sometimes when her husband expounded on his favourite topics interminably. They were a wonderful couple, more like family than neighbours.

"Mrs Finch," — the Viscountess finally interrupted Mr Anderson's mundane conversation — "doesn't your eldest son reside at Brampton Manor?"

"No, my lady, it's just Eleanor and me at this house. Godfrey prefers our estate in Kent. It's the larger of our estates and is newly acquired, so it requires careful management. He also administers the family agriculture business and needs to be in

London frequently. My second son, Henry, has recently purchased an estate in Hampshire, so he is needed there, and Bevan, my youngest, is a Commodore in the Navy, but he and his wife have a small estate near Plymouth. Of course, they all return home when they can, but with young children it's sometimes difficult to travel, don't you think?"

Lady Heyer nodded approvingly. "And what of your daughters? Mrs Anderson said you have three older daughters; do they live close by?"

"My eldest daughter and her husband, Lord Ratcliff, have an estate in Derbyshire, but he is, of course, busy with Parliament, so they stay in London most of the year. My other two girls, Lily and Gillian, live in Warwickshire and Northamptonshire, so, closer than the boys, but they're busy with their families. Lillian has four children and Gillian is expecting her third."

Eleanor felt like cheering. Her mama had imparted the family's wealth, prestige, and fecundity in one small speech. Eleanor looked up to see that, while Lady Heyer looked as if she'd bitten into a lemon, her son looked intrigued by the Finch family history. "How many grandchildren do you have, Mrs Finch?" he asked quickly, his mother's face presaging a likely change of subject.

Eleanor flashed a shy smile at the Viscount. It was her mama's favourite topic of conversation. Her expansive family was a source of great pride.

Mrs Finch replied, "Good Lord, I think it must be twenty at the moment, twenty-one if you wish to include Gillian's current condition."

Lady Heyer reached for her glass, took a swallow of her champagne, and coughed rather alarmingly. It surprised Eleanor when she looked up to find the Viscount's eyes upon her, and shocked her when he winked. Whatever was going on between them got interrupted when a footman opened the door and announced that dinner would be served.

Mama had selected the smaller of the dining rooms for the meal. It was a warm, inviting room which comfortably sat ten. As the lesser of the dining rooms, it was most often used for luncheons and small family dinners, and her mama had allowed her to fill the walls with her own paintings and family portraits. Eleanor loved that her portrait of her dear papa, the first portrait in oils she had ever completed, hung over the fireplace. She'd always felt like he was smiling down on her when she dined. The portrait raised her fondest memories of her papa. She had painted him in their park, beneath a large oak tree: a favourite place where they'd had family picnics when she was little. She'd painted him with a brace of birds in his hand and surrounded by his beloved dogs. In her opinion, it was the best painting she'd ever done. She felt she had captured her father's good humour and his love of the countryside.

The guests were seated informally in the middle of the table so that conversation could flow between everyone, rather than the traditional expectation that you conversed only with the person on your right or left. Despite the small scale of the dinner, the table groaned under a plethora of silver cutlery and accompaniments, and each end was lit by huge candelabra and pots of greenery and white roses. Roses also snaked down the centre of the table, providing a wonderful scent and a pleasing arrangement.

Eleanor found herself opposite the Viscount and felt her stomach flutter as she wondered if she'd need to take the lead in the conversation, but her mother's foresight in arranging her guests was inspired. The conversation flowed most agreeably and Eleanor found she was listening far more than speaking. Though it was rather odd that the Viscount also remained quiet, only responding when someone asked him a question. The weather, hunting in Scotland, the paucity of game after a harsh winter kept the exchanges to banal topics interspersed with pauses as the party digested the delicious food. It wasn't until the lull between the main course and dessert that the tone of the evening changed.

Lady Heyer smiled charmingly at her hostess. "Mrs Finch, I must ask who you employ for your decorations? I noticed your parlour and this room have a certain style, which I find very pleasing. Is it someone local or from London?"

Eleanor noted that her mother, who'd been looking tired, sat up with a smile. "Neither, ma'am, I do it myself. It's a diversion that I have found I've a minor talent for and it keeps me busy, especially during the winter."

Lady Heyer nodded. "I've been searching for a decorator for some time to refurbish several rooms in my house in Surrey. I would've wished for a name and recommendation, Mrs Finch, but I applaud your tastefulness and selections. Your rooms reflect a person of discernment and an artistic temperament."

"Why, thank you, my lady, but I'm not as talented as Eleanor here. She's our true artist. She has painted most of the paintings in this room."

As the guests looked around the room, Eleanor felt herself blush at the unexpected praise. Most of the paintings were portraits of her nieces and nephews, done in water colours. Eleanor had caught the children at play, or informally posed with their favourite cats, dogs, ponies, and even a couple with rabbits. It had been a style and medium she had enjoyed before she had discovered oils.

"Delightful." Lady Heyer nodded in Eleanor's direction. "And such a pleasant occupation for a young woman. Your brothers and sisters must keep you busy indeed with requests for portrayals of their children."

"They do, my lady. It's sometimes hard to keep up. But I do larger portraits now of the entire family, and I work in oils."

"Oils!" Lady Heyer recoiled almost in horror. "Oils, like a proper artist?"

"Yes, ma'am." Eleanor smiled sweetly and was pleased to see that the Viscount shared her amusement at his mother's astonishment.

"That's an unusual occupation for a young lady. Do you approve, Mrs Finch?"

Eleanor prayed silently for her mama's support. "I was a little perturbed at first." Her mama shook her head. "But when we had my dear husband's portrait painted by Mr James Green, Eleanor's talent astounded him and he persuaded us we should encourage her. He even offered to provide her with lessons, and did so for nearly a year. Mr Green still corresponds regularly with her about her paintings."

"Oh yes," Mr Anderson agreed. "Eleanor has done my portrait, and that of our son and his wife. I am hoping to persuade her to do another of our daughter and family, but she also does the most wonderful landscapes. I just love her trees set in fields at sunrise. Oh yes, we have a rare talent in Miss Finch."

The Viscount actually got up and studied the portrait of her papa above the mantelpiece. "Did you paint this, Miss Finch? Is it of your father?"

"Yes, sir." Eleanor was starting to like this titled guest who appreciated her art. He had a sense of humour and was not as stuffy as his mother. "It was my first portrait in oils, but I had considerable help from Mr. Green, who was very patient and kind. He did the portrait that hangs in the gallery, but Papa said he liked mine better and insisted it hang in here. That was before he became ill and..."

The Viscount returned hurriedly to his seat and, unexpectedly, took her hand across the table. "I'm sorry to have distressed you, Miss Finch. The painting is fine indeed. I cannot say if it is an accurate likeness, as I didn't have the pleasure of knowing your good father, but I can see his character in the portrayal. His eyes are alive with humour and his bearing is proud, in the best sense of the word. I'll look more closely at Mr Anderson's paintings with great pleasure, now I've met the artist."

Eleanor swallowed hard; it wasn't often she found her hand in that of a gentleman. In dancing, it was, of course, acceptable, but her age and isolation had afforded her little opportunity to dance. Mr Anderson's occasional hugs were as much physical contact as she'd had with men since her father's death. The Viscount's hand was warm and dry, and she could feel the hidden strength in his grasp. It made her feel a little breathless, and was relieved when the footmen arrived with dessert and her hand was her own again.

Mrs Finch was renowned for her desserts. Mr Finch had a sweet tooth and Mrs Finch had indulged his appetite by creating an expansive menu of delectable desserts and puddings, which she now offered to guests. Lady Heyer was impressed and requested several recipes to pass on to her own cook in Surrey. Mr Anderson then regaled the small dinner party with a detailed description of local landmarks and places of historical interest.

Eleanor ate her dessert without noticing its flavour or texture. Having Lord Heyer hold her hand, and be so sensitive about her Papa and admiring of her work, had made her feel shy. It was easier to just listen to Mr Anderson's profuse description of the surrounding district and occasionally cast surreptitious glances at the gentleman opposite. He did have an interesting face. A rather narrow face, good cheekbones, a straight nose and well-shaped brows. He didn't look as old as Godfrey, or even Henry for that matter, so Eleanor estimated he'd be in his late twenties. While he had an olive complexion and white, near-even teeth, he did not fit the usual description of handsome. However, Eleanor found herself attracted in some ways. She imagined him in a portrait. She'd dress him in bold colours and put him in a park full of trees, with his stately home in the background. It would give him gravitas, and she had a feeling he enjoyed the countryside.

"Perhaps Miss Finch would like to join us? What say you, Miss Finch, to a ride up to see the Nine Ladies tomorrow? She's painted them, you know, the Nine Ladies. Did a splendid job. I must show you when we return home. And your governess — Miss Smith, is a mine of information about local history. She must come too and we can always bring the trap for her if she declines to ride." Mr Anderson's question had interrupted Eleanor's wool-gathering and made her jump.

She blinked as she brought her mind back to the conversation and glanced at her mama, who gave a brisk nod of approval. "Yes, yes, of course. I cannot answer for Miss Smith, but I believe she'll be agreeable. We often venture out with the trap when the weather's good. Will you be coming, Ma'am?"

"I think not, Miss Finch. I've had quite enough of carriage riding over the past two weeks." Lady Heyer sniffed. "And I'm not sure Julian is ready to venture out into the wilds after such a long journey, but he'll make up his own mind; he usually does."

"I can think of nothing more pleasant, Mr Anderson." Viscount Heyer spoke to Eleanor. "I've heard that the Peaks are magnificent at this time of year. It'll be most agreeable to ride, although my mother is correct. I've had quite enough of carriages for a while. I presume it's not far, sir?"

"About two miles to Birchover, and then another half an hour after that. The track to Stanton Moor is not too steep for a good horse, and I believe you can get the trap up most of the way. Is that not so, Eleanor?"

"Yes, Mr Anderson. Miss Smith and I often take the trap up, and the views are magnificent from the top. The stone circle is very picturesque. Of course, the heather isn't flowering, but it's very pretty in the woods, and there may be bluebells."

"Will you bring your paints, Miss Finch? Will we see you in action?" the Viscount asked.

Eleanor shook her head. "No, sir, to paint outdoors would require an entire day and much preparation and equipment. But I'll bring my sketchbook, pencils, and watercolours. It sometimes helps to catch the perspective and hues of the day, then complete the painting out of the wind, dust, and rain in the attic, eh my studio."

"Then I'll ask to see your attic, too. I find it fascinating, Miss Finch, and I'd like to see you at work. If that's allowed, of course."

"Yes, of course, sir." Eleanor blushed again.

Lady Heyer glared at her son, then turned to her hostess and pointedly changed the subject. "I wonder, Mrs Finch, if I could prevail upon you to offer a tour of your delightful house. As I explained earlier, I have several rooms that require refurbishment. They are rather poorly lit and I'd very much appreciate your opinion on what colours and lighting would improve their ambience. If I can impose, maybe a visit again tomorrow, while the others are out riding, so I can see your rooms in daylight."

"I'd be honoured, my lady." Eleanor noticed her mama flushed pink at the request.

All three ladies then entered a lively conversation about decorating, which prompted Mr Anderson and the Viscount to depart to the library for their port and cigars. Eleanor joined the ladies in the parlour, but found herself ignored pointedly by Lady Heyer, and wondered what on earth she had done to earn the lady's censure.

It was also strange that as soon as the men returned to the parlour, Lady Heyer complained of a sudden headache brought on by the fatigue of too much travel. The lady didn't look tired or ill, but she did look cross. Eleanor wondered what had brought on such obvious displeasure that resulted in their guests leaving so early.

As the guests departed, Eleanor once again found her hand in the Viscount's while she bobbed her curtsey. "Miss Finch, it's been a pleasure. I'm very much looking forward to our excursion tomorrow. We'll have to pray for a fine day, don't you think?"

"Yes, sir." Eleanor felt her cheeks heat again. It was quite discomforting to receive so much attention from an older man. Her mama had looked on fondly as the Viscount took his leave, but Lady Heyer gave her a cursory nod and turned on her heel, seemingly hell bent on leaving Brampton Manor as swiftly as possible.

"Well," her mother exclaimed as they returned to the parlour, "the evening went well, I believe, Eleanor."

"Yes, Mama."

Eleanor wished she had the courage to ask her mother about the Viscount's consideration, and Lady Heyer's obvious displeasure. But mama would no doubt scold her for impertinence, for even noticing a guest's demeanour, and then excuse her manner because of her stated poor health. But Eleanor didn't believe that was the real reason. She'd just have to sort it out with Bertha in the morning and hope it didn't spoil what promised to be an interesting time with the increasingly handsome Viscount Heyer.

Chapter Two

May 14th 1818

Eleanor frowned as she stepped back from the painting and half closed her eyes. It was a practice that was second nature now, though it had sounded strange when Mr Green had introduced the idea. She could still hear him saying, "You have to stand back, squint and look, really look, at every part of the work. Look for anything that leads the eye away from your point of focus. Look at the brush strokes you've just completed, then look at the whole painting. Have you captured the light? Are your contrasts strong enough? Is your perspective correct? Is it conveying the image and mood you wish to present? If you can answer all these questions positively, put down your brush and put the painting away for a while and then look again."

With half-closed eyes, Eleanor looked at her finished painting. The contrasts of light and shadow were enhanced, and the shapes emerged from the background. Colours were stronger in front, softer and cooler behind her mother's likeness. The new brush strokes blended well into the painting and there was no hint of tonal variations where none was required.

Opening her eyes, Eleanor nodded. It had taken little to change the disgruntled image of her mother from yesterday to the grand, benevolent lady captured today. Tiny strokes to lift lips and brows, pale paint to remove darkness under the eyes, black strokes to raise and straighten slumped shoulders and tiny points of light to brighten eyes and give her humour. A few alterations and the entire portrait lifted in tone. Oh Mama, if only I could wave my magic brush and take away your grief and pain so easily. I would be in London by now.

Eleanor grimaced and set down her brush. It was finished. She picked up her brushes and swirled them in the jug of turps. She would need to take them down to the stables and give them a scrub with hard soap. Brushes were scarce in the wilds of Derbyshire and needed assiduous care. A damp cloth over the pallet would preserve her oils for a few weeks, in case the painting needed further adjustment.

The old kitchen clock set in the corner of the attic showed it was just on nine. She'd have plenty of time to clean her equipment, clean herself, and be ready for eleven when Mr Anderson and the Viscount would arrive. Butterflies bounced in her stomach as she thought about the day ahead. The Viscount had been interesting and, what was bizarre, had appeared to be interested in her. He'd spoken to her as if she were an adult, held her hand, even winked. That showed some interest, didn't it? Miss Eleanor Finch, all of seventeen and an eligible spinster, was the focus of a gentleman's attention. Eleanor chuckled as she walked carefully down the servant's stairs. She'd wear her blue riding habit; it would contrast well with Merry's cream, dappled coat. Merry was the larger of the two riding ponies, and the prettiest, and was less inclined to stop to eat grass than the old brown gelding, Jasper.

Her father and brothers had taught Eleanor to ride as a young child. But after a couple of falls, she'd found she didn't enjoy it. Now she saw riding as a necessary way to get from one place to another rather than enjoyable recreation. She preferred to walk, and then she could study the shapes of a tree, reflections in a puddle, clouds and softening mists as they cloaked the nearby Peak District. Derbyshire was a magical place for an artist, the tors and craggy outcrops a constant source of inspiration for landscapes, though she also enjoyed painting the gentle rolling farmlands surrounding Brampton Manor.

Eleanor had persuaded Bertha that a trip out in the governess trap would be enjoyable. It was a fine morning, perfect for a good outing. And she was interested to get Bertha's opinion of the Viscount.

Jane was waiting for her in her bedroom, and Eleanor realised the importance of the occasion. The assiduous maid had polished her riding boots, brushed the blue habit, and had selected a pretty matching top hat with feathers.

Jane tutted as she inspected Eleanor's hands and sniffed at the smell of caustic soap and turps. "Well, we haven't time for another bath, Miss Eleanor, but some lavender soap and a bit of lotion and perfume should help. And I'll brush your hair and put it in a bun, seeing as you'll be out riding most of the day."

"Did you see the Viscount last night, Jane? Did you think him handsome?" Eleanor couldn't contain her curiosity any longer.

"He looked a right gentleman, Miss. Not too tall, mind you, but he dressed well and had a noble bearing. How did you find him, Miss?"

Eleanor had thought no-one would ever ask. "He was attentive and amusing, Jane. I also thought his stature was not to be commended, but he has acceptable features, a good complexion, and very fine eyes. I liked his hair colour, and he dressed well. But he was so kind to me, and Mama too — a perfect gentleman."

"What did you talk about, Miss? He's a widower, so Mrs Penn said. Was he sad and despondent?"

"No, not at all. I passed on my condolences, of course, but after that the matter didn't come up during dinner. Actually, Jane, we didn't talk that much. Mr Anderson was rather verbose, as is his wont, and other conversation was sparse. But the Viscount admired my portrait of Papa and was most interested in seeing more of my paintings. He's asked to see my studio in the attic, and Mr Anderson was going to show him my works at Pelton Court. He was interested and kind, Jane, and that's all." Eleanor realised she was being too effusive and that she shouldn't say more. Jane, although friendly, was a servant. For the first time she understood her mother's caution about talking too openly with staff and realised that warning might have some merit. Oh, how she missed having sisters with whom to share her thoughts and her inexperience.

"What about the Dowager Viscountess, Miss? She looked right proud to me. We all said she was very grand and felt sorry for your mother having to entertain such as her."

Eleanor prevaricated between sharing her severe reservations concerning Lady Heyer and keeping her opinion from the gossipers in the servant's hall. Discretion, she decided, was required. "Lady Heyer was grand, but she was very complimentary to Mama. She was full of admiration for Mama's décor and the food. She even asked for some recipes and will return this afternoon to look around the house with Mama, to get some ideas for redecorating her house in Surrey. It was a very pleasant visit, Jane."

Jane was wise as well as talented. She nodded approvingly, and the rest of the time spent dressing Eleanor occurred in silence or with small conversations about her grooming requirements, the intended ride, and the weather. When Eleanor looked in the mirror, she saw herself as a well-turned-out young woman, and for the first time, she realised she had incorporated the training required to see herself as a young gentlewoman as well. It made her feel proud and provided a strange but welcome cloak of confidence.

Mr Anderson and the Viscount arrived promptly at eleven and paid their respects to Mrs Finch and Eleanor in the parlour. Eleanor, in her cerulean blue riding habit and matching hat, enjoyed the Viscount's appreciative smile.

"Ma'am." The Viscount bowed low to her mother. "With your permission, we'll leave immediately. The day is fine now, but there are low clouds on the horizon and Mr Anderson's steward has predicted rain by late afternoon, but be assured we'll be back by three, at which time, I believe my mother and Mrs Anderson will be here for afternoon tea."

"Yes, of course, sir." Mama turned to the footman. "Jenkins, please ask Cook to give Miss Smith the packed luncheon. And get the maid to pack a cloak for Eleanor, in case the rain arrives early."

Eleanor kissed her mama on the cheek and turned with a bright smile to the visitors. "My friend, Miss Smith, is most delighted to accompany us. She's waiting with the trap out the front. I must say, this is such a treat. I hope your steward is correct, and the rain holds off till after we return."

As she walked past Mr. Anderson, he gave her a wink. "You look beautiful, Eleanor. The sun will surely shine to ensure that we've the pleasure of seeing you smile." Eleanor grinned. Mr Anderson's effusive compliments were a regular and welcome form of banter. She took her neighbour's proffered arm to walk outside.

Bertha was standing beside the small governess trap. It was designed to carry a single person on the front seat and had another small bench in the back for small charges or one large one. Bertha preferred the trap to riding. She was fond of saying, "Sitting on a horse is fine, but getting up and down is now beyond my capabilities."

The tiny cart was small and nimble. It could easily traverse the narrow riding tracks, some of them quite steep, that Eleanor favoured when out looking for vistas to draw and paint. Mostly Bertha would drive herself, with Eleanor in the back or walking at the side. The trap had proved to be a wonderful means of escape for both of them in fine weather.

Eleanor turned to the Viscount, who was following her and Mr Anderson. "My lord, may I present Miss Smith, my former governess and now my friend and companion."

The Viscount bowed. "Miss Smith, I am delighted. Mr Anderson has mentioned that you're an expert on local history and I'm looking forward to hearing your commentaries."

Bertha wasn't one to be obsequious to the aristocracy, but she blushed at the Viscount's warm compliment, much to Eleanor's amusement.

Mr Anderson led Eleanor to the mounting block, and she mounted onto Merry's back with a degree of elegance. The light blue of her new habit did indeed look fine against the warm cream coat of the small mare. Comfortably seated, Eleanor could turn her attention to the Viscount.

Today, he looked more relaxed. He was wearing grey buckskins, an olive-green, double-breasted coat, and very shiny black hessian boots. He didn't wear a hat and his cravat was tied loosely. It impressed Eleanor when he declined the mounting block and leapt lightly onto the saddle. His horse was a finely appointed small mare with a rich, dark-chestnut coat and long black mane and tail. The Viscount gathered the reins, and the horse whipped around and reared at being let free from the groom. The Viscount grinned at Eleanor, keeping his seat with ease. "She hasn't had a good run for a few days, but she'll settle down soon."

Mr Anderson laboured mightily to mount his large grey, even with the help of the groom and the mounting block, but eventually settled in the saddle, grimaced breathlessly, and the party was off.

The ride to the village of Birchover was exciting for Eleanor. The Viscount rode at her side, while Mr Anderson rode alongside the trap and enjoyed a robust conversation with Bertha about new agricultural innovations. Mr Anderson had gone with his steward to attend a three-day conference at Holkham on new ideas on land management. Bertha, who was always interested in education and inventions, was pleased to listen to Mr Anderson's voluble account of the event.

Initially the Viscount had trouble settling the chestnut mare, which snorted and pranced, stepped sideways, and even made placid Merry skittish.

"So sorry, Miss Finch. She's a breed from Spain. Has Arabian bloodlines and a turn of speed most don't believe. I may need to give her a gallop. If she gets it out of her system, she'll settle after that."

Eleanor was rather enjoying watching the Viscount manage the rumbustious mare. He looked as if he'd been born in the saddle, hardly moving as the horse darted and danced beneath him. It was an impressive show, but wouldn't be conducive to conversation.

"Sir, I do not mind. I'd enjoy indeed seeing her 'turn of speed.'"

The Viscount grinned and touched his heels to the mare. She streamed away, mane and tail flying, her rider crouched low in the saddle. It was a wonderful show. Eleanor stopped Merry and watched in delight as horse and rider sped away, jumped a small log, and then cantered back almost demurely. The Viscount's cheeks had colour. His hair was falling across his brow, and his face was a picture of pure joy. Eleanor wished she had her sketchbook to hand. It would make a wonderful addition to a landscape. A small, fast rider amidst a tree-scattered park with a clear blue sky and morning sunlight. She would call it the Galloping Horseman. She visualised the painting and knew the image was there in her head and that she could use it later in the attic.

The Arab mare settled well and plodded along contentedly beside Merry. Eleanor found herself tongue tied, unsure if she should open with a new subject or leave it to the Viscount. It was confusing being a young adult; even with her mama and Bertha's copious instructions, uncertainty reigned. It was a lack of practice, she supposed. Her lonely life was proving to be a disadvantage. She'd so little experience at being a gay and lively companion.

"Miss Finch." The Viscount finally broke the increasingly difficult silence. "Mr Anderson led me to believe you intended to go to London this summer, but I understand your sister's condition has delayed your plans. Will you be going to London next year?"

Eleanor sighed and relaxed. "Oh, yes, sir. I'd so hoped to visit this year, and Gillian had it all planned, but she's confident I'll be coming out next year."

"Are you looking forward to the balls and dancing, making a mark with the ton, and visiting Almack's, Miss Finch?"

"Well, yes." Eleanor pondered the question and answered honestly. "But I must confess, it was Mr Turner's exhibition at the Royal Academy I was most excited about. And, of course, it won't be on display next year. I believe he intends to visit the continent again, now the war is over. But I suppose I will endure my disappointment, and perhaps the balls and dancing will lift my spirits next year."

"You don't enjoy dancing?" The Viscount's tone was teasing.

"I've done very little of it, sir. Mama doesn't entertain much and isn't able to travel to Matlock, where the local assemblies occur. It's difficult to miss something you've never really experienced. I enjoy music, though. I was keen to attend the theatre and concerts, and see an opera at least once."

"One should definitely see an opera at least once in their life." The teasing tone continued. "But I agree. I can do without dancing and balls, but I enjoy concerts and plays while in London, and I've been to ten different operas, so have had more than my fair share of those. But, Miss Finch, surely, it's the social life that draws you to the Season. The prospect of finding a young man to fall in love with, to marry and have a family of your own.

I'm told that most young women attend the Season for romance and matrimony. Is that not your aim?"

Eleanor flashed him a smile. It was a risqué and enjoyable topic. "My Mama has repeatedly informed me that finding a husband is the only reason I should contemplate a season in London. But I'm not convinced I want to go hunting for a husband. It seems somehow..." Eleanor paused as she stumbled to find the right word, "... desperate."

The Viscount raised a brow. "You don't want a husband and a family, a house to call your own, children you can coddle, and servants you can command. I'm surprised, Miss Finch."

"Oh, my lord, I do want marriage and a home of my own, and I'd love to have children. And I'd love having them while I'm still young, so that I can play with them, take them out, and show them off. It would be wonderful to teach them, show them the world, and make them curious and brave. But it's the finding of that husband that causes me concern. If it means I must suffer bruised toes and inane conversations in smelly, packed ball rooms, I'm not so keen. No, sir, I think I'll enjoy being settled, but I do not believe I'll enjoy the hunt."

The Viscount laughed again: a warm, amused laugh that lit up his eyes and caused his mare to startle. "I think, Miss Finch, you'll take London by storm and find many young men treading on your toes."

They settled into amiable silence again. Eleanor wondered if she'd been too bold discussing her concerns about finding a husband. Her mother would no doubt think so, and would scold her for being forward and indiscreet if she found out about it. Bertha would probably be surprised too, but possibly proud. Bertha was a vigorous advocate of being honest and putting forward your own views, even if you were only seventeen. Eleanor sighed and decided that a more neutral topic would be safer. The village of Birchover came into view with its grey gritstone cottages climbing up the hill. It gave her inspiration for a more suitable subject for conversation.

"I hope, sir, that we'll have time to see Rowter's rocks on our way up to the moor. They're strange indeed and quite the talking point in this area."

The Viscount nodded, "I believe that Mr Anderson has planned to see the rocks, Miss Finch, but tell me about them, please."

Lord Heyer continued to rise in Eleanor's estimation. He had humour and a confidence that made being with him easy and enjoyable. She informed him of the history of Rowter's rocks in a lively, suitable manner and felt quite satisfied that she had extricated herself from too much personal disclosure. It was tricky conversing with a man when she'd hardly any experience with witty repartee. But Eleanor felt safe in the Viscount's company. She relaxed and enjoyed herself.

Rowter's rocks, with their twisting stairs, tunnels, and caves, proved to be an entertaining diversion for the Viscount, but as both Mr Anderson and Bertha struggled with the steep terrain and bending entrances, it was difficult to see all its secrets. The Viscount listened as Bertha recounted the strange facts about Reverend Thomas Eyre, who was said to be a magician, as well as a man of the cloth. It was the cleric's lifelong enterprise to have carved and constructed many of the features of the rocks.

Following the tour, Bertha pulled out the cheese and pickle sandwiches, chicken drumsticks and bottles of ginger beer cook had packed for a quick luncheon. They sat on the rocks and enjoyed Mr Anderson's lively account of the folly of some gullible visitors who believed the Rocks were an ancient Druid site. He cheerfully explained that the only connection to Celtic culture was the naming of the local public house, The Druid Inn.

The Viscount laughed at Mr Anderson's tales of how locals had hoodwinked visitors with ghastly tales of human sacrifices and hauntings, which were gleefully accepted by readers of popular gothic novels. They all talked companionably together as they ate the luncheon. Eleanor thought it was one of the most enjoyable outings she'd ever experienced.

The track up to Stanton Moor was steep and narrow as it wound around large, grey gritstone boulders, so further conversation was impossible. Clouds from the west were being pushed by a harrying breeze and the sky promised rain. They circumvented the Cork stone, a large, top-heavy outcrop of granite which resembled a cork for a bottle and then admired the views across the Derwent Valley. The track then led through an expanse of heather and gorse.

"It's so much prettier in summer, sir, when everything's in flower. The purple heather and the yellow gorse make for a wonderful foreground to the view of the farms below. It's quite magical in August," Eleanor commented as the track widened enough to allow two horses to walk abreast.

"Have you painted it, Miss Finch?"

"Yes, sir, it's a favourite view of mine. Mr. Green has also painted the scene. They exhibited his painting in the Royal Society and he sold it to the Earl of Chesterfield. It's on view at Bretby Park."

"Ah, I've met that gentleman on many occasions, even bought a nice thoroughbred mare from his stables. He's a man of taste and refinement, particularly in regard to horseflesh. But what about your painting, Miss Finch? Has that gone to Bretby too?"

"No, sir. It's nowhere near as good as Mr Green's, but it was one of my father's favourites and hangs in the library at home."

"Then I'll see it on our return, Miss Finch. I'll definitely pay it attention now I've been to the actual location."

The small opportunity for conversation vanished as the trail disappeared. Bertha brought the trap to a halt, and they made a quick decision to leave the horses with Mr Anderson while Eleanor, Bertha and the Viscount walked up the last bit of the pathway.

"Go ahead without me." Mr Anderson puffed. "I'll let you young people view the site. I've been here many a time. Most happy to mind the horses and get my breath back. But I think you should hurry Miss Finch. Those clouds are closer and that wind is indeed chilly."

The brown heather dragged at her skirts as Eleanor pushed her way along the overgrown path. The wind pulled at her hat and the clouds raced in great rolling bundles above the low bushes. It was exhilarating, and she glanced back with a grin at the Viscount, who appeared as if he was thoroughly enjoying himself. Bertha kept up despite her rheumatic knees and pushed her way through the undergrowth at a steady pace. She took her duties as chaperone seriously.

The Nine Ladies stone circle was on a well-cropped rise, surrounded by birches and woodland ferns. Their arrival startled a herd of sheep that fled into the woods with plaintive bleating.

"And these, my lord, are the Nine Ladies of Birchover." Eleanor spun on her heel and threw her arms open theatrically.

For one moment she thought the Viscount might join in her silliness, but Bertha coughed and the hilarity declined.

The Viscount removed his hat, strode into the centre of the prehistoric ruins, and slowly turned to survey the monument. "I'm not impressed, Miss Finch. They must've been very short ladies indeed."

Eleanor lifted a brow. "They may not be as large as the henge at Salisbury, but they are our Derbyshire stones and I won't allow for any disapproval mentioned in their presence."

Bertha nodded as she also took in the sight. "And what they lack in height, my lord, they make up for in beauty, you must agree."

"Indeed, Miss Smith. It's a pleasant aspect amidst the woodland. Is this, too, a favourite subject for a landscape, Miss Finch?"

"It is, sir; I've painted them many times. My sister Isabel has one of my first attempts, and my brother Henry also has one, if I remember correctly."

"And I have a wonderful watercolour in my bedroom," Bertha chimed in proudly.

"I would prevail on you to show it to me on our return, Miss Smith. If it's not too large and cumbersome to move, that is."

"No, sir, it is small and easy to carry. I deem it's one of Eleanor's best landscapes in watercolours. I'll be very proud to show it to you."

The Viscount again turned around and Eleanor realised he was spending time actually studying the stones. She'd been here countless times with family and, more rarely, visitors to Brampton Manor, yet the Viscount was the first of them who examined the landscape with appreciation. Eleanor walked quietly away to hide the tears welling in her eyes. She wouldn't cry. What would the gentleman think of her being so missish?

The Viscount pointed to the west, "I like this aspect the best, with the opening to the heather and the view beyond. As you say, Miss Finch, in the summer the colours would be spectacular. And the sun would bathe the stones in afternoon light, with shadows breaking up the green grass. Yes, it's my favourite view." He grinned at Eleanor, for some reason, she could only nod in agreement. "Now, will you be sketching my view? I've a mind to commission a painting from you. It'll take pride of place in my library at my London house, and I'll be wanting it by Christmas. Will that be long enough, Miss Finch?"

"Yes, of course, my lord, it should be fully dried by then. And you'll need to provide me with the dimensions of the place you intend to hang the painting. It won't do if it's too large or too small." Eleanor said.

"Phooey, Miss Finch, I want it as large as possible. I want it to dominate the room and be a constant reminder of a peaceful place and a splendid afternoon in good company. But surely, you'll need to make a sketch of my painting. Shall I return to the trap and bring you your sketchbook and pencils?"

Eleanor scanned the sky, where the ragged, dark clouds were quickly engulfing the small patches of blue. The wind had become fierce and the colour of the clouds to the west was a steel grey on the horizon. "I think it may be too late, my lord. The storm will be upon us if we don't get off the moor. But I've many sketches of this place; I'll be able to compose the painting with no trouble. I have your instructions, sir, and that must suffice."

The Viscount contemplated the sky and nodded. "You may be correct, my dear girl, but I insist on seeing your sketches this afternoon. I wish to get the perfect view."

"Of course," Eleanor replied, then caught Bertha glaring at her with one eyebrow raised. She wasn't happy, but Eleanor found she didn't care for her governess's censure. The Viscount was flirting with her and she didn't care a jot. Feeling very bold, Eleanor walked to the Viscount and tucked her hand into the crook of his arm. "I believe, sir, we had better run or the wind will sweep us away."

They arrived back at the horses breathless and laughing, much to the amusement of Mr Anderson. Bertha appeared less amused, especially when Viscount Heyer placed his hands on Eleanor's waist to hoist her onto the back of her mare. Bertha's scowl clearly conveyed her opinion of such forward behaviour. Eleanor knew she'd be in for a lecture about her lack of decorum sometime later in the day. But she experienced no shame. Viscount Heyer proved to be a lively companion, and he made her feel happy and attractive, and those were uncommon feelings in her humdrum existence.

They conducted the ride back to Brampton Manor at as rapid a pace as a pony and trap could endure. The wind became ferocious and bitingly cold, and plops of rain fell just as they reached the end of the driveway. Eleanor was cold and windswept and anticipated with pleasure changing into an afternoon gown and slippers and having afternoon tea before a large fire. She was starving.

The journey home had not been conducive to further conversation, but Eleanor had mulled over her entire day and was pleased with her conduct. It had been fun, but respectable, and the Viscount had certainly been flirting with her, which was unexpected and flattering. He'd expressed an interest in her as an artist, admired her riding, and engaged in enjoyable conversations. The Viscount presented as more relaxed today, and his love for the countryside was obvious. He didn't appear old nor present as bad-tempered or belittling, like many adults. She discovered she was finding her visitor more handsome and agreeable all the time. It was an exhilarating sensation to be drawn to such a man.

Bertha followed her up to her room, her opinion freely given while Eleanor changed. "You were far too forward, Eleanor. You need to learn that men will flirt with pretty young girls if there's no other suitable lady around. Don't think that the Viscount's attention was anything else but a pleasant diversion for him this afternoon."

"Oh Bertha, I'm not thinking any such thing. He's pleasant company, that's all. And he'll disappear without regret at the end of the week. Though I will regret it if he doesn't pursue his commission of the Nine Ladies. I'd like to paint them again and it would be fun if he truly wants it for his library."

"Be careful, Eleanor. You have little experience with men of the ton. He is certainly flattering, but I sense an underlying discontent in the man, and his mother would not favourably judge your forward behaviour."

Luckily, Jane's arrival ended the lecture. Bertha stomped off, announcing she would head to the kitchen for some hot soup and a large pot of tea with the cook. Jane watched Bertha depart, then helped Eleanor take off her hat and gown. "I hope you had a pleasant afternoon, Miss."

"Oh yes, Jane, it was splendid. But please hurry. I must go down and see how Mama has managed with Lady Heyer and Mrs Anderson, and I've promised to show the Viscount my paintings and sketches. He's most interested and has asked me to do him a painting."

Jane worked her magic, and Eleanor dashed down the stairs to re-join their guests. But something appeared wrong. The Andersons, Lady Heyer and the Viscount had gathered in the hall, and were being helped into their cloaks and hats.

"Ah, Miss Finch." Lady Heyer spoke. "Your mother isn't well. We'll not intrude on her hospitality any further. I thank you for your company today, but we must take our leave immediately."

Eleanor blushed at the cold reproach of the lady's address. She curtseyed as Lady Heyer marched away and then glanced at the Viscount's face. He seemed angry and nodded coldly, then strode to the door with no further expressions of regret and no indication that he would visit again. Bertha was right, Eleanor realised: she didn't have any idea how gentlemen behaved.

Mr Anderson, obviously perturbed, rushed off after his illustrious guests. Mrs Anderson managed a grimace that might have been a smile. "I hope that your mama recovers rapidly, my dear. Please send word if you require any assistance." And then she also left in a flurry of skirts and sighs.

It left Eleanor standing forlornly in the cold draft from the open door until she gathered her scattered wits. Mama must be very unwell to cause such a commotion. With a pounding heart, she raced into the parlour and stopped at sight of her mother looking comfortable and eating afternoon tea.

"Mama, are you well?"

"Yes, absolutely, my dear, but I believe I might benefit from a glass of Madeira, and you may have a small glass too. We both will benefit from some fortification."

"But... but what happened? Lady Heyer said you were unwell. I don't understand."

"Neither do I. It's most strange. One minute we were sitting down enjoying afternoon tea and the next Lady Heyer decided I was too ill for visitors and demanded the Andersons and her son take her home. Immediately. I was far too flummoxed to protest, and what can you possibly say when your visitors want to go? Now, ring for a footman, Eleanor. I rarely imbibe in the afternoon, but I will today."

Eleanor grabbed a slice of cake — she really was hungry — then rang the bell and waited as the maid arrived to gather up the remnants of the interrupted tea. They waited until the maid sent up a footman to provide them with two large glasses of Madeira and waited again until he left the room. The waiting was tedious indeed, but it gave Eleanor a chance to come up with some pertinent questions. Questions that were better answered without the matter becoming gossip in the servant's hall.

As soon as the door closed, Eleanor put down her glass and rounded on her mother. "Mama, what actually happened? It's so odd them leaving like that."

Her mother nodded. "Well, Lady Heyer and Mrs Anderson arrived at about two. We chatted in the parlour about nothing of consequence. Then Lady Heyer spoke about her desire to redecorate her breakfast room and morning room and explained that both rooms were on the south of her house and received poor light. I then took them to our breakfast room and the library, as both rooms face south too and needed bright colours and extra lighting to counteract the poor quality of the natural light. Lady Heyer then expressed a desire to see the gallery and passages upstairs, and I explained that I currently couldn't manage the stairs due to my ill health, so I called for Mrs Penn to show the Viscountess the upstairs rooms, while Mrs Anderson and I ordered tea."

Mama paused and took a large gulp of Madeira. "Lady Heyer returned for tea and we were enjoying a chat about decorating when Lord Heyer and Mr Anderson arrived, and then it all turned into a strange conversation indeed."

Eleanor frowned. "But what did they say that caused it so? I don't understand it at all, Mama."

"Neither do I, Eleanor. Mrs Anderson asked something innocuous about the weather and if the rain had ruined your excursion. The Viscount responded that you had all enjoyed a splendid outing, and he was most complimentary to you and Miss Smith for providing such excellent company. And then the Viscount mentioned you were, in his words, 'an interesting and amusing young lady'. Then he said he'd not had such an enjoyable day out for many years."

Eleanor's cheeks warmed at those words. "But what happened next? It doesn't seem a reason for such a hurried exit, and to blame your ill health when you are not unwell is most odd."

"I had the sense that the Viscount's mother was becoming agitated by his praise of your company, Eleanor. She frowned and went quiet until he said that he'd commissioned you to paint him a landscape and he looked forward to seeing your art work this afternoon. That's when Lady Heyer said, 'You'll do no such thing, Julian. We have imposed on Mrs Finch's time sufficiently today. Mrs Finch suffers from poor health and we mustn't burden her any longer. I insist we leave immediately.' She then got up and almost ran to the door. Well, the Andersons and the Viscount could do little else but comply. They were all astounded, and the Viscount shook his head as he passed on his apologies. It was most strange."

"And he said nothing else? He didn't make another time to visit?"

"No, Eleanor. Mind you, the poor man really had no time to even rally his thoughts. He seemed happy when he arrived, but his mother's manner of leaving caused him distress, I warrant. He went white in the face and his lips were quite blue. I wouldn't like to hear what his address to his mother would be when they're in private."

"Oh, Mama, it's such a sad way to end the day. Lord Heyer was the best of company. We had such fun, with Mr Anderson and Bertha joining in. It was delightful."

Mrs Finch sighed and shrugged. "Well, we'll probably hear no more on the matter. Mrs Anderson told me when we were alone that the Viscountess has said she'll be leaving for Surrey tomorrow, that she'd shortened her visit because of some business arrangements that needed the Viscount's urgent attention in London. It's a bit of a mystery for Mrs Anderson; they'd expected the visit to last until Friday. Mrs Anderson was most unhappy with the new arrangements."

Eleanor's stomach dropped at the news of the Viscount's imminent departure. She had enjoyed the afternoon and had been excited to be showing him her work. But could it be more than that? It had been pleasant to entertain the gentleman, to be judged attractive, gratifying she could gain the admiration of a man of such stature and intelligence. It'd been wonderful to be treated as a woman and not a child. But his attention to her was surely not something that would account for Lady Heyer's rudeness. It had taken the shine off the day. Eleanor decided she would talk it through with Bertha later, but reassuring her mother that she wasn't perturbed by this rejection was her priority now.

"Well, Mama, it has been a delightful diversion to have such visitors, but if Lady Heyer must leave, then I'm sure we'll survive our disappointment, don't you?" Eleanor said. "But it will be unfortunate indeed if I've lost the Viscount's commission for a landscape. I'll do one anyway and maybe he'll call again another year."

Her mama chuckled. "Trust you, Eleanor. Any excuse to paint."

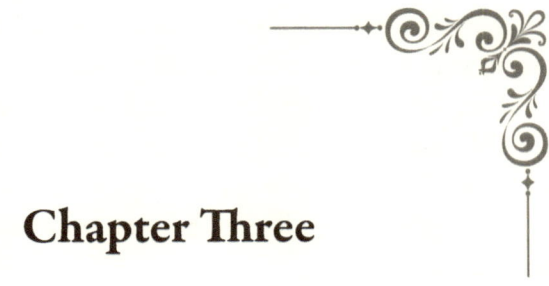

Chapter Three

May 15th 1818

Eleanor slept late the following morning. An unusual occurrence, but the idea of returning to the everyday routine of life, a life that was unlikely to change for maybe an entire year was dispiriting. Yes, that was a good word for her mood, dispirited.

Eventually, hunger goaded her to rise, dress in her everyday clothes, and clump downstairs to the breakfast room. Mama was already seated with a piece of toast in one hand and several sheets of paper in the other.

"Ah, there you are, Eleanor. I've just received word from Lily. She and the family are well, but Robert will be busy in June, so they'll not be coming up for the holiday. She writes that she'll not be going to London for a few seasons either, as her youngest daughter, Charlotte, is prone to lung disorders and the smoke in town is too much for the poor little poppet. They'll remain at the country seat. She's suggested we might join them there for the summer, but I don't think I'll be able to travel yet. It seems we may have a quiet time at home, my dear."

It was surprising how quickly dispirited turned into despondency.

Eleanor nodded, then realised she hadn't even said good morning to her mother. She must try harder.

"I'm sorry to hear that, Mama. Did you have a good night?"

"No, not really. I may go back to bed for a while. It's cold, and that doesn't suit me. Yes, a morning in bed will set me to rights. Ring for Jane, dear. I'll need her help to disrobe. I'll see you at luncheon."

Eleanor rang for the maid, then helped herself to some coddled eggs and toast and contemplated the now-empty room and the empty day ahead. It was cold. The attic would be bitter, and the thought of starting a new painting was not inspiring. It was a strange phenomenon that after completing a painting; it was difficult, even intimidating, to plan for the next one. It was something Mr Green also struggled with; he had mentioned it several times in their correspondence. If she were in London, she would dispel her inertia by going out to the shops, visiting friends, or seeing an exhibition for distraction or inspiration. With no pleasant diversions, Eleanor felt dispirited and bored.

Deciding a brisk walk outside might improve her mood, Eleanor looked out the window, but of course, it was pelting down with rain. She looked out at the grey, damp view, huffed, and resolved to retrieve her sketches of the Nine Ladies from the attic and bring them down to the parlour. There was a fire in the parlour, so she wouldn't freeze. And she would do a sketch of the Viscount as he galloped on his Spanish mare. She would draw the rider in a landscape, with the peaks in the background and a winter-grey sky and windblown trees. Feeling more enthused, she pounded upstairs.

It was far too cold to work in the attic. Huffing out white clouds on every breath, Eleanor grabbed some paper, pencils, watercolours and her sketchbooks, then descended to the parlour. She had Robert set a sturdy table near the fireplace and relaxed as she applied herself to mastering the shape, movement, and shading that best captured the dashing figure of the Viscount galloping through the rain. She lost herself in the task and had no idea of the time until Robert's cough brought her attention back to the room.

"Miss Finch, Lord Heyer has arrived. He apologises for not sending a note, but he was passing by and said he'd call in to pay his respects."

"Oh, oh. Thank you, Robert. Would you send Jane up to Mother and ask Miss Smith if she can join me in the parlour immediately? And... order some tea and cakes for our visitor. You may show him in once Miss Smith arrives. And please move this table and throw some more logs on the fire. Lord Heyer will undoubtedly be cold and will appreciate a chair near the fire."

Eleanor sent up a small prayer, hoping she had acted appropriately in dealing with an unexpected guest. One thing that Bertha had impressed on her was that, at seventeen, she should never, ever be alone with a gentleman. But did that rule apply when the visit was unforeseen and left a guest dripping in the cold hallway? Did it apply when she would be alone with a gentleman to whom she had been introduced? Did it apply when it would be only for a few minutes? Eleanor considered Bertha's dictates and realised, in Bertha's view, it would be totally unacceptable. She sent up another small prayer that Bertha would arrive soon, and she wouldn't have to leave her guest shivering in the hall for too long. Good Lord, who would have guessed that being an adult could be so complex.

As usual, Bertha was cognisant of the dilemma and promptly clumped up from the kitchen, astutely entering from the dining room. She gave Eleanor an approving smile. "Your mother is dressing and will join us shortly. But I'm here now, so you can invite your guest in and ring for tea."

Eleanor looked at her smudged hands and rather drab morning gown, gave Bertha an eye roll and a grin, and then stood, threw back her head and shoulders, and rang the bell.

The Viscount strode into the room, stopped, and made a small bow. "Miss Finch, Miss Smith, forgive the intrusion. I was out exercising my horse and was passing and... No, that won't do. I came here deliberately to make an apology and I'll not prevaricate with niceties. I wish to explain my mother's precipitous leave-taking yesterday. Will your mother be joining us, Miss Finch? I consider she also should be the recipient of my explanation and apology."

Eleanor curtseyed, then indicated a chair near the fire. "Please, sir, have a seat. My mama will be here shortly. Will you take tea, or perhaps coffee?"

The Viscount only nodded. He looked flustered. He was red in the face and his hair was wet and tousled so that it fell across his forehead and dripped onto his jacket. His brow was furrowed. His clothes looked dry, so Eleanor suspected he must own an encompassing great coat, probably with several capes, as was the fashion. The coat was no doubt dripping somewhere in the hall. He sat stiffly in the chair and held his hands out to the fire, but appeared to get little comfort from his actions. His brow remained furrowed. Eleanor rang the bell for tea.

Several minutes passed in an uncomfortable silence which needed to be relieved by some sort of conversation, but maybe not about his mother. "Did you ride over on your Spanish mare, Lord Heyer?"

The Viscount straightened and actually pursed his lips at the interruption of his reverie, but he nodded in her direction. "Yes, she's a horse that likes her exercise, no matter the weather. Also, my mother has returned to Surrey with the coach, so I'm riding at present, much to the animal's delight."

The Viscount's tone was clipped and cold, his posture unbending. His Lordship had a temper, it seemed, and was none too pleased with his mother. Luckily, the tea arrived and the task of providing refreshment distracted Eleanor until she got her turmoil under control. "Please, my lord, have some cake. It's our cook's speciality, made with walnuts, honey and carrots of all things. It's really delicious, sir."

Perhaps it was the hot tea, and cake, but the Viscount seemed to relax as he involved himself with the social rituals of sharing food. He took a large piece of cake and then another, licked his lips, and asked that his compliments be passed on to the cook. "The lemon icing is exquisite and sets off the sweetness of the cake perfectly." He smiled at Eleanor, with his effusive praise of cake, and she relaxed too.

"I notice you were working on some drawings, Miss Finch." The Viscount nodded towards the table covered in sketchbooks and papers that had been cleared to the side of the room. "Are they perhaps from our excursion yesterday? I'd like to see them, if I may. I've very pleasant memories of our trip to the Nine Ladies."

"Oh yes. I usually work in my studio in the attic, but it's freezing today, so I sketched by the fire. They are just scribblings, really — ideas for a larger painting," Eleanor stammered.

"Would you mind if I looked at them? I've commissioned the painting. I'd enjoy seeing the process of its creation."

Eleanor darted a glance at Bertha, who nodded approval. "Yes, of course, sir." She rose and blushed, well aware that her hair was in a plait down her back and she wore her faded moss-green gown, which was two inches too short for an acceptable morning gown. She swallowed a pessimistic sigh and hoped the Viscount was unobservant.

The sketch of the horse and horseman immediately caught the Viscount's attention. Though crudely drawn, Eleanor had put emphasis on form and movement, the pencil strokes delineating the speed of the animal by capturing the flow of mane and tail and the position of legs and hoofs. The Viscount stared, picked up the page and examined it thoroughly. His voice, when he spoke, was full of wonder.

"Why, Miss Finch, this is remarkable. You've captured the horse and rider perfectly. The proportions and movements are amazing. I've several paintings of my horses by Stubbs, but this, this is magnificent indeed."

Eleanor swallowed hard. To be compared favourably with the renowned Mr George Stubbs was breathtaking. She stammered, "I've heard of Mr Stubbs' work, though I've seen only one of his paintings, but it was so lifelike. You're too kind to compare my poor sketch to his paintings."

"I will compare it, Miss Finch, and compare it most favourably. You'll be making a painting of this figure, surely? I'd certainly like to commission a painting of my mare, Bella. I insist the rider wear no hat, mind you, so people will know it's me."

Eleanor blushed, and the Viscount's dark mood vanished. He picked up some of the other sketches of windblown trees, the peaks in the distance, and the horse and rider more crudely drawn within the landscape.

"Could you make the horse and rider larger, Miss Finch? Here they're disappearing into the horizon, but I'd prefer to make them larger, more like a portrait, but with the movement you have captured in this sketch."

"Of course, sir." Eleanor smiled as she contemplated the proportions needed to capture the Viscount's vision. "But I'd not make them so large that you lose the impression of freedom and speed. I think they must be a part of the landscape, or the essence of the subject will be lost."

"You wouldn't change your vision then, to suit the wishes of the buyer?" The Viscount quirked a brow.

"No, sir," Eleanor said with what she hoped was an appeasing smile. "I don't need payment for my paintings and I don't need to compromise what I consider is the best interpretation of the subject. I'd try to accommodate a person's preference, but not at the expense of my own artistic judgement."

The Viscount nodded assent. "Bravo, Miss Finch, bravo. And no doubt your paintings will benefit from your determination, even if it's at odds with the determination of the... eh, recipient."

What might have turned into a lively debate was interrupted by her Mama's timely arrival. The Viscount's light mood evaporated. He walked to Mrs Finch and bowed low over her hand. "Ma'am, I'm sorry, indeed, to have disturbed your morning. I should've sent a note, but I was out riding and passed nearby. My visit is unforgivably bad-mannered, I see that now..."

"But you're here now, my lord, and most welcome, sir." Mama cut off what may well have turned into an effusive and embarrassing apology. Eleanor was struck again by how well her mother managed difficult situations. Mama took the Viscount's arm and was escorted to the closest chair to the fire, where she sat and patiently waited for the Viscount to start the discourse. Her Mother looked regal and totally in control of any emotion that might have displayed her curiosity or temper. The Viscount was correct: his unannounced visit was bad mannered. Eleanor liked that he had the grace to blush.

Eleanor walked over to stand behind her mother's chair and adopted an expression she hoped reflected her mother's serenity.

"Mrs Finch, Miss Finch. I came to apologise for my mother's precipitous departure from your house yesterday. She's been rather tired on this journey and prone to headaches. She asked me specifically to relay her thanks to you, Mrs Finch, for a very enjoyable visit to your lovely home, and wished to convey her regards to you both for your hospitality."

"Thank you, my lord." Mama maintained her cool gaze and tone, which did nothing to aid the Viscount's discomfort.

"She's returned early to her house in Surrey to recuperate. She left first thing this morning, or I'm sure she would have visited herself."

Absolute nonsense, Eleanor thought. She was certain Lady Heyer had sent no apologies, nor her compliments, and had deserted her son after some frightful row that had no doubt lasted well into the night. She struggled not to grin at his discomposure. This was how polite society handled such situations, and she would learn from her mother.

"Lord Heyer." Mrs Finch said. "I'm sorry that Lady Heyer is indisposed, and we thank you for your visit. Now, I need a cup of tea. Eleanor, would you ring the bell for a fresh pot? Sir, please join me and my daughter."

"Of course, ma'am." The Viscount said.

So, it was done. A flustered apology, a poor explanation, and a return to the rituals of polite society. Eleanor would probably find out more about the whole sorry business from Jane, through the staff gossip, than she would from their distinguished visitor. She glanced at Bertha, who looked stony-faced and had remained steadfastly silent during this exchange. Eleanor wondered if Bertha had formed a poor opinion of their guest, having witnessed his polite but deceitful nature.

The Viscount resumed his seat by the fire, while Eleanor turned and rang the bell, then busied herself with offering the Viscount more cake. The poor man grimaced at the proffering of another slice, but accepted it with forced alacrity. He was probably full from his two previous slices, but he would refuse nothing after being let off the hook so graciously.

"My lord, will you be staying in the area?"

"Yes, ma'am. I have prevailed on the generosity of my aunt and uncle and will stay until Friday, as intended. I've also come with an invitation for yourself and Miss Finch to join us for luncheon tomorrow, and Miss Smith as well. Mrs Anderson is most insistent that she return your generous hospitality, and Mr Anderson will send his coach for you at twelve. If that's suitable?"

Eleanor wondered if her mother would refuse. Her mother's lumbago was often a convenient excuse to avoid travel. It surprised her when the invitation was received enthusiastically. "A quick journey in the middle of the day should be achievable, sir. And I'm sure Eleanor and I would enjoy an outing enormously. Please pass on our acceptance to Mr and Mrs Anderson."

"And, Miss Finch, I hope you'll be able to show me your paintings today, after tea perhaps." The Viscount flashed her a grin, then turned back to her mama. "Miss Finch agreed to show me her studio and some of her completed works yesterday. I'm very much looking forward to seeing her paintings, especially after seeing her sketches this morning. Would that be acceptable, ma'am?"

"If Miss Smith is free, certainly. I'd join you myself, sir, but I'm unable to manage stairs at the moment."

Bertha looked unhappy, but nodded agreement. Eleanor wondered if it was the prospect of touring the cold house, the attic stairs, or something else that was making her friend glower at the visitor. She hoped Bertha would get over her displeasure or it would put a damper on what looked like an interesting diversion for the day.

The Viscount continued. "Mr. Anderson gave me a tour of the paintings in his house this morning. I agree with him, your landscapes are beautiful indeed. I'm a man who enjoys the country rather more than London, I'm sorry to admit, so relish rustic scenes. What of you, Miss Finch? Do you enjoy the country more than town?"

"I have had very little experience of town, sir. I've only been twice, and I was just a child. But I remember visiting the cathedrals, and the Tower of London to see the wild animals. I liked the parks and gardens very much. I would like to have a season or two in town. Maybe I'll learn to enjoy dancing and attending balls and the other entertainments. It's the done thing, but I sense I'd miss the countryside too. I think I'd enjoy both."

"Well said, Miss Finch, well said. Now, Mrs Finch, with your permission, may I steal your daughter and Miss Smith away? I'm expected back for luncheon by Mrs Anderson at one thirty, as she's arranged for her sister to attend. It should give us a good hour, Miss Finch. If that's suitable?"

Eleanor rose and was horribly aware again of her shabby appearance. The Viscount didn't seem to notice and offered his arm after making his bow to Mama. It was an enjoyable experience to be escorted out of her parlour by a handsome, distinguished guest.

They started in the attic. Bertha stopped by her room first and retrieved a heavy woollen shawl for herself, and then they climbed the dark back stairs, much to the Viscount's amusement.

"Miss Finch, do you climb up here every day to paint?"

"Most days, sir."

"You're dedicated indeed."

The attic remained bitterly cold and was dark because of the low clouds and rain pouring down the panes of the dormer windows. It smelt of turps and linseed oil. Eleanor lit some candles to cast a little light on the portrait of her mother. She was pleased she had made the alterations.

"You've captured your mother so well, Miss Finch. What say you, Miss Smith? Do you think she's provided a fair likeness?"

"Yes, sir." Bertha remained taciturn, but humour had crept into her voice. No doubt she was remembering the earlier, less flattering portrait of Mrs Finch.

Eleanor was glad the Viscount was attempting to include Bertha in their conversation. She had noticed that many men, and some ladies, dismissed Bertha as just another servant. It made her angry. It incensed her when any of the servants were treated with disrespect. They were people, too. They had employment and circumstances different from that of the privileged, but they deserved recognition and consideration, and many of them at Brampton Manor were like friends.

The Viscount examined Eleanor's workbench. It was of rough wood, but had a smooth surface. Mr Wilson, the carpenter and handyman for the estate, had made the large table in situ as the steep stairs prevented any assembled structure from being brought in. Containers of brushes of all shapes and sizes, glass-stopped chemist jars of pigments, bottles of linseed, walnut and safflower oil, a stack of scraped wooden artist palettes, and a basket of old rags were arranged in neat order. The table surface was stained with a variety of colours, as were the stone mortars and pestles Eleanor used to grind down her pigments. A collection of prepared canvases leaned against the table leg on one side.

"Miss Finch, this looks a complex process. I didn't comprehend it was so involved. You have to grind the pigments then mix your colours. They don't come ready made, obviously. And these canvases, do you make these as well?"

"No, sir. Mr Wilson, our stable manager, knows carpentry and learnt how to stretch the linen over a wooden frame from Mr Green. I just ask for the standard sizes I need. I usually order a roll of linen, and then Mr Wilson spends a few hours on a rainy day preparing them for me. He also coats them with the painting surface, which is called the size. It's a smelly rabbit-skin glue, so I'm very happy for him to do it for me."

"But you mix the paints using these..." The Viscount waved at the jars of powder.

"Oh yes. I wouldn't have anyone else mix my paints. You can get mixed colours, but I enjoy making my own hues. Of course, I also mix the paints on the palette when I'm doing the finer touches to the painting. I use different oils for different parts of the painting. Linseed oil is for darker colours, but I use poppy seed oil for lighter colours, as it doesn't yellow so much as it dries."

"I didn't know, Miss Smith, that the process was so complicated. Your young charge is quite the expert, wouldn't you agree?" the Viscount said, turning to Bertha.

"Oh yes, sir, and very dedicated. She'll spend all day up here when she's working on a canvas, even in the extremes of winter." Bertha harrumphed. "But then she's very young and copes better with the cold than we would."

The Viscount was no doubt cognisant of the censure in Bertha's tone. He turned back to Eleanor and smiled. "Yes, Miss Finch is young, but I suggest we descend to the heated rooms, or else our noses, even Miss Finch's, will turn red and we'll sniffle alarmingly."

Eleanor giggled. "Oh yes. Sorry, my lord, Miss Smith. I'm used to working in the cold. I quite lose myself in a painting and only regret my enthrallment when I get chilblains on my fingers and toes. Come, sir, we'll explore the gallery quickly, then return to the parlour to warm up."

"Maybe Miss Smith could send for her painting of the Nine Ladies. I'm still very keen to commission a painting of those stone ladies from you. But I think it must be two paintings now that I've seen your sketch of my mare. You've a rare talent, Miss Finch, a rare talent indeed."

The tour of the house was completed in better comfort than in the attic, but the Viscount would not be hurried when contemplating her paintings. He was full of praise for the portraits, but seemed drawn to her paintings of local landscapes.

The peaks and dells, viewed through mists and rain. The brooding clouds and wind-bent trees captured his attention more than paintings of clear blue skies and sunny meadows. He expressed his praise carefully, commenting upon the colours used, the composition, and perspective. He was most interested in finding out when the painting had been completed and then commented on changes in style and technique as her work matured. By the end of the visit, Eleanor felt Lord Heyer was truly interested in her work as an artist. It was humbling and flattering, and she took her leave thinking she had made a friend in this proud but humorous man.

"Two commissions, Bertha, two. Can you believe it? And he really is interested in the entire process, don't you agree?" Eleanor said as she settled again to her sketching in the parlour following luncheon.

Bertha harrumphed and looked at the painting she had brought down from her bedroom. "I think he may also be interested in you, child. He paid you an inordinate number of compliments for your paintings. Be careful, Eleanor. He's a clever man and wise in the ways of the world."

Eleanor stopped work on the sketch of the Nine Ladies and looked up. Mother had gone for another lie down after luncheon, leaving her and Bertha to enjoy the parlour fire. "Me? He wouldn't be interested in me. No, Bertha, not in that way. He's just kind, and I like him as a friend."

"He's a man looking for a wife, Eleanor. You are now of an age to marry. He is interested."

"But... but he has said nothing."

"He has said a lot, Eleanor, but cleverly, so that you are flattered and take to him. He's courting you, Eleanor. You are an attractive young woman from an excellent family with a substantial dowry. He's interested."

Eleanor put down her pencil and walked over to the fire to warm her hands. She looked up at her friend. "I suppose he might be. That's possible, I suppose. I hadn't thought of him that way." She sighed as the thought now emerged in her mind. It left her befuddled and a little perturbed. "But what should I do, Bertha? I'm unsure what to do. I wish I had my sisters here. They never talked to me when they were being courted — I was always too young — but it would be good to discuss it with them now."

"Your mother will discuss it with you, Eleanor. You should talk to her."

"Hah, I think it would suit Mother if I married a Viscount. She'd encourage a match, I think. And it would be convenient. I wouldn't need to have a season in London, and she would have the entire business off her hands. She'd be for it without a doubt."

Bertha snapped, "You do your mother an injustice. She would be guided by your opinion and not taken in by a flattering man out to find a convenient wife."

"You don't like him, Bertha. I sensed that both today and yesterday afternoon. You've been quite cold towards him, even though he has tried to be friends with you. Why, Bertha? Don't hold back, please. I would value your advice, you know that."

Bertha took her time. She placed her embroidery down on the couch and looked at her hands before she spoke.

"I don't know, Eleanor. I've mixed emotions about him. He presents as kind and with good humour, but there's a sadness, too, which is to be expected in a widower. But he is sometimes angry, and he barely contained his anger this morning, or yesterday, when his mother left so hastily. I get a sense that he's troubled by something. I think he could be a difficult man to be married to, and he's so much older. It worries me that you have so little experience with men, Eleanor. You must also consider his mother. She's a fierce lady, and I have a suspicion she wouldn't look favourably on the match. She could make your life difficult. But what of you, my dear? What is your impression?"

Eleanor rubbed at a chilblain on her index finger. They itched and hurt when her hands warmed up. She thought through what Bertha had said. Was she drawn to the Viscount? Dear Lord, she hardly knew him, but he was a handsome man, aristocratic, rich, and would be considered an excellent match for a young woman from a genteel, but untitled family. And it could be argued that none of her sisters had known their husbands well before marriage either. A marriage, it seemed, was a matter of chance in high society. People were introduced at balls and assemblies, danced, dined with their families a few times, and then the contracts were arranged with little input from the bride. Romantic novels might extol the virtues of a love match, but Eleanor was sensible to the fact that most marriages were not about love.

But could the Viscount love her? Would she fall in love with him?

Lord Heyer was attentive to her as a person and as an artist. He hadn't given her paintings a cursory glance and followed up with effusive praise, but had asked questions and looked at the paintings carefully, had been fascinated by the process. She felt certain he would encourage her to continue her painting.

Another man might be affronted by her unusual passion, wanting a more conventional wife. He could relegate her art to a pastime status. Without support, her painting time could be limited to accommodate a social calendar of his making. A life without painting would be intolerable. Eleanor knew she needed more time to contemplate her future — a future she hadn't really considered before, except as a child drawn to the bright lights and excitement of London.

"I don't really know, Bertha. I like that he's interested in me as a woman and an artist. He's funny, even silly at times, and I like the way his eyes light up when he smiles. He's easy to talk to and is neither dismissive nor demeaning to you, Bertha. In my opinion, he's neither ignorant nor arrogant and he's an excellent horseman. The Viscount is also drawn to the country, and in that we are suited. I've seen he has a temper, but he is a man, and men need to have a strong disposition, especially when you consider his mother. There's much to like, but I expect nothing more will come of his interest once he's departed for London, so I'll give it no more consideration."

Bertha laughed and nodded. "Sometimes, Eleanor, I think that all my efforts in giving you an education have been put to good use. You are likely correct that it will come to nothing more than a gentleman amusing himself with a young lady for a few days in the country. He'll probably leave for London on Saturday, to find himself a suitable bride, and it'll be the last we ever hear of Lord Heyer."

"Oh, I hope not, Bertha. He's commissioned two paintings."

They both laughed.

That night Eleanor struggled to sleep. The Viscount's visit had raised so many new ideas to consider. Her thoughts spun, but the contemplation was not unwelcomed. London had been her goal for so long she had forgotten why she was going there. London was excitement, new experiences, dancing, new friends, social occasions, an end to loneliness. And for her, the chance to meet other artists and visit galleries.

But in society, the Season was a marriage market. Girls came out in London and were paraded around all the pleasant entertainments by hopeful parents seeking a husband for them. The primary purpose of the Season was to find the best, most suitable match. And for many young women, the meeting, wooing, and marriage all took place within a few months. Certainly, Lily and Gillian had both been introduced to their husbands in London and both had married before Christmas the same year. Lily had been just eighteen and Gillian nineteen when they wed. Isabel was different; she had married at seventeen but had known Baron Ratcliff most of her life. He was a local man and regularly dined either at Brampton Manor or with other local families. He was much older than Isabel, but they now had five children and seemed happy enough. Love really didn't seem to be a prerequisite for an advantageous marriage.

What did she really want? A funny, kind, and attentive man. Someone who would not stop her painting. Who would encourage her, be involved, and fascinated by her need for art. A husband who would visit galleries with her, who had commissioned works by Stubbs, who had commissioned works by Eleanor Finch. Yes, she wanted children, to run her own household, to entertain and enjoy being married, but her art was essential, indispensable, as necessary as breathing. So, did she need love?

The luncheon with the Andersons the following day was full of laughter, good conversation, and excellent wine and food. Mr

Anderson was the best of hosts and remained his garrulous self, keeping everyone amused with his droll anecdotes and accounts of local history.

Even Mother laughed at his buffoonery, and the Viscount was hugely entertained and encouraged his host with loud guffaws and pertinent questions. Eleanor joined in occasionally, but she spent a lot of the time observing the two men. It was obvious they had become firm friends over the past week. Eleanor admired and trusted her neighbour, and it was encouraging that he accepted his aristocratic visitor.

After luncheon, Lord Heyer suggested they take a walk in the garden, as the rain had cleared and there were even a few patches of sunshine breaking through the billowing clouds. The Andersons agreed a walk in the fresh air would be splendid. Eleanor was pleased that Bertha didn't have to chaperone her and could stay with her mother by the fire.

A playful wind cooled the air. Eleanor was thankful for her pelisse and hat. Both were in a honey-coloured velvet that complimented the soft cream of her day dress. She felt elegant and grownup, and smiled as the Viscount offered his arm and they stepped outside. They strode out while the Andersons ambled along behind, and it was only a few minutes later that Eleanor knew she and the Viscount had put enough space between them and their chaperones to converse privately.

Eleanor had always been told that young ladies should open a conversation with a non-intrusive, impersonal topic. The weather was usually a good place to start. "The rain has cleared nicely, my lord. That must be a comfort to you for your ride south tomorrow."

"Yes, Miss Finch, but I'll be most reluctant to leave Derbyshire. I've enjoyed this past week enormously."

Eleanor turned and replied with a smile, "Yes, Mr Anderson is a consummate host. But I hope that will encourage your return, my lord, so you can enjoy the Dales another time, preferably when we have better weather."

"And when the heather is blooming, Miss Finch. I trust you'll add the heather to my painting of the Nine Ladies?"

"Of course, my lord. I won't forget."

They walked along in silence for a few moments. Eleanor felt a fluttering in her stomach. She sensed that Lord Heyer was about to say something important, but that could just have been her fancy. It was so difficult to gauge this gentleman's behaviour. Eleanor's mouth was dry, and she could feel her heart beating. Eleanor had an urge to run away, to dispel some of the pent-up tension she was experiencing, and that made her cross. She was just being missish.

She was about to say something inane, just to break the growing tension, when the Viscount coughed and spoke instead.

"Miss Finch, I can no longer prevaricate. I've enjoyed my stay with Mr and Mrs Anderson very much, but I enjoy your company even more. I find you intriguing and refreshing company, and I've come to view you with a great deal of affection and esteem."

Eleanor felt her stomach actually squeeze uncomfortably. This shouldn't be happening. She glanced behind her as they turned a corner of the garden. The Andersons were a long way back, but still in full view, and that provided some comfort. She swallowed, but couldn't find any words at all.

"I'm aware, Miss Finch, that there's a great disparity in our ages and experiences, but we share many things in common. We both enjoy the countryside; we both want marriage and a large family. I beg you not to reply to me today, but I'd be honoured if you would consider my proposal of matrimony. I understand we've only just met, but I really have faith that I could love you, Eleanor, and I would strive with everything I have to make you happy."

As a proposal of marriage, Eleanor presumed it had sufficient sensibility. It wasn't the most romantic of proposals when compared to the flowery compliments of heroes to their beloved in novels, but he liked and esteemed her, and felt that friendship could blossom into love. A fleeting thought came to Eleanor, that the Viscount may have rehearsed this proposal, spent all night getting the words and tone of address just right, and that was comforting. As a proposal, it was nearly there, nearly a declaration of love, but was it sufficient? Eleanor needed time to think it through, to talk to her mother and Bertha. Could she love this man, live with him, have children with him, find the company and excitement she craved?

She turned and smiled with what she hoped was bravery and assurance. "Sir, I'm flattered and I thank you. I beg for some time to discuss this with my mother."

"Please, Eleanor, if we are to be nothing more, we can still be friends. Please, call me Julian. I would ask that you consider no more until the morrow. With your permission, I'll call on you and your mother in the morning, at eleven, and I'll eagerly await your decision. However, if my proposal is abhorrent to you, it will take only one word of dissent, and I'll prevail upon you no further. I'll leave for London with pleasant weather but a disappointed heart."

"I will consider your offer, Julian, and be pleased to talk again in the morning." Eleanor murmured, though her heart pounded in her ears.

Eleanor was glad that they had returned her to the steps of the terrace and she could rush to the Anderson's newly appointed bathroom to regain her composure. The rest of the visit was a blur. As the afternoon light was fading and her mother was tired, they left early. The leave-taking was full of sincere compliments to their hosts. Eleanor said nothing to Bertha or Mother in the carriage. She wanted time alone to sort out her churning thoughts and strange sensations. At seventeen it still felt like she was a child, yet she'd just received a proposal of marriage from a Viscount. It was all too much. She needed to think.

Eleanor had a good sleep, but woke to find that she still had not decided how she would respond to the Viscount's offer. She rose early, dressed in her oldest walking gown, and took the path alongside the brook to the small woodland at the edge of the Brampton Manor estate. The wind had died down during the night and the air was clear. A bright sun glinted on the dew drops strung along all the branches in the hedgerows. The grass was silvered, the sky a pale, watery blue.

It would be hard to leave this place, her home, since infancy. But Eleanor expected that if she stayed, her family would see her as a convenient companion for her mother. She would be the spinster, the slightly eccentric spinster who painted but had no other life.

Eleanor walked on, her attention on the beautiful rustic landscape. She imagined what it would be like to have children with her here. She imagined them dancing around her, shouting out as they discovered a bird's nest, or mushrooms, or some unnamed flower. They might come up with names, amusing names that would make them giggle deliciously, and then later they'd find the flower's real name in a book in the library.

She loved children, loved spending time with her nephews and nieces, seeing how much they had grown since she last saw them. Some of her happiest times painting had been while telling stories to wriggling children as she tried to capture their dear little faces on paper and canvas. Her recollections made her realise she wanted, no, needed children as much as art. It was a deep wanting in her body, a desire so strong she could not imagine a life without them.

And the Viscount shared that need. He was a man in his prime, bereft by sadness at the loss of his wife and their baby. He was childless and yearning for a family. And she, Eleanor Finch, could give him what he wanted more than anything else. Surely that was the essence of a good marriage and love.

Eleanor turned for home. She'd talk to her mother and listen to Bertha, but her own doubts were less pressing. On the walk back to Brampton Manor, Eleanor didn't notice the countryside. Her attention was entirely focused on the expected opposition of her best friend to the proposal, and what arguments she'd need to counter Bertha's well-intentioned doubts.

"The Viscount's proposed?"

"Yes, Mother. He asked me when we were in the garden after lunch."

"My goodness." Mother sat down heavily. "Are you sure, Eleanor?"

"Yes, Mother. He definitely proposed. I don't believe I missed his meaning." Eleanor chuckled at her mother's total disbelief.

"Oh my." Mrs Finch looked bemused. Eleanor glanced at Bertha, whose lips were pursed and brow creased.

Her mother appeared to recover by waving her fan violently for a cooling waft of air. "But what did he say, dearest? It's all so sudden, so unexpected. What are your feelings about this? About him?"

A barrage of questions made it difficult to know where to start. Eleanor decided to start with the facts, rather than her emotions. "Well, Mother, he said that he's been drawn to me over the past week, admires and esteems me, enjoys my company, and knows that he can make me happy. Oh yes, he also said we share many things in common and he thinks I'm a talented artist."

"No words of love then?" Bertha cut in coldly.

"He's only known me for a week, Bertha. He mentioned affection and assured me I am loveable; said with time he'd fall in love." Eleanor said.

"Oh, Eleanor, this is no time to be flippant," her mother interjected before a fight could erupt. "So, what's your response? How do you regard Lord Heyer's proposal?"

Eleanor swallowed. "I can't say that I love him, Mother, but I like him well enough. He's handsome and kind, and he makes me laugh. I love that he encourages me as an artist. He's looking for a wife, and I'll be looking for a husband, if I ever get to London. I have thought it through, Mother, and I'm considering saying yes, but I've some other concerns that I need to discuss with you and Bertha."

"You're thinking of accepting him?" Bertha exploded out of her chair and took three paces to stare, far too close for comfort, into Eleanor's eyes. "He's too old, Eleanor, and you're too young for him. You've no experience with life, no idea about marriage. He'll have you tied down with babies and you'll never have the joy of just being young and free. You don't need to marry now; you're only seventeen. For goodness' sake, child, I know you wish to go to London, but you'll get there next year. You don't have to marry a man near old enough to be your father to get your way."

Eleanor understood that if she lost her temper, she would lose her argument. Bertha had instilled in her the rules of debate. Stay calm, have your arguments clear and ready, consider all opposition and reflect on all the permutations of the subject. Be prepared to agree and then reason away the opponent's points of view. She would turn her training onto her mentor and friend. The early morning walk had worked well to rally her thoughts. She took a quick breath.

"He is older than me, I know. I am young and inexperienced, I know. But it's not only about going to London, Bertha. Lord Heyer likes me, and I like him very much. He'll make a good husband, I'm sure. He wants children, and so do I. I've been alone for the past five years, except for you and Mama. I want a family of my own, and I want them while I'm young and I'd like them close together. Of course, I want my own household and I want friends and company, as well as the company of artists and other creative people. Lord Heyer will give me all of that, and it's what I want for myself, for my life."

A fleeting spark of respect lit Bertha's eyes. She moved backwards, but maintained her stare before slowly nodding. "You've thought this through, Eleanor."

"Yes, Bertha, I have. But I'm not entirely determined. I need to be open to opposite views, and I have some conditions the Viscount will have to consent to before I accept his proposal."

"And those are?"

"That my best friend accompanies me as my dear and trusted companion. And I have a fire in all my art studios."

"Studios?"

"Yes, Bertha, I fully intend to have studios in London, in his country seat, wherever that may be, and in Scotland, too. Particularly in Scotland."

Bertha smiled at the lighter tone of the conversation, but her furrowed brow still radiated her concern. "But is this really what you want, Eleanor? It's so hasty a proposal. We know so little about him or his family. I've a notion that Lady Heyer was cognisant of her son's intention all of two days ago and that it may have prompted her hasty departure. You might well have made an enemy in his family, and that may not be an easy thing to bear."

Eleanor nodded. "I've thought about that, Bertha. I don't know what objection Lady Heyer might have towards me, but I'll not allow the mother's disapproval to mar my happiness. She is the Dowager Viscountess, but I'll be the Viscountess, and I consider that Julian's actions in staying here and proposing to me shows her opinion did not intimidate him. He is his own man, and I'm confident he'll support me. No, Bertha, it's my inexperience that worries me the most, not the judgement of Lady Heyer. So, I'll definitely need a friend. I'll need you to help and support me. I'll not have Mother to depend upon. I want to accept the Viscount's offer, but I'll not do so without your commitment and approval."

Bertha shook her head. "I'm just not sure, Eleanor. I want your happiness more than anything else. But, as I said, we know so little about him and his family. I just don't want you rushing into this."

Eleanor nodded; Bertha was wavering. "Bertha, I like and admire the Viscount, and I know I could easily fall in love with him. Yes, I could go to London and meet other men, but I may not find someone to like and love. Women often make marriages in haste, and even love can lead to unwise unions that don't always ensure happiness. I'm considering accepting his proposal."

"Are you really sure the Viscount will make you happy, Eleanor?" Bertha persisted.

"I consider that I've as much chance of happiness with him as I'd have with any other man. It is only a few days since we met, but I've spent many hours enjoying his company in that time. Having a life of my own and children is so important to me. And I want a man who appreciates that I'm dedicated to my art. He'll provide for all of my comforts; he is rich and titled, and our children will be well placed in the world. But I need you to come with me, Bertha. That will truly be my one condition of acceptance."

Bertha nodded. "If it's really what you want, I will accompany you, but your title, or your husband's, or his mother's will not intimidate me. I'll say my piece when and if it's needed."

"I would ask for nothing less."

"Then you'll accept his proposal?" her mother asked, still looking a little bemused and worried.

"Yes, I will," Eleanor replied with a smile.

"Oh my, Eleanor. Oh, my goodness. I'll miss you so much." Mother fluttered her fan violently. "But are you sure, my darling? You hardly know him. And we must consider Godfrey's view; he's head of the family now, Eleanor. He'll need to be consulted at the very least."

Eleanor walked over to her mother, knelt on the floor by her chair, and took her chilly hand. "Godfrey will be happy to see his youngest sister happily settled, Mother. And I'm sure I'm making a good move, as much as anyone can be sure about these things. If I'd gone to London for the Season, it would be much the same with any prospective husband. Miss Austen may write about love matches, but most marriages are arranged for mutual needs and the comfort of both people. I'm comfortable with this path, Mother, I really am."

Mama looked at Eleanor's face, then nodded. "Then I'll write to Godfrey and tell him to approve. And I must say, it'll be a blessing for me too. Godfrey's been pushing me to move to his dower house in Kent for several years. He plans to lease, or possibly sell, Brampton Manor, you see. But I've held off while you were at home. It will be nice to live in a smaller house with Godfrey, Catherine, and the children on hand if I need anything."

"I know, Mother. It'll be for the best for everyone."

"Oh my, I'll have a baroness and a viscountess in the family. I can hardly believe it."

Chapter Four

June 14th 1820

Eleanor grimaced and squeezed the hand of the nurse. The poor woman sighed heavily but said nothing. Eleanor presumed she was used to being abused by patients.

It was horrible experiencing some strange man's fingers poking and prodding her stomach, then entering her body and poking and prodding in there. Tears sprang to her eyes, and she felt like sobbing, but that wouldn't do at all. The examination seemed to take forever. Eleanor forced her mind to contemplate her unfinished portrait of Elizabeth Riley. It was going well, despite that lady's rather mannish face and propensity to wear the most unflattering gowns imaginable. Eleanor had asked that Lady Riley come for the sitting this afternoon in the gown she'd worn at the Thornton's ball. The cerulean blue gown suited Lizzy's skin tones, and she could then dress her subject up in lace and feathers to detract from the woman's long face and small eyes. She was rather looking forward to this afternoon's session and making the unattractive, but very humorous, Lady Riley look her best in a portrait for her besotted husband's birthday.

The doctor moved and pushed further into Eleanor's body. She gasped and would have kicked the man, but her ankles were securely enclosed in what could only be described as stirrups.

"Sorry, Lady Heyer, we're almost done."

Eleanor refused to answer, but silently cursed her husband for her current embarrassment and discomfort. Julian had sprung the appointment on her just this morning, over breakfast, no doubt thinking that any earlier warning would have allowed her to find an excuse not to attend. "He's highly recommended, Eleanor. He studied in Scotland and is an associate of Dr Baillie, who cared for the Countess of Richmond."

Eleanor was fairly certain that Dr Baillie was one of the doctors involved in the sad death in childbirth of Princess Charlotte. That tragedy had happened several years ago, but it remained the topic of hushed conversations among ladies and considerable anger in the higher ranks of the aristocracy. But there was no point arguing with Julian. He was convinced that the medical profession could find the reason that, after two years of marriage, there were no children, not even a sad miscarriage. Julian was convinced it was her fault. He'd decided she was barren and must be subjected to this mortification.

None of her sisters or sisters-in-law ever needed the services of a dubious accoucheur. They'd all been content with the services of a good midwife and they now had twenty-two healthy children between them.

The doctor withdrew his fingers and washed his hands. Eleanor thought it a pity he had not done so before the examination. "You may get dressed now, Lady Heyer. The nurse will assist you and I'll discuss my findings with you and Lord Heyer in my office." At least this doctor deigned to include Eleanor in the discussion about her intimate health. The last one hadn't.

The doctor's office looked out over a small park, and sunshine streamed in through the window, softening the dark wood panels on the wall. Eleanor took a seat in front of the mahogany desk. She refused to look at Julian and glowered at the doctor instead, expecting another useless diagnosis and admonitions to improve her diet, light exercise and no horse riding. It was the standard advice. Good God, she'd heard it from the last three doctors, and all the light exercise and fresh fruits and vegetables made no difference despite two years passing.

"My Lord, Lady Heyer." The doctor addressed them both, but he only looked at her husband. "My examination has revealed no physical reason conception hasn't occurred. Lady Heyer presents as a healthy young woman and, as you have informed me, you are engaging in regular marital relations. Lady Heyer has confirmed what you told me in your letter, that her courses are regular and present with no unusual symptoms."

Julian nodded encouragingly. Eleanor looked out the window at the lemon green leaves of the elm trees swaying in the spring breeze.

"However, sir," the doctor continued, "as you've queried in your letter, there is the matter of your wife's pastime and the inherent dangers of working with strong chemicals. I tend to agree that such a dangerous pursuit could be detrimental to a young woman's health and could very well adversely affect fertility."

Eleanor lost interest in the pleasant view as the doctor's words sank in. "Dangerous? What do you mean, dangerous? I'm an artist, sir, and art is surely no more dangerous a pastime than knitting."

"I beg to differ, ma'am. Research shows that watercolours are of little consequence, but oil painting requires the use of thinners, oils, and pigments, many of which are full of poisons. I know that some colour pigments are poisonous and most paints contain lead and mercury. A learned friend has treated some artists for lead poisoning. He has speculated that this is the reason ladies should not be allowed to paint with oils, as they're just too dangerous and can have adverse effects on the weaker body systems of women, including the reproductive organs."

"That's such nonsense. I have many friends who are artists and I've never heard of any such a thing."

"Ma'am, I can only report on my research. You've been barren for over two years, and I believe you were painting with oils for a few years prior to your marriage. It's my informed opinion that your inability to conceive is most likely due to you being poisoned by the oil paints, particularly those that contain lead. Your husband says you use oil paints daily. My advice, Lady Heyer, is that you stop painting with oils immediately."

Eleanor stood up and walked to look out the window. Poisoned by own her paints. It was ridiculous, wasn't it? It was all too much to take in. But it explained the inexplicable. She had no children after more than two years of marriage. Oh, she needed to ponder this possibility. She needed more information, and she needed it now.

"But, sir." She turned with a rustle of silk from the window. "I find it hard to comprehend. Why, I... I met with Mrs Mary Moser just last year, before her sad passing, and she'd painted all her life with no ill effects."

"I cannot answer that, ma'am. Did the lady have children?"

"No, not that I recall, she married later in life."

The doctor shrugged annoyingly; his argument confirmed.

"Well, what about men? I've met many artists at the Royal Academy. They're healthy and have achieved elder status with no ill effects from their profession. And many have families and children."

The doctor looked over at Julian with a quirked eyebrow before returning his attention to Eleanor. His voice became oily. "Madam, men are of a more robust constitution. They're less likely to be affected by poisonous substances. But I believe some artists succumb to the effects of lead poisoning. I've read up on this subject for this consultation. There is a condition called Painter's colic, which can manifest itself in madness. Michelangelo and Caravaggio succumbed to health problems because of their art. No, madam, the condition exists, and my recommendation is that your husband stops you painting and takes you to the country for rest, and that you, madam, ensure you get a wholesome diet and gentle exercise. I have considered that sea bathing or the waters of Bath may be proven beneficial. That is my recommendation."

It was the fact that Julian looked relieved and rose from his chair that made Eleanor return to her own seat, straighten her spine, and glower at the physician. "Thank you, doctor. I'll consider your recommendations. But what of my husband? He was previously married for six years, yet has no children. I have no children after a further two years. Is it possible that he has the problem?"

The doctor — oh, she wished she could remember his name — bristled, and she saw her husband's thigh muscle actually tense, as if he was managing a rebellious horse. There would be another argument after this session, but, by God, she'd asked the question too many times in the silence of her own thoughts to let the opportunity go by now.

"Madam, in all cases of infertility, inevitably, the fault is found in the female. It's only where there's an obvious injury that a man cannot father children. Your husband has informed me that his first wife was sickly in constitution, endured several miscarriages, and then died in childbirth, so his fertility is not in question. No, I've no doubt that the problem lies with your unhealthy pastime and that, with time and the recommendations I've made, the poison's effects will be mitigated and you will have children. Now, good day, madam. I have another patient."

The ride back to their London house was uncomfortably silent. Julian looked pale and stared at the plush walls of the carriage. Eleanor looked out her window, watching the busy streets and elegant houses go by without registering what she was seeing, or even what she was thinking. A knot of misery tied up her stomach and radiated into her groin. Had she made a fool of herself with her impertinent questioning? Made a fool of her poor husband? He'd changed so much in the past year. He was tense and surly much of the time, drank more, and spent much of his time while in London at his club. They'd developed two separate lives, coming together only for shared evening entertainments and the duties of the marital bed. The relentless duties of the marital bed. Eleanor could not remember when she'd last heard Julian laugh.

The Heyer townhouse was on Half Moon Street. One of the newer buildings it was narrow and tall. It comprised four stories plus an attic for servants, with the kitchen and storage in the basement. She loved the little house, loved London, its parks and galleries, its palaces and grand buildings.

They'd been happy that first summer. Julian proved to be attentive, kind, and funny. Even his mother thawed a little after their small wedding in Kent and presented Eleanor at court before graciously retiring to her manor in Surrey. They'd seen very little of the Dowager Viscountess Heyer since then.

They'd waltzed at Almack's, visited Vauxhall Gardens for a masquerade, dined with Julian's small but welcoming group of friends, and settled into London life. It was a disappointment for Eleanor that the Royal Academy did not admit ladies to their ranks, but she enjoyed meeting with James Green again, and he quickly introduced her to other artists.

Also, in that lovely honeymoon year Julian informed her he'd bought Brampton Manor. "I have the estate in Devon, Eleanor, but the house is closed, so it doesn't serve as a country residence for a family. The Brampton estate and house are a good size, and the land is arable and will provide good pasture for my horse breeding business. And I thought you'd like to keep your childhood home in the area you love so well. I hope you're pleased."

Eleanor had squealed with delight and thrown herself into her husband's arms, and they'd ended up in bed in the middle of the afternoon. It was a relief to know she could return regularly to her beloved Dales and the wonderful scenery. She also knew her mama would be so pleased that her home was to remain in the family and that they would retain the servants and estate workers when she moved down to Kent. It was a delightful surprise, and Eleanor felt blessed in her choice of husband.

But her greatest joy occurred when Julian took her for "a surprise" for her eighteenth birthday. He'd walked her around to a newly built mews in Bruton Place and produced a key with an enormous bow tied around it. The building was a carriage house with attached stables, and Eleanor initially guessed she would be given a new horse, or even a carriage and pair. But Julian had led her around to a steep but serviceable outside staircase. The room at the top was huge, flooded by light from the dormer windows. "Your new studio, madam." He laughed and bowed with a mocking flourish. In that moment Eleanor had fallen in love with her husband.

Lady Heyer's studio became the hub of London's art set. It was the place to be seen. Julian provided a maid and a footman who ensured her guests were served the finest wine and food. Eleanor purchased chairs and sofas in bold colours and placed them around the large fireplace. The walls were hung with gifts of art, and sculptures sat in corners. Eleanor painted there, entertained there, and, when in London, spent the best part of every afternoon working in its welcoming space. And now it would be closed, if Julian had his way. Eleanor felt her heart would break.

The silence of the carriage ride continued over luncheon. Eleanor had no intention of disagreeing with her husband in front of the servants, though she knew many couples had no such qualms. The silence gave her an opportunity to work through the devastating information from the doctor. It was in the privacy of the parlour over tea that Eleanor voiced her plan.

"Julian, I'll be at the studio this afternoon, finishing Lady Riley's portrait. I'll write to my other clientele to say we will leave for the country for health reasons. Could you make the arrangements for us, or just me and Bertha, to travel to Derby sometime next week. We can let out the mews. I'll ask around to see if anyone wishes to lease the space. I trust these arrangements are suitable for you." Eleanor spoke calmly with effort. She really wanted nothing else but to burst into tears.

Julian looked surprised, as if he had expected more arguments. "Madam, there's no need to rush; we can finish the Season in London. We'd planned to return to Brampton Manor next month."

"No, Julian." Eleanor spoke firmly. "I'd prefer to leave London as soon as possible. I will close the studio when I've finished Lizzie's portrait. It's what I want, sir."

"I'm sorry, Eleanor, truly sorry."

"No, Julian, it's I who must apologise, it is my fault we have no children, though my error occurred in total ignorance." She took a breath. "You know I want children, Julian, as much as you do, if not more. The doctor has given us a reason we've not been blessed. I'll heed his advice and do all in my power to start a family."

He rose and came around and kissed her, and there was such relief in his face that Eleanor couldn't hold back her tears. He pulled her close and held her gently until the sobs quietened and she dabbed at her eyes with his handkerchief. "It won't be forever, Eleanor."

"No, it won't be forever.

March 5th 1823

Eleanor woke alone in the huge four-poster bed. The air was freezing, as only an early Scottish spring could be freezing. It was first light, and the maid had not yet arrived with her tea or to build up the fire in the grate.

The pillow beside her still had the imprint of Julian's head, but he hadn't stayed. She missed waking up with him in the same bed, but that had rarely happened in the past three years. He had been drunk last night: a habitual state of affairs since arriving in Scotland in October. He'd been impatient and rough. There was none of the pleasuring and wild delight of their honeymoon year, and now she felt the cramps low in her abdomen, a sure sign that she'd be bleeding again. The monotonous regularity of failure. It was three years since she'd fled London and her courses had never altered. Eleanor bit her lip to stop herself from crying. Julian hated it when she cried.

She arrived late to breakfast, always tired and wretched when she was bleeding. Julian was reading the paper with a large cup of coffee. He took one look at her and his face fell into a stony mask. He was well aware of her cycles, and the tell-tale signs wouldn't have escaped his notice. Eleanor took some toast, and the footman poured tea.

"Julian, I would like to go south earlier this year," Eleanor said. Anything to remove herself from the freezing cold of this winter season and the cold discomfort of her marriage. She missed Bertha.

Julian sighed and put down the paper. "I'm not sure. I'll think about it, Eleanor." His voice broached no further discussion, and Eleanor knew better than to push. Julian was wrapped up tightly in his own misery, and today could trigger an unravelling, which would cause a horrible row and tension for the next week. The last time she had her courses, Julian got drunk every day for the week and became more and more insulting and cold. At one point, she feared he would hit her, but at the last moment, he'd walked away. It left her shaken.

Eleanor went back to bed. She felt more despondent than tired, but there was little to do in the large, cold house to provide distraction. Bertha remained at Brampton Manor; she said that the bitter cold of Scotland made her bones ache. In past years, and better weather, Eleanor had adored Scotland, loved the walks, the snow on the mountains, the light and shadows. Julian hunted, and Eleanor walked and sketched through the day and painted the hauntingly beautiful scenery in watercolours and inks later in the afternoon and into the evenings. They dined with neighbours once a week, and entertained in their turn. They even attended the ball at the New Year — Hogmanay, as it was named — and Eleanor enjoyed learning the jigs and country dances.

This year the weather was colder than usual and very wet, and the weeks passed by in tedious isolation. Eleanor found herself unusually irritable and despondent. Her thoughts revolved more and more on their childlessness. It was getting harder and harder to console herself that she would get with child. She blamed herself. She'd poisoned herself and ruined their lives. Guilt was a heavy burden, and she sensed her life and love slipping away. She needed Bertha's acerbic wit, some sunshine, good company, and something, anything, different to lift her spirits.

It was several days later that Eleanor received a small pile of mail. Her mama and sisters wrote long, descriptive letters detailing their everyday lives. They sent recipes, synopses of books they had read, what bloomed in the garden, and who had visited whom. Eleanor read with delight and sadness their accounts of the children's activities, and cried when she learned that another of her sisters or brothers had increased their family yet again. She and Julian visited her family assiduously for the first year of their marriage. They didn't visit at all now, and Eleanor didn't push Julian. Seeing her large family made them both more aware of the absence of children in their own lives.

Julian came into the parlour with a letter in his hand. She knew he'd spent much of his morning answering correspondence relating to the business of the estates. It was unusual for him to receive a personal letter.

"I've had a letter from Mother. She's asked that we visit her in Surrey as soon as possible. Apparently, my brother Robert is unwell and has come to stay with her. She fears he's more unwell than he lets on. She doesn't say so, but I sense she's struggling with him; he's always been a difficult man."

"Oh, yes, of course, Julian." Eleanor looked up with a frown. "He's back in England then?"

"Yes, he returned from Spain last November, but he's always suffered with his lungs in England and he found that his rooms in London were not conducive to recovery. He visited Mother at Christmas and has been there ever since. She sounds quite worried, which is unusual for her. I believe you'll get your wish and we will travel south early this year."

Robert was Julian's twin brother: a twin brother she'd never met. Julian said Robert had lived abroad for many years and corresponded irregularly. He was unwed, and Eleanor sensed that his family disapproved of him, but she'd never been appraised of the particulars. Maybe she'd learn something of the family from Robert, because Julian certainly proved to be reticent on the matter. It was another thing that disappointed

Eleanor in her marriage: Julian was secretive, and had proved to be an expert at prevarication when it came to discussing his family history. He would become defensive and angry whenever she asked about his childhood or his family. It was just another topic that Eleanor learned to avoid in order to maintain at least a semblance of conviviality in their marriage.

"When do you wish to depart, Julian? I'll need to inform Mrs Cullen."

"Is Friday too soon? We can stop at Brampton Manor on the way to Surrey to break the journey, and Miss Smith can join us there, if she's so inclined."

Eleanor smiled. She was missing Bertha, and it would be good to see the Andersons again. She looked outside and grimaced. It was raining again. It wouldn't be a comfortable passage south, but good company and sunshine would be a welcome escape from this sombre winter.

April 2nd 1823

The Dowager Viscountess Heyer sat as straight-backed and stern as usual, but Eleanor saw that her face was grey and drawn. She had dark circles beneath her eyes, and her mouth was set in a thin line. She greeted Julian with an unexpected rush of affection, and then turned more coolly to Eleanor.

"Welcome, my dear. You're looking a little peaky. Are you well?"

Eleanor recognised the euphemism, and the underlying censure, for not having produced an heir. "I thank you, ma'am, I'm well, but a little tired from the journey."

The Dowager Viscountess nodded and turned her attention to Bertha. "Miss Smith."

Bertha gave a cursory curtsey. "My lady."

Ashfield Manor was near the little village of Ash, in the far west of the county of Surrey. It was a small house set in pretty woodlands and at the top of a gentle rise. The front of the two-storey house presented as modest, but two wings stretched out at the back, adding several extra rooms. The gardens at the rear were extensive and led to rolling hills and meadows, which were accessed by a delightful small wood. Eleanor had enjoyed exploring the countryside on previous visits and had presented Lady Heyer with two paintings of local views which were well received.

After a stilted afternoon tea at which Lady Heyer had spoken of the weather, the state of the roads, and asked Julian about his hunting in Scotland, Eleanor decided she was unlikely to learn anything interesting about her sickly brother-in-law from his mother and brother over tea. She glanced at Bertha, who nodded conspiratorially. They would need to learn about Robert from the servants.

"Ma'am, with your permission, I'll withdraw. A hot bath and a lie down will see me right for dinner."

"Yes, of course, Eleanor." Lady Heyer looked relieved. No doubt it allowed her time with Julian to provide a private update on the health of his brother and to work out just how much Eleanor was to be informed of Robert's history and illness. Lady Heyer could be every bit as circumspect as her son, with family secrets.

Bertha didn't ask permission but rose, curtseyed, and followed Eleanor out the door. She raised an eyebrow and winked. "Looks like I'll have to interrogate the servants again."

Eleanor chuckled. Thank goodness Bertha came with her to mitigate the coldness of her marriage.

Eleanor returned to her usual suite of rooms and was extremely grateful that a hot bath was in front of the fire. A new maid curtseyed as she entered the room, and she proved to be efficient at stoking the fire regularly and replenishing the hot water. Eleanor relaxed in the hot bath and had the maid wash her hair, rinsing away the dust and tiredness of the journey. Mary, her own maid, unpacked her trunk, laid out her favourite lavender evening dress, and put away her other gowns. It always fascinated Eleanor to watch Mary pack and unpack her trunks. The pretty, young, red-haired maid had a knack of folding and placing clothes so well that when they were removed from a trunk, they looked freshly ironed. Mary had been with her since her first year of marriage. She proved to be discreet, efficient, and kind, and in the situation of a troubled marriage, those were desirable attributes indeed.

Bertha knocked and entered long before Eleanor finished drying her hair.

"You're looking better, Bertha. Did you have a bath too?"

"I did indeed, and it was glorious. Lady Heyer is most accommodating to her guests."

It was a running joke between them. Bertha, like many governesses and companions, was a gentlewoman, but of no means or title. Many of Eleanor's acquaintances and friends seemed unsure what to do with Bertha: pack her off to the servant's hall or treat her as a guest. It often provided the hostess with a dilemma and gave much amusement to Eleanor and Bertha as they compared the comforts provided to each other by their hosts. Bertha was sometimes placed in the attic with the maids, while at other establishments she was given a small guest bedroom with a maid of her own. To her credit, Lady Heyer always provided Bertha with her own room and the status of a guest. Eleanor sometimes wondered if this kindness had more to do with stopping Bertha's access to the gossip in the kitchens.

Bertha looked quite flushed, and Eleanor guessed she might have some information to share. She smiled, remembering Bertha had been severe about listening to servants' gossip as a governess, but as a friend she was much more inclined to heed downstairs chatter.

"Mary, take a break and have some tea downstairs. I'll manage with Bertha for half an hour."

Bertha only waited until the bedroom door was closed before whispering, "It's syphilis! Robert Heyer has got syphilis, and he's dying of it."

"Oh, my goodness, Bertha. That's terrible. Poor Lady Heyer. No wonder she looks so strained."

"And why she was less than forthcoming in her letters. You know about syphilis, don't you, Eleanor?"

"Of course. It's been mentioned by some of the younger artists, but I know little of the details."

"And you shouldn't. It's a horrible illness that's often the result of blatant immorality. It's not usually a subject of discussion among well-brought-up young women, but it's rampant in the baser elements of society." Bertha spoke with pursed lips. "The contagion is spread through carnal behaviours.

It can take many years to become life threatening, but apparently your brother-in-law is severely ill and likely to die soon."

Eleanor was unsure what to say. She had no particular emotional attachment to Julian's brother. She knew very little about him. But if it had been one of her own brothers, she would have been devastated.

"Poor Julian. It must upset him. It's his twin brother, and even if Robert has been estranged from the family for years, they must've been close once."

"Not according to the maid assigned to me." Bertha came and sat by Eleanor near the fire. "Sweet girl, young but with sharp ears and a proclivity for gossip. From what she's heard, Robert Heyer was a nasty tyrant as a child and made Julian's life a misery. Robert apparently grew up very wild and, as a young man, settled into a life of depravity and drunkenness. My little maid said that some fifteen years ago, a serious incident occurred at Heyer House in Devon, and that forced Master Robert to remove himself overseas. As far as she knows, he's been abroad ever since."

Eleanor experienced a moment of panic. It was bad enough that Julian's brother was unwell, but such an embarrassing illness would make her husband's inclination to secrecy even more pronounced. "Oh, Bertha, I don't know what to believe or what to do. What should I say to Lady Heyer and Julian? It's a family matter, surely. I must pass on condolences as a matter of course, but what do I say to them that will be of comfort?"

Bertha leaned forward and took her hand. "Say as little as possible, Eleanor. Be polite and circumspect and keep your ears open. I've long considered that your husband has kept you in the dark for far too long. This family is full of secretes and recriminations and it's making you despondent."

"What do you mean?"

"Eleanor, for the past five years, I've seen you become more and more unhappy. You've withdrawn, lost your love of life. You've even stopped painting, and I know you take all the blame for you not having children. It has to stop, Eleanor. Something has to change or I fear for your health."

Eleanor shuddered and nodded in agreement. Bertha, as usual, recognised her mood and her situation. "But what can I do Bertha?"

"What have I always said about what to do when you're uncertain in difficult circumstances?" Bertha's voice took on the quality of the challenging governess.

"If in doubt, get more information." Eleanor parroted a well-learned lesson.

"Exactly, and we know next to nothing about Julian and his family. You've never talked about his brother, and I suspect your husband never talks about him or his childhood for a reason. Think, Eleanor. Why is he so guarded? The Heyer family has secrets that may bear on your chances of having a family."

Eleanor nodded. "I think that Julian experienced an unhappy childhood, but I've always respected his privacy. I judged it might be too painful for him to talk about. But what has his childhood got to do with us having a family?"

Lowering her voice, Bertha leaned forward, even though there was no-one else in the room. "Robert, according to the gossip, has never married and has no children, not even illegitimate children. One would suspect that, with his history, he'd have some natural children somewhere. I've understood that the younger brother, Christopher, is unmarried and childless too, yet he must be all of thirty by now. Julian blames you for the childless state of your marriage, but when you examine the history of this family, it's significant that none of the Heyer men have fathered children. Even the mother only managed two pregnancies: twins and then the youngest son, five whole years later," Bertha stated flatly.

Eleanor blinked and swallowed. The thought that their infertility might be Julian's problem had been squashed by the doctor in London three years ago. But that was three years ago, and she remained barren despite doing everything the doctor recommended.

And Julian was adamant it was all her fault, and was pitiless in his belief. Eleanor suddenly realised it was her guilt that made her accept fault. That doctor had said it was her oil painting that caused her to be barren, that she'd poisoned herself, and she'd childishly accepted his assertion.

Holding her hands out to the fire Eleanor felt her temper rise for the first time in years. She'd been angry with the doctor for that opinion, but then had meekly succumbed to Julian's wishes. She had closed her studio, lost her friends, lost her art, and for what? Three years of isolation and despondency and still no children. And now there was a possibility that infertility was a factor in the Heyer family. She'd been kept deliberately in the dark and it needed to change.

"You might be right, Bertha. I need to find out more about this family. But how? Julian is hardly likely to be forthcoming."

"Then you must talk to his mother. Talk to his brother, if you have to, while you have the chance. I'll try to get more information from the servants. If you have some information, you can confront Julian and get to the truth."

Mary's return prevented further discussion, but for the first time in years, Eleanor's spirits lifted. She spent the next hour getting ready for dinner, and her mind whirled with a thousand questions, none of which were going to be easy to ask. But she was determined she would stop being so hopelessly compliant, and that was a good first step.

Dinner was held in the breakfast room: an informal setting for just Lady Heyer, Julian, and herself. Eleanor was apprised by Lady Heyer that "Miss Smith sent her apologies. She asked that she take her meal in her room as she was tired after the journey."

Eleanor thought it more likely Bertha was taking her meal in the servants' dining room. "And Robert, will he not be joining us? I'm so looking forward to meeting him."

Lady Heyer glanced at Julian and then put down her cutlery. "Robert keeps to his room. He's far too unwell to come down to meals."

"Truly, I'm sorry to hear that. I'll endeavour to visit him tomorrow then. Is he better able to receive visitors in the mornings or the afternoons?" Eleanor asked.

Julian frowned, set down his knife, and snapped, "Eleanor, Robert's very unwell. He's not well enough to have any visitors."

Usually, Eleanor would have murmured something inane and complied with her husband's direction, but she was not so inclined anymore. She straightened her spine and turned to look her husband in the eye.

"Then he must be very ill indeed. Pray, what is his illness? What is his prognosis?"

Julian looked so surprised at her questions, she nearly laughed. It took her husband half a minute to respond. "I don't consider my brother's illness is any of your concern, Eleanor."

Eleanor stared at her husband, then found a coldness of tone she'd never realised she could achieve. "I beg to differ, Julian. Robert is your brother, and thus my brother too. He's family. I would appreciate being able to visit my brother, and I believe I can comprehend the nature of his illness and not be excluded from providing any meaningful support to you and your mother."

Lady Caroline nodded when Eleanor glanced in her direction. It was a surprising acknowledgement, and it gave her hope of support. Julian went quite red in the face and frowned at them both. "Eleanor, I don't want you bothering Robert. His illness is such that he is disfigured and in pain. His mind wanders, and he's often heavily sedated. I don't consider it's appropriate for you to visit."

Eleanor snapped, "I've been informed that he has syphilis and is dying. I wanted this to be confirmed by my family. I'm not a child to be protected, Julian. I'm a part of this family too."

Julian glared at her, and she glared back.

Lady Heyer rose from the table and said, "I believe Eleanor is right, Julian. The truth is better coming from us, rather than from servants' gossip. It'd be wise for you to discuss this together in the privacy of your room. I'm tired and will see you both in the morning."

Julian didn't come to her bed until near on midnight. He had been drinking and clearly wanted nothing more than a quick coupling and a return to his own bed. Eleanor knew that Julian, in a temper, could be cuttingly cold and dismissive. He'd never hit her, but she found herself shaking at times. He exuded determination and power and expected submission. In the past, Eleanor would have succumbed, but her talk with Bertha, and the unexpected support from Lady Heyer, gave her courage.

"Julian, I want to see Robert. I can go with you or your mother, but I want to be supportive and offer prayer and solace if I can," she whispered as he left the bed.

Julian was putting on his robe, but he turned back to look at her with a sneer. "You. You want to offer solicitude. I would think, madam, you have provided me with enough grief that you would have little regard for the additional burden of a brother whom I've never liked. He's dying. I'm here to discharge my duties as head of the family and nothing more. I believe, madam, your interest is more about prying and avoidance of your own sad state of affairs than it is about any concern you harbour for me or my mother."

"That's untrue, Julian. I want to be a part of this family, but you always reject any support I offer." Eleanor felt tears welling; she swallowed them hard. "But I will offer my support to your mother, and I will see Robert. I'm a member of this family and I'll not be treated as a child, not anymore, Julian."

For a moment, Eleanor feared she'd gone too far, too fast. Julian's face drained of all colour, all emotion. His eyes narrowed and flashed a frozen, dangerous despair. His hands clenched into fists, but then he seemed to gather some rationality. He turned abruptly and stormed to the door, shouting over his shoulder.

"My brother was always a monster, Eleanor; he now looks like a monster. I wanted to protect you, but if you insist on subjecting yourself to my brother's malicious nature, then visit him by all means, but do not reproach me when you're distressed by the encounter."

At the door, he turned and glared directly at Eleanor with a hatred she'd never encountered before. Then he seemed to contain his emotions, drew himself up, and added, "You've been warned, madam."

Chapter Five

April 3rd 1823

Eleanor woke with a headache the following morning. She lay in bed long past the time she usually rose. When she rang for the maid, the sun was high in the sky. Sipping hot chocolate, she regretted her tardiness and wished she had gone for a brisk walk in the early morning sunshine to clear her head.

A note from her mother-in-law arrived with the chocolate, requesting Eleanor to meet her for morning tea at eleven in the parlour. She expected it would be an interrogation about her infertility. The headache got worse; it was much easier to stay in bed. It was close to ten o'clock by the time she got dressed. She decided to forgo breakfast and take a walk instead. The chocolate would suffice, and she hoped fresh air and exercise would relieve her sore head and set her up for an unpleasant meeting.

Eleanor felt a little better when she entered the parlour, but almost dropped her shawl when she saw Bertha already seated by the fire, nursing a cup of tea. "Good morning, Mother. Good morning, Bertha."

"Ah, there you are Eleanor." Lady Heyer looked pale but sat tall and spoke with her usual snap to the footman. "That'll be all, Wilson. We'll ring if we need anything else."

Eleanor took the chair opposite her mother-in-law and smiled as Bertha leaned forward and poured her a cup of tea handing over the cup with an encouraging smile. Eleanor helped herself to a slice of cake and waited for her mother-in-law to start the conversation. She would not make this interrogation easy.

"I've wanted to talk to you for some time, Eleanor, but Julian has thwarted my efforts at family gatherings for some years. Robert's illness is distressing, but I'm thankful for this opportunity to converse with you in private." Lady Heyer glanced at Bertha and frowned. "I've included Miss Smith. I'm sure that she can be discreet, and I'd prefer she hear what I have to say from me and not from the servants, so here she is."

Bertha had the grace to blush.

Lady Heyer sat back and sipped her tea; a frown left a deep crease in her brow.

"As you are no doubt aware, Eleanor, I opposed your marriage with Julian. I considered, at the time, that you were far too young. You presented as a lonely child enticed by the notion of marriage and the bright lights of London. On reflection, I don't think I was wrong. I've watched with misgivings as you have endured a difficult, childless marriage for the past five years. It concerned me that Julian would... No, that will not do." Lady Heyer put down her cup with a rattle and stared at Eleanor. "I must go back earlier than that. I must explain the entire history, including my own."

Eleanor could not have been more surprised by both the topic and the tone of the conversation. She tensed with anticipation and nodded in agreement at this unexpected revelation.

Lady Heyer looked into the fire. "I was married to my husband at just eighteen. Looking back, I now realise my parents pressured me to marry, told me it would be a good match and that I'd gain a title, that I would be happy. Like you, I was far too inexperienced and naïve. I should have refused, but I was a child and they had brought me up to be obedient. Julian's father, Eugene, wasn't much older than I. He was a handsome man, but he drank heavily, enjoyed the company of his friends, and left me alone in the country for much of the year. I became unhappy in my marriage, lonely, and I yearned for a family. I didn't conceive for nearly six years."

Eleanor took in a shaky breath and received a sharp look from her mother-in-law. "Suffice to say, Eleanor, I understand what you're going through."

Eleanor bowed her head, unable to do anything else.

"My husband proved to be a selfish man and, of course, blamed me for our childlessness. He became cruel in his demands and, at times, violent. He threatened divorce, or annulment, even though he knew it would ruin my reputation and relegate me to the status of a barren divorcee. It was a miracle that I finally conceived. My relationship with Julian's father improved considerably after the birth of the twins. Having produced an heir, and having a second son, my husband spent even more of his time away in London or Scotland. But I had children to care for and found true happiness in being a mother."

Lady Heyer paused, as if she needed to give herself permission to continue with her painful history. "Julian was a joy as a child. He slept well, had a robust appetite, and was active and happy. Robert was very different. As a baby, he screamed much of the night. He appeared sickly and refused food. They

101

deemed colic caused his problems, but as he grew, it became apparent there was more wrong than a stomach disorder. He was late crawling and walking, never said a word until he reached the age of three. And he had such a temper. He would bite his nurse, and me, throw toys. He hated loud noises, and going outside would cause terrible distress for him. It was sad for him; he was a difficult child to love."

"As he grew, he improved. He loved the water, and we spent most of the year at Heyer House in Devon, which is on the coast. Both boys loved to be in the sea. He and Julian learned to swim, and as they played together in the water, Robert started to talk and even smile. He still had a temper, but he learned to master his moods. After five years, I hoped he could be happy and lead a normal life."

Lady Heyer paused and looked as if her thoughts took her far away. "The boys were five, and I hadn't been away from them for many years. I had word from my mother that my father was dying and she couldn't manage because of her own illness. She begged me to return home, to this house, and help her see to his comfort. They died within three months of each other. My mother left me this estate, as it had been her marriage settlement and was not entailed to my late father's assets. It was a generous gift and I've always appreciated having my own home. My husband attended the funeral. He and I went to London afterwards, spent time together. It was with great joy that I found out I was expecting another child."

Eleanor would have liked to ask if her mother-in-law had other siblings, or if she had been an only child as well. It was another reminder that Bertha was right: she really knew nothing about the Heyer family history. Eleanor cringed inside at her cowardice, but she appreciated the history now and would not interrupt its telling.

"I returned to Devon and had Christopher. Again, I was blessed with an amiable child. Julian appeared entranced with his baby brother, but Robert... I believe, was jealous, and he either ignored Christopher or would pinch or hit him to make him cry. We had to ensure someone was with the baby at all times.

"Julian had changed while I was away. He'd become more and more unhappy. Robert proved to be sly and destructive. Julian's toys would disappear or get broken. A kitten in the stables, that Julian loved, died mysteriously. Julian and Robert got into terrible fights and both often ended up scratched and bruised. And Robert would deny any responsibility, always blaming Julian for the misdeeds and causing the brawls."

Lady Heyer grimaced, and a tear trickled down her cheek. "It was a testing time, but I tried hard to help both Julian and Robert, but I just... just couldn't stop Robert's destructive nature. I tried to love him, but nothing worked, so I gave up. When I look back, I realise I should've done more with him, helped him, but I had a new baby and I left it to the governess and servants to deal with the older boys. It's something I regret to this day."

Eleanor leaned forward and took Lady Heyer's icy hand. "Mother, it's a hard story. Are you sure you can continue?"

"Oh, don't stop me now. I would have you know the truth, and it's better done in one difficult telling than for me to distress us both with dribs and drabs. No, I can continue."

Bertha, of a more practical nature, rose and returned with a glass of sherry, which earned her a rare genuine laugh from Lady Heyer, who took a large swig before setting the glass on the table.

"I became desperate about Robert's difficult behaviours and wrote to beg my husband's attendance. Like many men, he had no genuine interest in raising children, he considered it women's work. He was next to hopeless, too. When he eventually came to Devon, he thrashed Robert and berated him for being a fool, but he thrashed Julian too, claiming he was weak and pathetic for not standing up to his brother. He then engaged a brute of a man as a tutor. He adhered to the philosophy of 'spare the rod and spoil the child.' That finally cowed Robert enough to understand he needed to behave, or at least he became less inclined to be openly defiant. Julian, my lovely, happy, sensitive boy, was profoundly unhappy, but he stood up to Robert more and found he could escape by riding and hunting. It was a harsh lesson to learn, but one perhaps he needed. It made Julian stronger.

Eleanor nodded; this history explained so much about her husband: his coldness and withdrawal when overwrought, yet his sweet, sunny nature when his life was without pressure.

Lady Heyer took a second swig of wine and then another, finishing the glass. "I struggled on alone for another three years with no further help from Eugene. It was when Christopher was five that I finally had to act." She sniffed and took out her handkerchief. "Early one morning, when it was just light, I heard shouts coming from the nursery. I ran up the stairs to find the room full of servants and my poor little Christopher unconscious in his cot. The nurse had blood running from her nose as she tried to revive my little boy. She had heard some noise and had entered to find Robert leaning over Christopher, pressing a pillow over his face. Robert had to be dragged away from his brother and he hit and bit the nurse repeatedly. She, good woman, fought him off and he ran away when a footman appeared. That nurse picked up Christopher, blew into his mouth, and rocked him until he groaned. Her actions saved Christopher's life. The doctor came but found that, thank God, Christopher had suffered no lasting harm, though he had nightmares and was terrified of the dark for years after the experience."

Lady Caroline brought her hand to her mouth and appeared to struggle to calm her emotions. She continued, though her voice shook. "They found Robert in the stables. He had stabbed Julian's new pony to death and was covered in blood."

Lady Heyer started to take gasps of air. Eleanor found she was crying herself. Bertha walked over to the cabinet and returned with three large glasses of sherry, which they consumed in silence. Lady Heyer rose and walked around the room. She appeared to get her emotions into order, then returned to her chair and took a deep breath.

"I sent for my husband from London. Our local doctor was a good and sensible man. He sedated Robert and recommended an asylum. He deemed Robert too disturbed and dangerous to be around other children. My husband arrived and refused to place Robert away from home. He could not countenance that his second son was mad and dangerous. We fought repeatedly, but my husband remained adamant that Robert would remain at home and the tutor would continue to work with him.

"It became too much for me. Eugene and I separated. Christopher and I moved into this house. I begged and begged that Julian come with me, but his father blamed me for Robert's problems and refused to let Julian leave with us. He said I'd been too lenient and boys needed a firm hand. I persuaded him that Julian should go to a school, and he went to Eton from that time, and then went on to university. I had no contact with Robert after the incident, but Julian wrote to me from school and would visit me when he could. When I look back, I'm ashamed that I abandoned Robert. I should have fought his father more, insisted on another doctor's opinion, but I was exhausted and vulnerable. My husband was a cruel man, Eleanor, and, when pushed, would threaten to remove Christopher from my care. I checked with a lawyer who confirmed it was not an empty threat. I was lucky to keep this house and Christopher. Legally, my husband could have cast me out from here and barred any contact with the children. I believed I had no other recourse than to accept my husband's direction."

The room remained silent except for the sibilance of the dying fire. Eleanor found she couldn't move or find any words to offer comfort, so she swallowed her tears and raised her head to meet the pale, stricken gaze of her mother-in-law and offer silent solidarity instead.

Lady Caroline Heyer nodded. "Two days ago, I wouldn't have shared this history. I believed you still too young, too innocent. But yesterday I saw you had a strength of mind that surprised me."

Eleanor realised she was being assessed. She straightened and returned her mother-in-law's steely gaze. "Thank you, ma'am."

Lady Caroline seemed to deliberate for a moment, then her face returned to its usual impassive mask and the pain in her eyes was replaced with steely determination. It was as if she had pulled a curtain over her tragic recollections and assumed the stately bearing of stoic nobility.

"Do you still wish to meet Robert?"

"Yes." Eleanor said.

"He'll be difficult, Eleanor. His illness makes him angry at his fate and cruel to everyone around him. Expect to be taunted and insulted by Robert. He's ugly and disfigured, and uses that to provoke rejection and despair."

"He's my husband's twin brother. I will survive."

"Then we'll attend to him now, Eleanor. Miss Smith, do you wish to meet my son?"

"Not particularly, ma'am."

Caroline Heyer smiled. "You're a good friend to Eleanor. I wish I'd had a good, wise friend when I was younger. I could've used one."

The sick room was overheated, dimly lit, and smelt of bodily waste. They had propped Robert up with pillows on the large bed. A swarthy-looking man rose from the side of the bed and laid down a book before bowing to Lady Caroline and Eleanor.

"Has he been awake, Mr Perez?"

"Yes, lady. He have a good day." The man spoke with a strong accent.

The sheeted figure moved slowly on the bed. Eleanor looked at her brother-in-law. Her heart pounded and she felt lightheaded. It was a good thing the room was poorly lit; one glance had revealed a thin face with a large sore instead of a nose beneath sunken eyes. Thankfully, a beard covered the rest of his face. His eyes glinted in the ravaged visage. Eleanor lowered her eyes to the sheets. It was hard to comprehend that the ancient-looking, decimated man still lived at all, but he had a strong voice.

"Ah, Mother, you've brought me a visitor. So young, so pretty. This must be Julian's second barren wife. Welcome, my dear, welcome."

The words were cruel and delivered in a cutting sibilance. Eleanor wanted to turn away and leave the room as swiftly as she could, but that wouldn't do. She should've expected such a reception. This was the evil twin. She took a shallow breath and looked the sick man directly in the face. "Robert, my name is Eleanor. I'm pleased to make your acquaintance." She dropped a small curtsey.

"And so polite. But, Mother, why is she here? To see the dying monster? Have I become a circus attraction to scare young ladies now? Or does she seek the truth about my dearest brother, the heir who cannot conceive an heir? Well, I can't help you with that either, but ten years ago I would've tried it, and given you some pleasure in the process."

"Robert, this is unnecessary." Lady Caroline turned to Eleanor. "We should go, my dear."

Eleanor wanted nothing more than to leave, but this dying travesty of a man didn't deserve her fear or condemnation. "No, I'll stay. Robert is correct. I have no children, so I am possibly barren. I would have it otherwise, but he is correct. But I'm intrigued, Robert, about your interest in my marriage. What is the truth you hint at? Or are you just speculating, enjoying my discomfiture?"

"The young lady has courage." The eyes narrowed, and Eleanor wasn't sure, but his horrible face might be smiling. "You'll need it, my dear Eleanor. My brother is delusional, quite mad, you know. Drove his first wife to absolute despair. She killed herself. My brother put it about that she'd died in childbed, but I have friends in Devon. I learned the truth of it. She threw herself off a cliff, or down the stairs, or some such thing. Wouldn't take anymore blame for my brother's infertility."

"Robert, you know no such thing," Lady Heyer loudly cut in. Then she grabbed Eleanor by the arm and started pulling her towards the door. "Come, Eleanor, Robert is unwell. His nature and his illness make him malicious. I'll not hear such lies. Come, we'll leave him to his ramblings."

Eleanor turned back before being dragged out the door. A noise that could have been a gurgling laugh arose from the bed. His voice flowed after them. "Go to Devon. Find out what happened there. And find Mrs Wilson and ask her. She knows all about your husband and his lies."

The afternoon presented as fine, but cold, with a sharp wind. Eleanor understood Bertha would prefer to stay inside by the fire. She experienced guilt as her friend limped beside her around the garden.

"I'm sorry Bertha, but I don't trust Caroline Heyer's servants and wanted, no needed, absolute privacy for this conversation."

"Yes, I can understand that. What did you find out from your brother-in-law?"

Eleanor took a deep breath. "Robert said that Julian was infertile and that his first wife, Emily, killed herself. That she'd never conceived and had been driven to despair and took her own life. I find it horrifying to imagine Julian's wife being so desperate and alone that she killed herself."

"Good Lord." Bertha drew her shawl tighter around her shoulders. "But is that possible? Wouldn't Julian have told you?"

"No, he's never spoken to me about his first wife. I've always respected his silence, believing it genuine grief. But now I don't know what to believe."

"But do you suspect that what Robert said is true? Lady Heyer said it was lies, and he sounds malicious enough to make something up to upset you and Julian, too. He obviously hates his brother and maybe, even now, wants to cause him more grief."

"Yes, but I sensed Robert had some knowledge of Julian's first marriage and that, while malicious, there could be an element of truth to what he said. He claims he has friends in Devon who informed him of the truth about Emily's death."

"Did Lady Heyer say anything after you saw Robert? Did she confirm any of his accusations?"

"No, she just reiterated that Robert is a liar. She wouldn't accept his version, and she counselled me to do likewise."

"So, do you consider that Lady Heyer may be lying, or at least hiding the truth?"

Eleanor frowned. "No, not really, but I don't think she knows what happened to Emily, either. When I questioned her further, she couldn't give me any reassurances that she had the truth of the matter. She admitted Julian had never told her any more than that Emily had conceived, then died in childbirth. She said she had very little correspondence with Julian or Emily, and they'd hardly met over the last few years. And she stated Julian got angry when she tried to talk to him about Emily's death. She'd always presumed grief stopped him from discussing his wife's demise. And, she believed, he closed Heyer House because of all the sad memories it raised."

Bertha tutted. "Well, it's a reasonable assumption. Julian had a terrible childhood, Eleanor, and then lost his wife and a much-anticipated baby. I can understand a man finding it hard to return to the scene of such tragedies. It's more understandable to me now why he purchased Brampton Manor and uses that as his country seat. But surely you can talk to him about this, Eleanor. He's your husband. Surely, he can explain and give you reassurance."

Eleanor bit her lip. The problems in her marriage had been insidious — so long standing and grave that she realised she'd even stopped confiding her fears to Bertha. She'd wrapped herself in guilt and despair for so long it had become an impenetrable cocoon of misery. Eleanor had contemplated asking Julian for a divorce, to free him and let him find a wife who hadn't poisoned herself and ruined their future? Sometimes she'd experienced some fleeting thoughts that death would be better than continuing. If Emily had taken her life, she understood that type of hopelessness. And Julian could be so cold. He closed up, refusing to accept any responsibility or offer any comfort. Oh yes, she easily imagined Emily killing herself. It would be an escape from a life of misery.

Eleanor shivered, but then she looked at Bertha and her resolve firmed. This had to stop. She needed to talk through her fears and share her dark emotions, and, unlike Emily and Lady Heyer, she had a strong, sensible friend to lean on.

"He won't listen, Bertha." Eleanor's voice shook. "I've tried. We hardly ever talk; we hardly spend any time together anymore. I sometimes consider he hates me, or at least hates that I'm unable to provide him with a child. His childhood remained a mystery until yesterday. He didn't even tell me what illness

Robert had contracted, and I would probably never have got that information if Lady Heyer hadn't decided that I'm old enough not to faint at the telling. Julian doesn't even talk to his mother. Since that contemptuous doctor put the blame at my door, he's just closed down and won't talk to me or anyone."

They walked on in silence. Eleanor pulled her own shawl tighter. The wind blew as bitter as her thoughts.

Bertha stopped abruptly and turned to face Eleanor. "How bad is it, Eleanor?"

"I can understand why Emily would want to die!"

"Have you told Julian how you suffer? Wouldn't he listen if he knows you're so desperate?"

Eleanor sniffed, and then continued to walk, not sure she'd want to betray her husband even to Bertha, but then she realised she must talk, honestly and openly, or she'd surely go mad. "I told him once that I wished I was dead. He found me crying when my courses had begun again. They had been late, and I had convinced myself I was with child. The disappointment, the sense of failure, nearly drove me mad, and I broke down and told him I wanted to die."

Bertha limped to catch up, took her arm, and turned her to a face full of sympathy and concern.

Eleanor knew what question was being asked without the words. "He said *he* wished I was dead too, and then he left to go to London for a week."

It was good to have Bertha's arms holding her shaking body. Good to share the despair of her existence. For several minutes, Bertha murmured words and sounds that offered comfort somehow. Eleanor sobbed. The moment was pure emotion and cathartic. As she pulled back, the image of Lady Heyer came to mind. The shutting off of the pain, the stiffening of the spine, the steel in the eye. Eleanor recognised she had to lose the last of her childhood. She straightened, stepped back, took a deep breath, and realised that, by crying out her pain, she had found another emotion.

"Damn Julian, Bertha, damn him." The unexpected anger felt good, felt right.

If Bertha was surprised by the cursing and sudden change of mood, she didn't say so. She passed over a clean handkerchief, took Eleanor's arm, and they headed towards a small summerhouse set on an incline at the end of the garden. Eleanor took in deep breaths of cold air as she walked, her mind still empty. She looked at the woods, the racing clouds, the weak sun sparkling on the rain-soaked grass. It was a magnificent view, the colours muted, soft with greens and greys. Three years previously, the view would've taken her breath away and she would have captured its beauty on a large canvas. Eleanor realised her grief was not only for a child she could not bear, it was for the art she had sacrificed, all her life sacrificed for an unattainable dream.

Eleanor appreciated Bertha's warmth and support as she surveyed the garden. She dashed away the tears and lifted her head.

"I've been foolish, Bertha. Stupid and naïve. I just accepted everything I've been told. But I'll not succumb to those lies anymore. I'll find out the truth, Bertha. I need to find out the truth about what happened to Emily. Robert is a horrible man, but I don't believe he lied."

Bertha harrumphed. She did it so well. "Well, madam, it's about time you found some gumption. It took a dying madman to make you see sense. But you need to work this through, Eleanor. You don't know that Julian is lying."

Eleanor bit her lip. Bertha was correct. "Oh, dear Lord, Bertha. I do suspect that Julian lies, but I have no proof. Maybe he lies to himself. Some people can convince themselves that their inventions are true. Robert called him delusional, said that he's mad. But where does that leave us, our marriage? I'm not sure what to think or what to do."

"Stop this, Eleanor. Work out what you want. How are you going to get it? I didn't educate you to be a bird-witted fool. Think, girl."

Eleanor sniffed, then blew out a breath. "I can't, Bertha."

"Yes, you can."

Eleanor dragged her shawl closer. It really was cold, even in the summer house, out of the wind. Thoughts swirled in her brain like the leaves on the trees in the garden. She remembered back to the school room at Brampton Manor. Bertha challenging her, asking questions, demanding answers. Her thoughts coalesced into some sort of order. "I need more information, Bertha. I need to know if our childlessness is really my fault, or if it's Julian."

"Why?"

Eleanor grimaced and paced around the small enclosure before stopping in front of Bertha. "I can't accept, Bertha, that I've poisoned myself by painting with oils. Yes, I painted for several years, but only for a few hours a day, and then not every day. And it's been three whole years since I stopped. That doctor said I should recover with time, but I'm still not bearing after three years."

"So, if you're not at fault, why do you suspect Julian?"

"Because he was married to Emily for six years with no children. That he's adamant that Emily died in childbirth, but refuses to give me, or his mother, the particulars. And everyone in my family is fertile except me, and there's a history of infertility in the Heyer line. And now Robert has said that Julian is both mad and infertile, and that poor Emily killed herself in despair. I need to find out what is the truth, Bertha."

"And if you find out the truth, what then? It seems a hopeless cause to find the truth unless you work out what you'll do with it."

Eleanor was about to reply, but then stopped. What would she do? Something had to change in the marriage. Both she and Julian were trapped in a union of misery and despair. There was nothing between them anymore, except a need to have children. An obsession that seemed more and more unlikely to result in success. It was an obsession that had consumed the fun, the enjoyment in each other's company, the intimacy, the love. Yet, she remembered the good times. A part of her still loved Julian. And a marriage remained a marriage. They'd made promises to God to love and honour each other in 'sickness and in health'.

Did she want a divorce? Society was unforgiving when people divorced. Women, in particular, would be shunned and shamed and returned to their family, expected to be dependent on a relative's charity. But she would have her art. The words came to her slowly, forming at the same time as her thoughts.

"I believe, Bertha, that if it's my problem, I'd ask Julian for a divorce, or an annulment, if that's possible. My family will support me and I will have my art. It would be better for Julian to marry someone else, to have the children he craves. He's had such a sad childhood; I understand better now his fixation on having a family. He'd make a good father, I'm sure. Yes, I'd offer Julian that chance."

"You still love him, Eleanor?"

"Yes."

Bertha nodded and gave her a moment to settle around that disclosure, then she ploughed on relentlessly. "And what if it's Julian's problem? What would you do then?"

Eleanor turned to look out at the windswept garden and found she had tears in her eyes. "I really don't know if he'll ever be able to accept it's his problem. His belief is absolute. He's adamant he's not to blame, but I don't understand why. Maybe he's got a child with someone else. That might explain his determination. But I don't know. And now Robert has spoken about this Mrs Wilson."

"Did you ask Lady Heyer about that? Does she have any information about a Mrs Wilson?"

Eleanor recalled the coldness of her mother-in-law's response when she'd asked the question. "I enquired, but she said that Mrs Wilson had been the wife of the steward at Heyer House and she was left a widow with a child, but she revealed nothing else. She might know more, but I had the impression she's not ready, or able, to talk to me about Mrs Wilson. It seems only Robert knows anything about this mysterious woman."

Bertha harrumphed again. "This family thrives on secrets, it would seem. You're probably correct, Eleanor. It doesn't sound as if Caroline Heyer would be more forthcoming, even if she had the truth of the matter. So, what will you do?"

Eleanor shivered. "I think we should go to Devon, Bertha. The answers lie there."

"But Heyer House is closed, Eleanor, and Julian will hardly approve of you opening it up for one visit."

Eleanor took a breath and made a decision that was likely to change her life completely. "I'll tell him you and I have decided to take the waters at Bath. You need some relief from the pain in your joints, and I wish to try the cures for infertility. We'll go to Bath, and then a Mrs Smith and a Miss Smith will journey on to Devon to get some sea air, perhaps even some sea bathing. And we'll visit Heyer House while we're there. We can stay at a local inn or a guesthouse, talk to the local people, and learn what we can about the history of the Heyer family. With the house closed down, there will be disgruntled former servants who are likely to gossip. The answers will be in Devon. That's where we'll find out the truth."

Chapter Six

June 2nd 1823

Viscountess Heyer and her companion, Miss Bertha Smith, descended on Bath in the Heyer touring coach on a fine, sunny Monday afternoon. The Heyer crest and the deep-blue livery of the servants caught the attention of many of the genteel residents and visitors, and gossip soon spread. Lady Heyer was in town and staying at the prestigious York House Hotel on George Street.

Mary, Eleanor's maid, and Victor, a footman, accompanied the ladies. Mary frequently travelled with Eleanor and knew much of her mistress' business. Her loyalty and discretion were accepted, but on this journey, she had additional tasks that would truly test her commitment to Lady Eleanor Heyer. Victor was Mary's 'young man' so Eleanor had no concerns that Victor would prove as discrete and loyal as Mary. The carriage was sent back to Surrey for the convenience of Lord Heyer, who had business in London. It would return to convey the ladies' home at the end of their three-week sojourn at the health spa.

Lady Heyer and Miss Smith walked to the Upper Assembly rooms the following morning, signed the subscription book, and were introduced to the Master of Ceremonies. He assured Eleanor he understood completely that she and Miss Smith were there for the waters, but would not be joining in the assemblies and balls on offer. The Master then escorted them to the impressive Pump Room and appraised them of the benefits of drinking and bathing in the waters.

The Master introduced Lady Salford, and Lady Sherrington to Lady Heyer and Miss Smith, and Eleanor enjoyed being reacquainted with Lady Riley and Mr and Mrs Moore, friends Eleanor had not seen for several years. They spent an enjoyable couple of hours conversing and drinking the waters brought to their table by servants known as pumpers. Lady Riley persuaded Bertha to try a hot bath. The Queen's bath seemed to be the most suitable for unaccompanied ladies. Bertha found that bobbing around a large pool of hot mineral water was so enjoyable she didn't want to get out.

"Oh Eleanor, I never realised how pleasant it is to have all my weight off my knees. I'm refreshed indeed, quite invigorated."

Following their afternoon at the pump room, Lady Heyer and Miss Smith visited Milsom Street and bought several books from Duffield's bookstore. Lady Heyer and her maid were later seen walking in the fields below the Royal Circle. The ladies then retired for the evening. It was well known by this time that Lady Heyer and Miss Smith, who had "terrible knees", were in Bath for the curative waters and would not be attending entertainments.

They spent the following days in the same comfortable routine until Thursday, when Lady Heyer attended the pump room with Mary, her maid. She responded to several enquires, saying, "Miss Smith has come down with a severe infection of the lungs and she's taken to her bed on doctor's orders." Lady Heyer coughed herself and admitted to several people she felt unwell. On Friday, Lady Riley received a note from Lady Heyer.

My Dear Lady Riley,

Please accept my profound apologies. Miss Smith and I are both poorly with an infectious disorder and will recuperate in our rooms at the York House Hotel for the next few days. We unfortunately cannot accept your kind invitation to dine this Saturday. I will write again when we have recovered from this confounded illness and arrange to meet.

Eleanor Heyer

At eight o'clock on the Friday morning, Mrs Bertha Smith and her daughter, Miss Eleanor Smith, exited the York House Hotel by the side door, rarely used by guests. Both wore plain, faded day dresses and carried well-used carpet bags. Victor met them, driving a shabby, rented Landau pulled by an ill-matched pair of horses.

"Oh, my goodness, Bertha. I'd never have believed subterfuge could be such fun." Eleanor giggled as she took her seat in the small conveyance. It smelt dusty, and of horse manure, but the seats were reasonably well sprung and there appeared sufficient room to find a comfortable position.

"I just hope Mary can keep up the ruse, so the hotel staff don't twig to the fact that their honoured guests have run away." Bertha snorted.

"Mary's a clever woman and she's well versed in explaining that Lady Heyer's contagion is highly infectious. I don't expect our ploy will be discovered. And we'll have several days to poke around in Devon and try to discover the truth about poor Emily and Robert's Mrs Wilson."

The rigors of the journey quickly tempered the enthusiasm Eleanor had for the enterprise. She discovered that, even though Victor was a competent driver, their schedule of driving for nine hours a day proved to be exhausting. Eleanor had always travelled in the comfort of a well-sprung, softly padded carriage. Her nights had been spent in the best rooms of posting inns, with private parlours and servants to provide baths and help with luggage. Travelling as an ordinary person proved to be uncomfortable and difficult.

After two nights of sharing a bed with Bertha, who snored most of the night, Eleanor was extremely grateful when Victor pulled up in front of a newly built guesthouse in the village of Lynton just in time for a late luncheon. Their hostess, Mrs Allcombe, had received their letter and proved to be most accommodating. She showed Mrs Smith and her daughter into two small, but clean, well-appointed rooms with large windows on the first floor, as requested. The rooms overlooked a small walled garden and had glimpses of the sea. After eating a cold collation in the comfortable dining room, Eleanor returned to her bedroom.

Eleanor unpacked her clothes, trying to remember how Mary managed the task. She then lay down and slept for two hours. She felt a little more energetic on rising. Bertha, who was snoring in her bed, couldn't be roused. Eleanor decided a walk through the village was just what she needed after the long, uncomfortable journey, but hesitated at the front door of the guesthouse. Was it the done thing for a poor but respectable woman to walk alone in a strange place? Certainly, the

Viscountess Heyer would not venture out without her maid in a new town, but what happened if you didn't have a maid? Phish, she was ignorant. Eleanor resolved she would walk on the main thoroughfare and look at the shops before returning for a cup of tea.

Lynton proved to be a small, attractive town set in a narrow valley. There were a surprising number of shops in the winding streets and quite a few new guesthouses and inns, no doubt accommodating rich visitors attracted to the seaside for holidays. The cool wind smelt of salt, and the air was filled with the raucous cries of seabirds. As she walked, Eleanor became aware that people passed by her without the deference or muttered comments that a well-dressed member of the aristocracy usually aroused. It was liberating to be walking alone, looking ordinary, acting ordinary. She wondered what Julian would say about her enjoying such freedom.

On her return, Mrs Allcombe happily shared a cup of tea with her young guest. She proved to be a curious woman, and Eleanor's constructed story was opened up for examination with a pleasantly conducted, but thorough, interrogation.

"So, Miss Smith, you knew Lady Emily Heyer as a child, before she married?"

"Oh yes, we lived near the family in Surrey. My father's a lawyer and did a lot of work for dear Emily's papa. I used to go with him and played with Miss Emily in the nursery. She was such a pretty girl, and we were friends for many years, but, of course, we came from different social circles and I lost contact with her when she came out and married."

"So, you didn't meet the Viscount?"

"Oh no, I've never met Lord Heyer. And Emily moved to Devon after her marriage and I lost contact with her entirely."

"But you still have fond memories of Miss Emily? You wrote in your letter that you hoped to visit her grave." Mrs Allcombe raised an eyebrow, making Eleanor wish she was better at lying.

"Well... yes, mother and I were travelling in the area anyway and I wanted to put some flowers on the grave and offer prayers."

Eleanor decided she needed to start her own investigation. "It's so tragic that she died so young, and that she had no children. It was always her fervent wish as a child to have a family. I was quite bereft when I heard of her passing. I felt the need to see where she'd come to, Mrs Allcombe, to walk in her footsteps, as they say. Did you know Lady Heyer at all?"

"No, not really, though I knew of her, of course. She was the Lady of Heyer House, and I imagine the entire town knew about her and the Viscount. I used to see her at church every Sunday, and I must say that I worried about her health, Miss Smith. She appeared happy when she first arrived, entertained most of the local gentry and attended the village fair every year. But as the years passed, she looked quite poorly. Became thin and pale. The whole village was concerned, and I know Dr Mailman, our local doctor, went up to the house most days during that last winter. But come the spring she seemed to improve. She came back to church, had roses in her cheeks, and looked as if she'd put on weight. There was talk that she may be expecting, and everyone in the village was most happy for Lord and Lady Heyer." Mrs Allcombe shook her head sadly. "But then we learned she'd had a dreadful accident and died. We were all devastated, Miss Smith, absolutely devastated."

Eleanor found herself about to jump in and ask about the "accident", but stopped herself. Too much curiosity would trigger alarm bells in even the most irrepressible gossip. She bit her lip and looked to the floor, as if contemplating her grief.

"Is the grave on the estate?" Eleanor asked, hoping that it would give her a good reason to visit.

"Oh, no, Miss Smith. They buried Lady Emily Heyer in the local church. There's a family plot. The old Lord and his parents are in the same place."

"Thank you, Mrs Allcombe. I'll visit it tomorrow."

Eleanor went up to her room to change for dinner and contemplate the information she had received from the garrulous landlady. She now had the name of the attending doctor and some disturbing gossip that Emily had died in an accident, not childbirth. She knocked and woke Bertha with her garnered troubling information. They would need to plan their next stratagem carefully.

The following morning dawned sunny and bright, and as it was unlikely Bertha would be awake for another hour, Eleanor decided to walk down to Lynmouth Harbour. The road down proved extremely steep and winding. Eleanor was glad she had come alone; Bertha would never have managed the descent. The harbour itself proved delightful, with twisting lanes between white-washed cottages. It smelt of salt and fish. Eleanor found one of the two rivers which spilled swiftly into the ocean. The walk back up to Lynton was horrendous. As she struggled for breath, Eleanor wished she'd paid the tuppence required to hire a donkey to make the ascent.

On the way up, she picked some spring flowers from the hedgerows and then found Emily's grave in the churchyard. It was a peaceful place, dappled by sunlight filtering through the trees. Eleanor knelt in the grass. "Rest in peace, Emily. I pray you've found the happiness that eluded you in this world."

Eleanor, flushed by her walk, was starving when she returned to the guesthouse.

"Ah, there you are, Eleanor." Bertha beamed up from a plate of eggs and sausages. "I thought you might have walked down to the harbour. Mrs Allcombe said she'd recommended it, but if the stroll has left you in this state, I won't be following in your footsteps."

"It's quite a climb, even compared to some mountains in Scotland."

Mrs Allcombe looked quizzical. Eleanor had to dissemble quickly. "But it's a pretty fishing village, is it not, Mrs Allcombe?"

"Aye, my lovely, very pretty indeed."

Eleanor, concerned Mrs Allcombe may ask awkward questions about Scotland, added. "I've also walked to the church and seen Lady Emily's grave. But is it possible to visit the Heyer estate? I'd like to see where Emily lived. Is the housekeeper amenable to visitors?" Eleanor flushed as she wondered if it was usual for ordinary people to ask to visit the houses of the gentry. She really wasn't good at subterfuge.

"Oh no, Miss. Lynton House has been closed these past six years. After Lady Heyer died, Lord Heyer went to London, then to his other estate somewhere in the north. He hasn't been back in all that time. A steward manages the estate but the house itself is closed."

"That must've been difficult for the local people. Many would have found employment in a great house, and the local shopkeepers would have missed the trade with a large country estate," Bertha put in shrewdly.

"Oh, aye, ma'am. Put many people out of work. Caused some anger in the village. We had hoped his Lordship would return when he remarried, but we've seen neither hide nor hair of him, or his new lady, for many a year."

"Oh dear, I'd so hoped to see the estate." Eleanor realised she wanted to see what would have been her country home in different circumstances. "Can we drive out there, see the house and grounds from the outside?"

"Aye, that's possible. It's about five miles west of here, but the road's good and it'll give you a chance to see the Valley of the Rocks on the way. That's a lovely spot, Miss Smith. People come from all over to look at the coastline and hills near Lynton. The views have become quite famous."

"Well, we can go this afternoon. What say you Mother?" Eleanor nodded to Bertha.

"Splendid idea. We'll need the carriage though," Bertha said.

Eleanor was just about to ask that Mrs Allcombe send a servant to inform Victor they would need the Landau in an hour's time, when she realized she didn't have a servant to send. It was certainly difficult being without servants to do one's bidding. She'd just have to walk to Victor's inn and deliver the message herself. And she would need Bertha's help to braid her hair again. Eleanor found dressing without a lady's maid more challenging than she had imagined.

Mrs Allcombe was amenable to providing a packed luncheon for the trip and included a rug to spread over the rocks.

It was a fine spring day and Eleanor enjoyed the walk to the local coaching inn. She found Victor in the stables, talking to an old man with an indecipherable accent. Victor rolled his eyes when he saw Eleanor and seemed grateful for the interruption to the conversation. "Aye, Miss Smith. I'll be at the guesthouse at eleven."

Eleanor nodded her thanks. She felt so lucky with both Mary and Victor. Victor had fallen into the role of a general manservant easily and hadn't once referred to her by her title or given away her identity by too much deference. He also appeared to be successful in engaging the locals in conversation. They were both proving to be assets. Eleanor decided that, when she returned to Surrey, she'd suggest a pay increase, or even a promotion, for both. She'd also do all in her power to help them marry, if that was what they desired.

The views of the cliffs and hills in the Valley of the Rocks were spectacular. The dark-grey granite contrasted against the early summer-green grass, and the cobalt sea sparkled in the sunlight. It presented a magical, majestic landscape, and Eleanor, for the first time in many months, yearned to paint. They found the road in good condition, and Victor put the horses at a steady trot. They had decided they'd have a quick look at Heyer House, then stop for a late lunch at the cliffs on the return journey.

Following Mrs Allcombes directions, it was easy to find the avenue of oaks that indicated a substantial estate. The driveway appeared neglected, with weeds and rain-filled potholes in places. Set back several miles from the coast in a wide valley, the Heyer land was flat and well fenced. Most fields contained sheep and cattle, but a few were newly planted with crops. The valley was several miles long and surrounded by low hills. They passed two hamlets with well-tended cottages for farm workers and their families. The drive took them beside, and over a small, fast-flowing river. To Eleanor, it was beautiful and reminded her of Derbyshire.

Heyer House was a large Georgian building with a pale stone facade, impressive steps, and a southerly aspect. The river was dammed to form a small lake in front of the building, which reflected its grandeur. Despite its appearance Eleanor saw, even from a distance, it was empty and unused.

"It's beautiful Eleanor. Sad that it's been shut up for so long," Bertha commented as Victor brought the carriage to a halt so they could view the imposing structure.

Eleanor found it difficult to reply. She swallowed hard. "Yes, but understandable. Julian spent such an awful childhood at Heyer House. And after losing his beloved wife, I can see why he finds it impossible to return here."

Eleanor's eyes brimmed with tears and she experienced an urgent need to leave. A flush of shame made her stomach roil at the thought that she had pried into Julian's private grief.

"Thank you, Victor. We'll stop at the Valley of the Rocks for luncheon."

"Aye, ma'am."

Eleanor found her mood lighten as they left the estate. She realised she was hungry, and was grateful when Victor pulled the coach over into a wide spot that afforded some fallen boulders for seats and a view of the cliffs and sea.

Victor spread the blanket over a low, flat rock and brought out the hamper. Eleanor had asked Mrs Allcombe for food for three and she invited Victor to join them, fully expecting that he had some local gossip to impart. The packed lunch comprised fresh bread rolls, cheese, cold ham and some delightful pickles, along with fresh fruit and a delectable current pastry. The hamper also contained bottles of cordial and cider.

"I'm sorry, ma'am, but I've heard very little about Lady Emily. There was some belief that she might have been expecting a child, but then died in an accident. Some of the gossip was cruel, ma'am, and I won't repeat it. I spoke to several of the older gentlemen and a lass serving in the inn, but I don't think the locals know what happened. There is still discontent about Heyer House being closed. The estate had employed lots of the younger folk as maids, grooms and gardeners, and after the estate closed, many had to move away to find work in the factories and mines further north."

Eleanor nodded her thanks. It matched the limited information Mrs Allcombe had imparted, and Eleanor had a notion that if Mrs Allcombe didn't have the particulars, it was unlikely anyone else in the village did, except perhaps Dr Mailman.

Victor interrupted her reverie with a polite cough. "I heard one other story about the family, if you don't mind me saying, ma'am. It concerned Mr Robert Heyer."

Eleanor nodded her approval. Mary knew about the purpose of their visit to Lynton, and no doubt had alerted Victor to keep his ears and eyes open.

"That old gentleman I talked to at the stables had a lot to say about Mr Robert Heyer. Said he was a right handful as a youngster and grew up quite wild. He told me the final straw was when he tried to seduce the young wife of the steward, Mr Wilson. Apparently, a duel occurred and Mr Robert shot Wilson in the back. It got hushed up, of course. The local magistrate got called in and told Mr Robert if he stayed in England, he would have him arrested and sent off to Australia. Mr Wilson was a local man and highly regarded and folk around here were angry he'd been murdered. Mr Robert got sent overseas along with his tutor and no one saw him again."

Eleanor looked out at the wonderful view as she digested this piece of gossip. It certainly explained why Robert had been sent overseas and supported Caroline Heyer's sad summation of her second son's character. But why had Robert brought up the name Mrs Wilson when she visited his sick room?

"Did the gentleman have any information about what happened to the wife, Mrs Wilson?"

"Just a little, ma'am. He said she was a lot younger than Mr Wilson and a comely lass. She had a babe in arms when left a widow, but the old gentleman wasn't able to say what happened to her."

"Thank you, Victor. Please let us know if you hear anything else concerning Mrs Wilson. The lady may be a local. I trust that the Heyer family would have ensured she was well cared for, given the sad circumstances of her loss."

As Victor packed up the dishes and rug, Eleanor took Bertha's arm and set off for a short stroll, giving them a chance to talk privately.

"It appears we've learnt little, Bertha. We only have gossip and innuendo about the death of poor Emily, and no clear idea if she was with child. I suspect the only person who may know the essentials is Dr Mailman, and I'm not sure how we can approach him. It's a delicate matter indeed." Eleanor sighed. "I'm afraid we've had a wasted journey."

Bertha snorted. "I think you must approach this doctor. You've put it about that you are a childhood friend of Emily's and you can say you've heard different accounts about her death. You could ask him to settle your unease about her passing."

"And he'll tell me to mind my own business. A doctor's not likely to break a confidence to someone so solely unrelated to his dead patient. And I'd worry that he might write to Julian about such an unlikely enquiry, and that would cause no small amount of trouble."

Bertha pursed her lips. "It is difficult, I agree, but we've risked so much and travelled so far to get some answers. We'll talk it through this evening and maybe come up with a plan. But at least we have some information about Mrs Wilson."

"But not enough, Bertha. We only have Robert's assertion that Julian knows Mrs Wilson and little else. It's a hopeless cause. We don't even know the woman's whereabouts. It's disheartening."

The return journey provided different perspectives of the coastline, and despite her discouragement, Eleanor relished the beautiful views. While Bertha dozed, Eleanor allowed herself to contemplate her future. As a divorced lady, she would have no income, no status, and would depend on her eldest brother. She might return to her art, but that would require her to beg her brother for money, for supplies. They would relegate her to another attic, most probably both living and working in it. And it would be unlikely she would ever remarry with her history. It presented a miserable prospect, but she would ask for a divorce, for Julian's sake. He deserved some happiness after his own bleak childhood and she suspected that, with children, he would return to the happy, funny man she had married. There was just too much grief and disappointment in his life, and her infertility added to his misery. But if it wasn't her fault, what would she do then? It proved to be a difficult and confusing dilemma. As Bertha would no doubt advise, she needed more information, and that clearly meant talking to the man who had been Emily's physician — Dr Mailman. But how to proceed?

Eleanor felt tired after the day's excursion. That afternoon, she and Bertha talked through approaching Dr Mailman, but they could find no acceptable approach that did not present as unwarranted prying. That evening, Bertha loudly complained about her knees as she descended the stairs for supper, and this prompted Mrs Allcombe to advise her to consult Dr Mailman. The landlady gave an enthusiastic account of his competence.

"He's highly regarded, Mrs Smith. Such a kind man, and he knows his potions and pills. We're lucky to have him here. A man like him could have been drawn to Exeter, or even London, but he says he likes his fishing here and he'll never leave."

To Eleanor, it sounded as if the good doctor could be a sensible and agreeable man, but wondered if he could be trustworthy. Would he gossip or inform Julian of her prying? It was becoming more tempting to consult with him, given the current lack of information about the Heyer family history among the villagers. When Eleanor retired for the night, she remained undecided about if she would approach the one person who could shed some light on Emily's demise.

The following day dawned bright with sunshine. Eleanor rose early, refreshed after a good night's sleep, but still undecided about the best course of action for approaching the local doctor. She dressed herself in her walking gown and got her hair into some semblance of a chignon. Then she donned her pelisse and hat and walked up to Hollerday Hill.

"It's a steep climb," Mrs Allcombe had advised the previous evening, "but the view over Lynton and the Valley of the Rocks is fine indeed." Eleanor packed a small sketchpad and pencils in her satchel, determined to get at least one sketch of the local area.

She gathered a couple of apples from a bowl in the breakfast room and headed out with nothing on her mind except an enjoyable excursion before breakfast. The walk was steep, but not as steep as the one up from Lynmouth. She soon became warm and out of breath, but the pathway wound through woods, which cooled her down. She ascended a series of steps to the crest of the hill. The view was indeed glorious, and Eleanor took advantage of a rough bench set at the peak of the hill to regain her composure and enjoy one of the crisp, sweet apples.

Sketching was relaxing and helped to clear her mind. Eleanor decided she would talk to Dr Mailman. He was a doctor, and she would prevail on his ethics to provide her with the answers and discretion she needed. And she would do it honestly. It would be Lady Heyer who would speak to the man, tell him about her infertility and despair, and beg his opinion. She would be brutally honest and explain that she needed to know if it was her problem or that of her husband, so she might decide the future of her marriage. The worst the doctor could do was inform her husband, and at least that information would raise the issue of her unhappiness. Julian would then have to talk about their problems.

Over breakfast, Eleanor informed Mrs Allcombe that she would visit Dr Mailman herself, feigning a headache as her excuse. She learned that the doctor consulted in his home between the hours of one and three. She declined Bertha's offer to attend with her. If she was going to be thoroughly humiliated, she would prefer to do so without even a sympathetic witness.

The doctor's house was a large cottage. A sign on the gate announced "Doctor Mailman, Consulting Physician". Mrs Allcombe had given specific directions to follow the path around the back of the house to a small outbuilding where the doctor saw his patients. Eleanor found that her heart beat like a drum as she entered a small waiting room containing an elderly couple.

After fifteen minutes, a young mother with a baby emerged from a room that looked like a library with a large desk. An imperious voice shouted "Next", and the elderly couple rose together and disappeared into the office, shutting the door behind them. Murmured voices could be heard, but it was impossible to discern what transpired. Eleanor sent up a prayer of thanks that no other patients had arrived by the time the doctor called out "Next" again.

Dr Mailman presented as a tall, spare man with grey through his hair. He wore thick, round glasses that rested on the bridge of his nose. He sat upright in his chair and had a tanned face and arms. Eleanor imagined him striding through the countryside with a net and rod, seeking fishing spots. He looked carefully at her posture and face as she walked over to the desk. He took up a writing pad and pencil as she sat down.

"New patient, eh? I will need a name, your age and a place of residence. The fee is one shilling and I require payment in advance."

Eleanor nodded, pulled her purse from her reticule, and placed a two-pound coin on the desk. She looked up, straightened her spine, and spoke with a cool tone.

"My name is Eleanor Heyer, Viscountess Heyer. I'm twenty-three years old. I have homes with my husband, Lord Heyer, in London, Derbyshire and Scotland, and, of course, he owns, but no longer lives at Heyer House near Lynton. However, I'm currently residing at the guesthouse run by Mrs Allcombe on Church Street. I'm known there as Miss Eleanor Smith. I am happy to pay you for an extended consultation, but I'll require your assurance that what transpires in this room remains completely confidential."

The doctor looked bemused for a few seconds, then straightened and nodded. He rose, saying nothing, and left the room. On his return, he gave her a brief smile. "I've closed the outer door. We will not be disturbed. Now, how can I be of assistance, Lady Heyer?"

Eleanor immediately liked the man and felt confident enough to continue. "I have been married for five years. I've not been able to conceive in that time, which has been of great distress to my husband and myself. We've consulted with several physicians who have all stated it's my problem. The last doctor said that I'd poisoned myself because I'm an artist and painted with oil paints. He believed that lead poisoning was the reason I couldn't conceive. I stopped painting three years ago and have followed all the doctor's recommendations, but nothing has helped."

Doctor Mailman removed his glasses. He had grey eyes, which were kindly without the thick lenses obscuring his character. "Lead poisoning. I know something about lead poisoning. A colleague sought my opinion when they opened up a new tin mine near Combe Martin. The mine had high levels of lead and many of the miner's children and the miners themselves showed symptoms of lead poisoning. I sent a request to Guy's Hospital for information so I could provide my colleague with some recommendations for treating the disorder."

Eleanor nodded, but her heart sank. Was she just going to learn that it was her fault again?

"Madam, when you were painting with oils, did you experience problems with heart palpitations, stomach disorders, joint pains, headaches?"

"No, sir."

"Did you experience problems with your cycles?"

"No."

"Any problems with concentration, dizziness or melancholia?"

"Not when I was painting. I could concentrate extremely well and did so happily. I experienced no ill effects from my pastime."

"And may I ask how long you used oil paints and how much exposure you had to the fumes?" Eleanor must have looked confused, because Doctor Mailman smiled encouragingly. "For how many years did you paint?"

"Only four."

"And did you paint every day?"

"No, but most days, especially in summer, though less in winter. I painted in our attic at home and it wasn't heated. And then I had a studio in London after I married. But while I wished to paint more, entertainments and other duties often distracted me."

"Were your studios well ventilated? Were they large spaces?"

"Oh yes, my art tutor made me well aware of the dangers of fumes from the mineral turps and paints. I was instructed to always have the windows open. I remember I had terrible chilblains on my fingers for much of the winter."

"Hmm." The doctor nodded and looked down at the blank piece of paper on his desk for nearly half a minute. He seemed to decide, put his glasses on, and again carefully examined Eleanor's face. "Madam, lead poisoning is an insidious disease. The mineral enters the body and can affect a number of organs. In my experience of the families at Combe Martin, the women had a higher rate of miscarriages and a lower rate of conception, but then the village had been heavily contaminated with dust from the mine over a period of ten years. I've read that some of the eminent artists had symptoms of lead poisoning because of their exposure over many years. I cannot rule out the possibility that you've ingested lead, and it may still be in your body. My information is that, in acute cases of poisoning, the lead leaves the body after two to three months and symptoms can improve after that time. However, even small amounts of lead can be harmful, and if it's in the bones, it can take many years before its effects are mitigated."

Eleanor's eyes welled with tears. Her despair must have shown on her face. Dr Mailman removed his glasses again. "However, you are young, your exposure was limited, and you have provided me with no history of symptoms of acute lead poisoning when you were first exposed to the contaminant."

The doctor paused, as if seeking the right words. "Lady Heyer, it's possible there are other factors at play. I believe, Madam, you didn't come all this way to Devon to get a confirmation of what you already know. I ask, therefore, what other reason you have for visiting your husband's local village, incognito, and without his knowledge or approval."

Eleanor looked up. The doctor's face betrayed no condemnation; his tone was neutrally curious. She swallowed hard, lifted her chin, and hoped she could emulate the proud bearing of the Dowager Viscountess, Caroline Heyer. "You're an astute man, Dr Mailman. You correctly assume that my purpose was not another opinion. I came because I believe that our childlessness may not be solely my responsibility. I question if my husband may also have difficulty conceiving children."

"May I ask why?"

Eleanor gripped her shaking hands together tightly in her lap, glad that the high desk would not reveal her nervousness to the doctor. She took a breath and looked directly into the doctor's eyes.

"My husband was married to Lady Emily Heyer for five years. He has been adamant that she died in childbirth. He refuses to discuss his grief and will brook no mention of her death. I've recently learned that my husband's mother also had difficulties conceiving, and I've learned from local people in Lynton that Lady Emily died in an accident, not as a result of childbirth."

Eleanor took a shaky breath, praying she could convey both her deep sorrow and her need for answers. "Dr Mailman, my husband, is deeply distressed by our childless condition. I've suffered enormous guilt and worry that it's my fault, to the extent that I'm considering asking my husband to end our marriage, so that he can marry again and beget the children he craves. I'd do that for Julian's sake, and, yes, I'm clutching at straws, but I think, if I have all the facts, I'll better accept the sad course I must take. But knowing if Lady Emily had conceived and died in childbirth would give me surety about accepting the blame and ending my marriage. I need to know how Lady Emily died."

The doctor looked down at his blank notepad. Eleanor waited with knotted fingers for some sort of response. The doctor rose and walked to his window to look out on his garden. He spoke while continuing to stare through the glass.

"Madam, I can readily understand your distress at your childless state. Lady Emily certainly became distressed for the same reason. What I'll impart to you, I beg you to keep my knowledge and beliefs in this matter to yourself. Lady Emily was my patient and, like you, she desperately wanted to provide an heir for her husband."

Dr Mailman paused, as though needing time to access his memories. "She was a pretty, lively young woman, and well-loved in the village, but over the years she became more and more despondent. In the winter prior to her death, I feared for her very life. She suffered a severe bout of melancholia. She stopped eating and kept to her bed in a darkened room, but rarely slept. Lord Heyer was distraught himself, and I visited several times a week and recommended a nurse stay with Lady Heyer. I feared she'd do herself harm. She became weak and thin, but just when I believed she would die from starvation, she reported her courses had stopped. The poor child truly thought she had conceived."

Doctor Mailman returned to his seat and steepled his hands on his desk. His fingers trembled. "I foolishly let her entertain this fiction. She started to eat and sleep, managed to walk out of her bedroom, and even got to go to church for a couple of weeks. I honestly couldn't exclude the possibility of pregnancy, and both she and Lord Heyer were so happy, so I did not subject Lady Emily to an examination. It's something I deeply regret to this day. I was a coward and, I believe, if I'd been honest with them, I could've better protected the dear lady."

This information was much worse than she'd expected. Her heart broke for Julian, and for the sadness of her predecessor's life and demise.

After a pause, Dr Mailman continued. "I was summoned to the house at dawn one morning. A footman galloped into my yard, saying Lady Emily had fallen down the stairs and suffered dreadful injuries. She'd passed away before I arrived. I again failed to conduct a thorough examination. They'd taken her to her room after the fall and there was blood on the sheets, but that poor, sweet lady..." The doctor looked at his hands. When he looked up at Eleanor, his eyes were full of tears. "I prayed, madam, that she'd not taken her own life upon discovering her courses had returned. I prayed that the fall was a horrible accident and not something worse."

The Doctor blinked several times, coughed, and seemed able to continue by rubbing his hands over his face and fixing his eye out the window again.

"Lord Heyer was distraught. I've never seen a man so bereft. He didn't know what to do with himself. He couldn't settle at all. I feared for his sanity, madam. In the end, he took his horse and galloped out. He rode away for most of the day. On his return, he appeared more settled. He wanted, of course, answers about Lady Heyer's death. I found I could not share my worst fears. I truly believed it would be kinder to agree with him that Lady Emily had been expecting and that an unfortunate accident had caused the death of his wife and child."

Eleanor found herself frozen. She could understand completely the good doctor's kind explanation about Emily's death. An explanation that, at best guess, was a lie. But that lie now fuelled her husband's conviction that she was to blame for their childless marriage? Eleanor found her cheeks were wet with her unnoticed tears. Finally looking up at the doctor's face, she saw he was tense and pale. She wanted to flee, to run out into the late afternoon sunshine and be free of Julian's dreadful history. There were no proper answers, but now she was burdened with a terrible knowledge about her husband's need for a child. Julian's desperate need to believe that Emily had been bearing his child and had not killed herself in despair.

Eleanor straightened and looked at the distressed man who had just shared with her his failings and fears. She had subjected this man to painful memories and powerful emotions when she had asked for this history. It was her duty to put him at ease, to take responsibility and act like a lady. "Sir, you acted with kindness. You did what you thought was right and necessary at the time. It's made my own circumstances more difficult, but your information has been edifying and will help me make some painful decisions about my marriage. I thank you, sir, for your time. You've given me much to think about."

Doctor Mailman looked as if he would say more, but then he shook his head as he acknowledged the futility of further discourse. He rose, bowed low, and murmured, "Goodbye, Lady Heyer."

Chapter Seven

June 11th 1823

Eleanor had never encountered the horrifying nature of suicide. As she walked away from Dr Mailman's rooms, she experienced such a mixture of emotions the thought of even talking about her experience was unbearable. She allowed her feet to lead her to the cliff path, walked alone in the sunny afternoon, and looked down at the churning ocean at the foot of the deadly drop. Her thoughts and emotions churned as ferociously as the foaming, pounding waves below.

Unexpected anger was as red as the lowering sun. How could Emily have been so weak, so pitiful, that death was preferable to accepting the truth? She may have not been pregnant, but she was alive. There were alternatives to death. Or were there? Eleanor stopped and looked down into the crashing waves, at the rounded boulders and sharp edges. If she walked out into thin air, she would end all her own misery now. She could become another young, gullible girl worn down by the pressure to produce an heir.

But she was more than that, more than a failed mother and wife. She was an artist, a friend, a member of a big and loving family who would be devastated if she took her own life. Bertha, her mother, and siblings, even Julian and his mother, would be as shattered as her own body would be on the unforgiving rocks below. Eleanor stepped back from the cliff edge and walked further along the path, now realising there was a terrible appeal in self-destruction.

Depression, hopelessness and guilt were powerful, painful emotions to bear. The blues of the rolling waves, the indigo depths of despair. Melancholia, the mind-altering illness that wiped away hope, that destroyed rational thought, that destroyed all love for life. Emily had experienced all of that, over years and years. Eleanor's heart ached for the dead Lady Emily Heyer. She knew how Julian would've acted. He would have withdrawn, being cold and spiteful, a man who would've been too wrapped up in his own misery to offer succour to a young woman he blamed. Eleanor had asked once what Emily was like. Julian's answer had been icy. "She was often ill and she was fragile in constitution." Emily would have needed someone strong to lean on, someone to wipe away her tears, to offer hope and give her a shoulder to cry upon. To give her an uplifting, powerful hug. Eleanor had Bertha, but if Emily had been isolated from her family, abandoned by Julian, Eleanor sympathised with her decision. But death was not the answer even when in the midst of such emotional pain.

Eleanor walked farther, no longer seeing the scenery but wrapped in a cold, grey mist of denunciation. Julian's callousness, his withdrawal, his obsessive need not to accept any responsibility, always to blame others. She hated that part of his nature. But Eleanor now understood her husband, was aware of his childhood misery, his abusive, unresponsive father and his insane, cruel brother. Relegated to the regime of a merciless, punishing tutor and a mother unable to offer any protection and love when he needed it the most. It was no wonder that Julian was incapable of offering comfort to his young wife. He'd never had it himself. Sympathy dispelled the cold mist of blame.

The cliff path met up with the track to Holloway Hill. Eleanor took a seat on a wooden bench, shut her eyes, rested there, feeling the warm sun on her face, the rough wood beneath her fingers. She inhaled, the air smelt of salt and grasses. Raucous calls from the swooping gulls filled the air and far away she heard the sweet trill of a lark ascending into the clear blue sky. Eleanor opened her eyes. The world was bright, colourful and beautiful, a world she loved and enjoyed and painted. Life could indeed be demanding, but there was always this world and friends and love to lead you down another path, not over a cliff.

Eleanor lifted her head and walked back to have tea with Bertha. They would talk, cry for the lost life of Emily, find understanding, if not forgiveness, for Julian. She would shore up her sorrows and decide about the rest of her life. And she, unlike Emily, could give thanks to God for having a trusted and loving friend.

The following morning, Eleanor and Bertha took a sad farewell from Mrs Allcombe. Three days of exploring the wonderful countryside, visiting the neglected estate of her husband and learning the sad, terrible fate of the previous Lady Heyer had left Eleanor with mixed emotions about Devon, but the talkative and attentive landlady would be missed.

It wasn't until their first stop at a coaching inn that Eleanor talked to Victor.

"Did you learn anything else about Mrs Wilson? Did she live locally, have family in the area?"

"Very little, milady. I spoke again to that old fellow at the inn. He said that Mrs Wilson's father was a harsh man who'd taken against her after the death of her husband. Wouldn't have anything to do with her, even refused to say her name. I got the impression that Mrs Wilson was blamed in some way for her husband's death, but the old fella didn't have the details, ma'am. He did say that when her father died, she didn't turn up to the funeral and she's never returned to Lynton at all."

Eleanor nodded her thanks. The information about Mrs Wilson was old and signified another hushed-up secret. It did not appear to have any connection to Julian's current life or the state of their marriage. She wondered if Robert's intimations were important, or just the malicious smears of a bitter, dying man.

"I'll have to talk to Robert again. Maybe I can prevail whatever goodness is in him to be more candid about Mrs Wilson." Eleanor said later to Bertha.

"From what you've said about Robert Heyer, I doubt he has any goodness in him. You may need to fox him in some manner, trick him into revealing more than he'd choose to do. From what you've described, he's an evil man, Eleanor, with little to do but cause misery and disruption. You'll need to approach him carefully. We must think of a plan."

Eleanor shook her head. "No, Bertha, I'll need to choose my words with care, but I'll not rely on subterfuge and misdirection. Those are his games and he excels at them. No, I need to demand answers. To bully him, if necessary, but I'll do so with veracity and authority. I am Lady Heyer. He will answer to me."

Another sojourn in Bath was much appreciated by the recovered Lady Heyer and Miss Smith. And Eleanor was most grateful to have Mary wash and dress her hair. The hot baths were even more enjoyable when one was recovering from a long journey in an inferior coach. Eleanor felt energised and refreshed as they travelled back to Surrey in the well sprung Heyer carriage. She also offered a prayer of thanks that no-one had guessed they'd journeyed to Devon during their period of convalescence.

June 23rd 1823

The journey back to Surrey gave Eleanor plenty of time to think and plan her confrontation with Robert Heyer. She decided she needed to be open and honest with her mother-in-law to get her support. Robert was in Caroline Heyer's care. He was her son, a guest in her house, and a dying man. The Dowager Viscountess had been dismissive and condescending towards Eleanor in the past, but that was over. Eleanor realised now that she was as strong as Julian's mother. She found additional strength in the realisation she had nothing to lose but a marriage that was already lost. Lady Caroline Heyer may be formidable, but Eleanor was her equal and now hoped she could make her an ally.

It was a relief for Eleanor to discover that Julian was still in London when she arrived late in the evening at Ashfield Manor. Lady Caroline had already retired, so Eleanor scribbled a note requesting they meet at morning tea for a private conversation, and then went gratefully to her own bed.

The room was the same, the weather outside was the same, but Eleanor realised she was a different person after her journey to Devon. Knowledge gave her assurance. She slept better than she had done in years.

The following morning, Eleanor told Lady Caroline the truth about her trip to Devon. She told her about the death of Emily Heyer. Bertha was present, but Eleanor had elected to do all the talking. She recounted the sad history using, as near as possible, the words used by Dr Mailman himself. By the end of the telling, her mother-in-law was pale and shaken.

"Good God, that poor, poor young woman. My poor son." Lady Caroline took a deep breath. "I should've realised there was trouble, could've gone there and been of some assistance. I should have helped her. But we don't, do we? We wrap ourselves up in our own selfish lives, not bothering to ask if our family and friends are coping with difficult circumstances. Women are told to mind our own business, not to interfere, to pray for our family in church every Sunday and then forget them for the rest of the week. I... I, in particular, should've known. I went through the same thing and I should've known."

"Mother, be kinder to yourself. If you'd learned she was ill, would you have attended?"

"Yes, of course. But I had no idea. I wrote to Julian, but his responses were always brief and uninformative. I wrote to Emily a few times, but she responded less and less as the years passed by. That should've warned me of her state of mind. I presumed that her own family was attentive and offering support, but I never checked, never asked the right questions. I assumed that Julian was there, and, as her husband, he would ensure her health and happiness. I should've realised he'd be struggling as well. His father bullied him as a child to hide his emotions. It's made him blind to other's pain."

Caroline Heyer paused, took a shuddering breath. "But that's the problem, isn't it? We're trained from birth to defer to our fathers, our brothers, our husbands, even our adult sons, told they are better than us. We're expected to submit to their acumen and position in family matters. But it's all a delusion, a fabrication. They know no more about the essentials in life than we know ourselves."

Eleanor moved and knelt beside Lady Caroline, taking her stiff hands. "You're right in that, Mother, but we've also allowed them to rule us. I won't do that any longer. But I'll need your help, Mother. Though you couldn't help Emily, you can help me."

The appeal broke through the grief and the Dowager Viscountess' more usual cold steel replaced emotion. "Do you really need my help, Eleanor?"

"Yes."

"Why?

Eleanor rose to her feet. She needed to persuade, not demand, a response from her husband's mother. It required asking Julian's mother to take her side against her natural inclination to support her own son.

She walked to the fireplace and then turned and raised her head. Keeping her voice low but strong, she stated, "I don't know if it's me or Julian who is infertile. I'd hoped to find that answer in Devon, but while Dr Mailman's account strengthens the idea that it may well be Julian's problem, he was not definitive. If it *is* my problem, then Julian deserves the chance to remarry, to find himself a wife who can bear him children. I'll ask, no, demand a divorce. It will mean that I'll lose everything. I'll be dependent on my family, and I don't expect I'd be an attractive proposition for any other gentleman. I expect my life will be that of a shamed, barren divorcee, but I'll gladly sacrifice my reputation and happiness if it gives Julian what he needs."

Lady Caroline nodded, never taking her eyes away from Eleanor's. "And if it is my son's problem, what do you propose to do?"

"I'll stay married to him. I won't allow him to destroy some other young woman's life with an unattainable dream. Yes, I'm stronger than Emily, but who is to say that his next choice could withstand the expectations and despair. Julian can continue in his belief that I'm to blame, I can live with that, but you must understand, that I'll need some confirmation of my belief if I'm to make the right decision."

Lady Caroline looked towards Bertha. "Miss Smith, we may need stronger refreshments than tea. Would you be so kind as to serve some sherry?"

Bertha's activity helped to reduce the tension in the room. Eleanor found that she'd been breathing shallowly and was dizzy. She returned to her chair and took a large swig of sherry, which helped. The restorative seemed to have a similar effect on the Dowager Viscountess. She, too, took a mouthful of the sweet, bronze-coloured liquor and then placed her glass down on the table.

"My dear, I've long suspected there's a condition within the Heyer line that makes the getting of an heir difficult. As you are aware, I didn't conceive the twins for many years. Julian's father was the only son and he had but one single sister. I waited another five years before I had Christopher, so your premise may have some merit."

Eleanor remained silent.

"I also applaud your intended sacrifice. As Julian's mother, I want nothing more than his happiness, and that will be secured with children. Julian needs an heir and he will make a good father. I also want some grandchildren to love. But, as you say, there is no definitive proof Julian cannot father a child, only assumptions. I'd ask that if you can't get absolute proof, you divorce him anyway. I'd wanted Julian to marry a widow with children, to test if he could father a child, but he was determined to wed you. He's getting older. He may listen to sense, next time. A woman who's proven to be fertile would've convinced even him he's incapable of having children and I reasoned he would come to accept that unpalatable fact. We had a dreadful row about it in Derbyshire, but Julian can be extremely obtuse and stubborn."

"I'm aware of that, Mother." Eleanor found a small smile.

"Hmph." Lady Caroline took another sip of sherry. "I suppose Robert's inevitable demise will make it easier for Julian to accept his childlessness. It terrified him that Robert would inherit. Julian predicted Robert would ruin the Heyer estates by gambling and squandering money if he had the chance, with no intent to produce an heir of his own. And I understand Robert hasn't produced offspring. He's taunted Julian many times with the fact that neither of them appears capable of fathering children. No, Robert's passing will ease that burden. But, of course, as second in line, Christopher will need to settle down and marry. As the youngest brother, he's led a life without responsibility or care. He's done well too. Owns three ships and a thriving business in China, built up all on his own. His father certainly did nothing beyond buying him a commission in the Navy. No, Christopher is a successful man, but if Julian dies childless, he'll be next in line. I consider he'd be a very successful Viscount too."

Eleanor couldn't help saying, "Then we must pray, Mother, that Christopher doesn't suffer the same disorder as the other Heyer men."

Lady Caroline looked daggers at Eleanor, then laughed. "Oh, but Christopher has children. He has a foreign woman in Shanghai who has provided him with two children. They're illegitimate half-castes, of course, but Christopher is quite besotted with them."

She took a large mouthful of sherry and cleared her throat. "But we get ahead of ourselves, Eleanor. You've asked for my help and that gives me the idea that you've some sort of plan on how to proceed."

"I do, Mother." Eleanor took a long swallow of wine herself. The liquid was sweet but bracing. She glanced over at Bertha, who nodded encouragement. They'd gone over and over this scheme and still it sounded ill conceived, ill fitting, but she couldn't think of anything else to try.

"For the past few years, I've pondered how Julian is so certain that he can father children. There can be only one explanation. He must have children already."

"An illegitimate child. Yes, that makes sense." Lady Caroline pursed her lips. "Yes, and he certainly would be loath to admit that fact to his wife, or to his mother. It makes sense, Eleanor and I hadn't thought of it myself."

"Hadn't you, mother?" Eleanor raised a brow. Lady Caroline Heyer was an astute woman, able to prevaricate and evade the truth. Eleanor had gained some respect, but she would have to gain more than respect to get to the truth.

"You accuse me of lying?"

"No, ma'am, but maybe you've been evasive. I'd like the truth about Mrs Wilson from you without prevarication. I learned a little about the death of Mr Wilson when I was in Devon, but the events surrounding his death have been suppressed, obstructed so that even that small and interested community has forgotten the particulars. I've learned that Mr Wilson worked for your husband as a steward and that he took a young wife. There was talk of a seduction and a duel, and that Robert shot Mr Wilson in the back and fled overseas to avoid the scandal. I don't imagine, Mother, that you're ignorant of this event and I would appreciate that you tell me all the facts."

"How dare you?" Lady Caroline rose to her feet, but then her anger dissipated. She sank back into her chair and looked away, out the window. "You're cruel, Eleanor. You ask me to disclose all the horrible truths about this family, but in this you cannot win. I know little more than what I've told you. Eugene, Julian's father, was alive then and I lived in Surrey with Christopher. Neither my husband nor Julian were forthcoming with information. The boys would have been nineteen or twenty and Mrs Wilson was of the same age. I can only surmise that Robert took a fancy to the young woman and was called out by her husband. Wilson's death couldn't be hushed up and there were plenty of witnesses who saw Robert kill the man unfairly. He was lucky not to be jailed. He might have been sent to the colonies, or even end up on the gallows. Eugene had to exert all of his influence to save Robert's life. But that's all I know."

"You didn't hear what happened to Mrs Wilson after the death of her husband?"

"No, I didn't ask."

Eleanor paused as she contemplated her mother-in-law's disclosure. "But I consider Robert has more information. He's directed me to find Mrs Wilson and ask her about Julian. He wouldn't have said that without a reason."

Eleanor thought through her incomplete and possibly erroneous conjecture. She had few facts and was surmising based on her knowledge of her husband's character and her own intuition. She took a deep breath and voiced her ideas. "In Devon, I learned very little about Mrs Wilson. She was a local girl and married an older man. She didn't return to the care of her family on becoming a widow. Indeed, the gossip showed her own father shunned her. It's reported she didn't attend his funeral. So, I ask, what happened to her? I can't accept that the Heyer family would abandon her. She had a child; her husband was a valued retainer of the Heyer estate. I can only surmise that Lord Heyer would have ensured her wellbeing and made some provisions for her and her son."

"My husband was just as likely to have cast her out, especially if she was of loose morals and culpable. No, Eleanor, I am not convinced of your reasoning," Lady Caroline interjected.

"Mother, neither was I, but Robert intimated we should ask Mrs Wilson and he revealed he was at least aware of her whereabouts and her current association with Julian. Your late husband may not have considered he had a moral duty to support Mrs Wilson, but I have confidence that Julian would do the right thing. I trust, in the absence of her family's support, he'd ensure the tragic circumstances that led to Mrs Wilson becoming a widow did not beggar her and her child."

Lady Caroline nodded. "Yes, Julian takes his responsibilities to his servants seriously." She stopped as another thought filtered into the story. "But you're thinking that Mrs Wilson is more than that, that she may be more intimately involved with the Heyer family."

Eleanor shook her head as she contemplated that her wildest imaginings about her husband and Mrs Wilson may be true. But she was not about to admit them, even to herself, without more information. "I don't know, but I credit Robert does. We must prevail on him to tell the truth of it."

Lady Caroline Heyer suddenly looked her age. Her face caught the light accentuating the deep lines around the eyes and mouth. Eleanor saw her sad life etched in her countenance. A life full of disappointment and regret. It felt cruel to push this woman to demand answers from her dying son. Then she saw the Viscountess straighten and her eyes snapped into life. "Yes, you're probably correct. I cannot guarantee the veracity of whatever he tells you, but you may ask. It was my intention to spare you from his hatred, but yes, I believe you must see him. I'll talk to Mr Perez. He'll inform us when Robert is lucid and awake, although those times are getting less and less frequent. I'll not attend with you, Eleanor. It's up to you to do the questioning. He may be more forthcoming if I'm not there to protect you. I will say this, you're aware of his nature. I'll not be responsible for your sensibilities."

It was two full days before Mr Perez said that Robert was alert enough to receive visitors. The day was overcast and the room was thankfully dimly lit. Robert was propped up with pillows and there was a flask of port on the table by the side of the bed. He looked thinner and frailer, his face disfigured by more dreadful sores, and Eleanor glimpsed bone through the space where his nose had been. She took a deep breath and nearly coughed as the smell of sickness and bodily waste entered her nose and mouth. She had a powerful urge to run, but that would not do when she needed answers from this travesty of a man. She looked him directly in the eyes.

"Good afternoon, Robert."

"Is it? I thought it a dreadful afternoon, madam. But then all my time is dreadful. I'm waiting to die, sister. I keep asking Perez here to hold a pillow over my face. It would be preferable to this. But the Spanish are far too devout to do murder, even if invited to."

Eleanor took a shallow breath as she decided how to respond. Robert might appear alert, but she had little faith in him being well enough, or sober enough, to answer her questions. Eleanor said a small, silent prayer for courage.

"I'm sorry for your illness, Robert, and I'll try not to keep you long, but I wished to talk about Mrs Wilson. You mentioned Mrs Wilson last time I was here and I wanted to ask what you meant when you said she has information about 'Julian and his lies.'"

She could have sworn that Robert's eyes lit up in his ravaged face. He gurgled, which turned into a cough, which deteriorated into a horrible coughing fit with bloody spittle and a wet burble that sounded as if he was drowning. Mr Perez jumped to his feet and pushed the dying man forward, rubbing his back and trying to get air into his lungs. It continued for minutes that seemed like hours. Had she killed the man with her curiosity?

The coughing finally subsided and Perez was able to get his patient to drink some of the wine, which proved to be a merciful restorative.

"I can leave if you wish, Robert. I don't wish to cause you any discomfort."

"No, no, my dear. Stay, stay," he rasped in a voice barely above a whisper. "Have had no entertainment for weeks, and you never know, you may be the death of me yet. Won't that be fun?"

Eleanor looked at Mr Perez, who nodded his agreement. She pitied the poor manservant. Caring for Robert Heyer must be an appalling duty.

"So," Robert whispered with glee, "how may I serve you, madam?"

Eleanor ignored the innuendo and took another shallow breath. To take a larger one of the fetid air would be overpowering, and she feared she would gag. "I ask you for the truth, Robert. I want to understand what relationship Mrs Wilson has, or had, with my husband?"

Robert gurgled again. "Ah, but what do I get in return? It seems an unfair arrangement that you get information, then leave without giving me a gift, a smidgeon of intelligence that I can mull over to keep myself entertained. I do like to learn of the follies of my family, and dwell on them. It keeps the mind sharp and Mother does so enjoy the odd titbits of gossip."

Eleanor's heart sank as she realised what Robert wanted. She prevaricated. "What do you mean, Robert?"

"I assume you and your companion travelled to Devon, dear sister, though you have been discreet and I've heard none of the servants gossiping. But if you want to know about Mrs Wilson's sad story, I want to know what happened to Julian's first wife.

What happened to Emily? I have long been curious about her sad demise. It's only fair, my dear Eleanor, that I spill the beans on Mrs Wilson in exchange for the story of Lady Emily Heyer." Robert gurgled.

Eleanor considered turning on her heel and not playing this sick game. She knew Robert would use her information to goad and hurt his mother, and even Julian, if he had the chance. It was sickening, but a miscalculation on Robert's part. Eleanor believed she could persuade Julian not to visit his brother, while Lady Heyer was already aware of the facts surrounding Emily's death. Hopefully, Robert would be dead before he might use the information to inflict further suffering on his family.

Eleanor nodded and, with a brief prayer to Emily for forgiveness, looked Robert in the eye and raised her chin. "I learned from Lady Emily's doctor that she'd been ill over the winter, had lost weight, and her courses had stopped. She thought she was with child and her health improved. Her death was caused by a fall down the stairs. The doctor deemed it to be a tragic accident."

"A tragic accident. How convenient. So much better than the truth for Julian. I hazard he could not get his wife with child and she killed herself after another disappointment. I'm not wrong, am I, sister? So, poor Emily suicided. To be expected after Julian had blamed her for years, just like he's blaming you. I told you my brother is delusional and infertile, didn't I, madam? Do you ever consider the sin of suicide, Eleanor?" Robert laughed.

Eleanor said nothing and stood her ground.

"But pray, madam, what did you learn in Devon about the wonderful lady, Mrs Wilson? I've little doubt you asked the locals. Come, it'll be fun. You can say what you learned and I'll endeavour to correct your misconceptions. Speak, dear sister, I want to see if you're as deluded as your husband."

Eleanor took another shallow breath, but did not look away. This was all he had left, this power to manipulate, but she would give as good as she could take. "I'll play your game, Robert, if it brings you enjoyment. I'll not begrudge you that. But, pray, let us be quick. I don't want to die before we exchange information, and the air in here is truly noxious."

Robert gurgled again, but thankfully did not have another coughing fit. It was enough to spur her on, to give Robert what he wanted. "I travelled to Devon, as you recommended, and I learned something of the sad demise of Emily Heyer, but I learnt little of Mrs Wilson."

"I'm surprised, sister. I always hoped it would have been part of the local mythology. A story for around a winter's fire when people yearn for tales of horror and woe."

"Perhaps your father was able to frighten the servants, sir. Perhaps he used his influence and money to subdue the truth."

"Hmm, you are probably correct, sister. He always was a frightening bastard."

"The little I learned was that Mr Wilson was your father's steward. He married a much younger woman who bore him a child. The man who imparted this news said he heard that you, Robert, had some involvement with Mrs Wilson, which Mr Wilson objected to. A duel occurred, and you killed Mr Wilson. The whole affair was hushed up and you were sent overseas."

"Was that all?"

"No," Eleanor gasped, but she was definitely struggling for air and suspected for the first time in her life that she might actually faint.

Robert giggled — at least it sounded as though it might have been a giggle — but whatever the sound, he proved to be observant. "Perez." He managed a hoarse command. "For God's sake, man, open a window and get Lady Heyer a chair. I think she's asphyxiating!"

A waft of delightfully cold and fresh air entered the room as Perez did as he was ordered. The servant also approached the bed and threw another blanket over the dying man.

"Sorry, my dear, can't smell my own shit." Robert pointed with a claw-like hand at his nose. "And Perez is immune to my stench and likes the room to be as warm as the south of Spain. I forget what fresh air is like. Are you fit to continue?"

Eleanor sank gratefully into the chair provided by Mr Perez. She looked at Robert, whose bright eyes encouraged further disclosure. She thought through her words, before continuing, "I also learned that, after her husband's murder, Mrs Wilson left the area and never returned. And, I learned she's been estranged from her family, who blamed her somehow, but I didn't get the particulars."

"Pathetic, Lady Heyer, absolutely pathetic. But I'm impressed you went to Devon to find the truth at all. Did the peasants stone your carriage? I've heard it riled up the locals when your husband closed down the estate. Put a lot of them out of work."

Eleanor realised that Robert might have been overseas for many years, but he'd obviously kept up to date with his family's affairs. He reminded Eleanor of a spider, who gathers gossip like

160

flies caught in his web, and then devours the corpses for his own edification. She shivered. His evil was palpable.

"No, Robert, they didn't stone my carriage." Eleanor decided that brevity might be the best way to curtail her brother-in-law's prying.

"Hmm." Robert snorted, but then his eyes lit up. "Well, madam, I suppose it's now my pleasant duty to enlighten you, to give you the full story of Mrs Wilson, without embellishments or tarradiddles. The whole horrible truth. How would that be?"

"Edifying, sir."

"You know, my dear, I start to like you. I just may become sorry to leave this earthly coil. You're providing excellent entertainment. Well, where to begin?" Robert paused theatrically. "It was summer, the last summer that my dear papa was to enjoy. Julian was down from university and we were having the usual fights and disputes to keep me happy. It was during July, I recollect. Mr Wilson had taken a fancy to a local lass, daughter of the butcher, as I recall. Wilson was an old man and she still a child, but he fancied her and would have her for his own. She was the prettiest little thing, slim and dark and desirable, but as silly as a bird. Green and gullible, but an attractive bit of muslin, nonetheless. Wilson was besotted and quite over the moon when she produced a fine young son. Trouble was, sweet Anna was less inclined to favour the stupid old goat, and she became quite mawkish. Julian found her crying bitterly one afternoon and, being the fool, he offered her a shoulder to cry on, and that, of course, turned into a full-blown dalliance." Robert chortled.

"All would've gone well if Julian — sorry, I appreciate he's your husband, but he's a fool — hadn't got deep into his cups one night. I goaded him into telling me how Mrs Wilson liked things in the cot. Well, what can one do but try the lady out? Julian and I were twins, and close enough in appearances then to bamboozle the general populace, so I plied Julian with more wine and then snuck off to his assignation with the delectable Mrs Wilson. Unfortunately, Mr Wilson returned unexpectedly from his rounds of the estate. I considered he'd been alerted that Julian was ravishing the trollop, and, of course, he found me in his wife's bed instead. She, the silly chit, had realised that I wasn't Julian. It had gotten a little rough, and she cried rape and had bruises to support her claim. Her affronted husband called me out."

Robert scrutinized Eleanor's face. "Sorry, my dear, don't mean to offend, but that's the way it happened."

"Don't give it a second thought, Robert. Pray continue." Eleanor spoke languidly, but experienced a sudden urge to smother the man herself.

"Well, the next day, Mr Wilson turned up with pistols. He was the best damned shot in Devon and I was still hung over. I did the only thing possible: I shot the braggart in the back. But his second took me down and all hell broke loose. I tried to implicate Julian, but he, being the heir, could do no evil. Father bullied and paid off the witnesses, leaned on the local magistrate and I got shipped off overseas. Little Anna's father proved to be a pious man and was determined she should give up her son to his care. He threatened to throw her in the poor house. Julian would have none of it, said he loved the hussy and that he'd put her up in London."

Eleanor swallowed hard. "You mean she became his mistress?"

Robert's eyes glittered. "Oh yes, still is. He provides her with a small house in Richmond and a housekeeper who has an expensive habit for gin. She's had two sons who she claims were fathered by your husband. The housekeeper is definitely of the mind that some manservant sired Mrs Wilson's brats. Said she chose a man who had similar looks to Julian. Your caring, stupid husband has been taken in and continues to support Mrs Wilson with a generous allowance and money for schooling the by-blows."

Eleanor felt faint again. She took a large breath and shook her head, totally aware of what pleasure she gave the dying man in the bed, but struggling to take in the information confirming her worst fears. "By-blows. You mean he has children with Mrs Wilson?"

"Oh yes, my dear. Two lovely boys. They must be about eight and seven now. Conveniently conceived when Julian had been married to poor Emily for about three years and had failed to produce an heir."

Eleanor heard the irony and hated this man even more. He was enjoying her discomfort, making light of her despair, and seeding doubts as he fed her the information that would've finally given her the courage to ask for a divorce. He must have sensed her anger even in the dimly lit room.

"Think, dear lady, think. It is something that my brother consistently fails to do. Do not be deluded, as he is, by her assertions that he's the father. They were involved for many years before Mrs Wilson had children. Julian was no doubt getting desperate and Mrs Wilson must have realised that her days were numbered, unless she provided him with a child. A delusion, my dear, but one that afforded that cunning woman with the continuing support of a generous benefactor, just when her charms were fading."

The fresh air in the room allowed Eleanor to take a deep breath, and that helped clear her thoughts and rally her judgement. Robert was sly indeed in the way he provided information. He wanted her to accept his nasty logic, to accept and provide the emotional disquiet he thrived upon. He wanted drama and denunciation. She was determined not to afford him that pleasure. She raised her eyes and challenged him in a cold, hard voice.

"Thank you, Robert. Your reasoning is sound and your assumptions fit your theory, but it is still only a theory. I can accept Julian cared for Mrs Wilson, and that she may even be his mistress. But given the way you both treated her, I'm glad he provided for her and that she is not in the poor house."

Eleanor exhaled, gathered her thoughts and selected her next words with care. "Regarding the parentage of the children, you've offered only speculation and no information based on facts. I cannot accept that Julian is mad or deluded. He wants children and has been possibly told by Mrs Wilson that he's the father of her two boys. His belief may be based on a lie, but it is a lie that is feasible. You've provided me with no conclusive evidence. I've gained little from your salacious telling of your evil actions. But, thank you Robert. I will pray Robert, that you remain alive for a long time. You deserve it."

Eleanor rose, nodded to Mr Perez and walked to the door.

Robert's voice rose like a bog mist from the depths of the bed. "Will you pursue the truth in Richmond, sister? Confront the lying Mrs Wilson in her den of iniquity?"

Eleanor turned with a serene smile and chose not to answer, a response not lost on her dying brother-in-law.

"You're more of a bitch than my mother, my lady," he shouted, then coughed horribly

Eleanor walked out, through the house and into the garden. In the shrubbery, she lost the contents of her stomach in a bed full of weeds.

Chapter Eight

June 26th 1823

Eleanor sat back in her chair and drank the Madeira. The fire burned bright and warm on her face, yet she felt deathly cold and tired. Robert's story still spun around in her head. She was sad and defeated, but also angry at her husband and his horrible brother. She had just recounted to Bertha and Lady Caroline the substance of her conversation with Robert. She'd made her report more acceptable for a mother and a lady. Even so, the recounting left her shaky and queasy.

Following her bilious attack in the shrubbery, Eleanor found she couldn't escape the dreadful stench of the sickroom. It had penetrated into her clothes and her hair. With every breath, she seemed to inhale the noxious aroma. She had returned to her room and taken a long, hot bath, washed her hair, and sent all her clothes to the laundry. By that time, it was dinner. Eleanor's appetite for food was diminished, but after two large glasses of wine, she felt steadier and able to talk.

Lady Caroline listened to Eleanor's account with a stern face. She'd stared into the fire as she took in the truth of her son's perfidy. She then turned to Eleanor with a penetrating gaze. "I'm sure, my dear, that you haven't given me the entire story. I know

Robert would have enjoyed baiting and offending you. He has a talent for it. I've fled his room in tears more than once."

"Oh, I was sickened, ma'am, truly sickened. But while he enjoyed disconcerting me, I think he told the truth, or at least his version of the truth. I have the impression he knows that the facts would be more distressing than any invention he can conjure. But one cannot be sure about Robert. I'm sorry, Mother, but he lies superbly and acts with no conscience, without care for anyone but himself."

Lady Caroline nodded agreement. "When he was born, he nearly died. His poor little head was bruised and misshapen. The midwife assured me he'd recover. She was of the opinion that Julian had squashed his brother in the delivery. I've always thought that Robert's brain suffered damage during the birth, and he's wreaked his vengeance on the world, and particularly Julian, ever since."

"Then I must pity him, Mother, but that doesn't help me accept his declarations as the truth. I've more information about Mrs Wilson, but still no definite answers. I'm at a loss to know what to believe," Eleanor said.

The room fell into silence, only the pop and crackle of the fire breaking the contemplative silence. Eleanor found that her head buzzed even as her eyelids fluttered. Oh, how good it would be to stop wondering, to just accept that she was at fault and leave it to Julian to do something about the childless state of their marriage. As a man, it should be his responsibility and duty to produce an heir.

"So, Eleanor, what will you do next?" Bertha asked in her governess voice. That always demanded an answer.

Eleanor sighed. "Oh, I don't know Bertha. I'm starting to believe that it's beyond my ability to work this out. I'm ready to accept that we'll have no children. But it's Julian's decision if he wants to divorce me and take on a new wife. I'll not stand in his way."

Bertha snapped, "Don't be a coward, Eleanor. You've come this far and learned much. You must learn more, and there is only one person who knows the truth of this sorry history. You must visit this Mrs Wilson."

Eleanor rose from her chair and walked to the fire, then rounded on her friend. "And what good would that do? That woman is hardly going to admit that she's fooled my husband into believing he's the father of her children. She faces poverty and ruin without him as her benefactor, and she has her children to protect."

"And you have the right to children, too. You have the right to save your marriage and reputation. She is a mistress and you are a lawful wife. You are Viscountess Heyer, you can demand a response," Lady Caroline interjected.

Eleanor harrumphed. "I can't demand anything, Mother, and I'll not ruin the life of that poor woman and her children. Goodness, she might have made a mistake as a young girl, but I can sympathize with her situation. Robert described her as little more than a child when she married Mr Wilson. And I doubt they gave her much choice in the matter. She was pretty but poor. He was old and rich, and while I don't condone her actions since, she was, and still is, acting to protect herself and her children."

"You're more generous than I would be, Eleanor." Lady Caroline sniffed, "But what if this woman has feathered her nest and lied to Julian? Given him false peace of mind. He's refused to accept that he has a problem, and subsequently has done nothing to get help. Maybe his infertility can be treated or cured, and then he could have children, legitimate children, with you."

Eleanor bit her lip. Her mother-in-law had a valid argument. "It would still need Mrs Wilson to admit the children are not Julian's. And she's unlikely to tell the truth of it. She has too much to lose."

"Then we must find out the truth some other way," Bertha added thoughtfully. "What did Robert say, actually say, about her situation? He must get his information from somewhere."

Eleanor dragged her mind back to the dreadful sickroom. She again smelt the stench, and it heightened her memory. "Robert said that Mrs Wilson's housekeeper had a drinking problem and liked her gin, but insisted that the Wilson boys were not fathered by Julian. She claimed a manservant had been selected for the purpose and Mrs Wilson was deceiving Julian to ensure she remained his mistress."

"Then we must discover the truth from her servants. Her neighbours may also have some intelligence about the comings and goings at Mrs Wilson's house," Bertha said.

Eleanor shook her head. "But it's unseemly, surely, to spy on that poor woman and her children. It's something I don't believe a lady would do."

"We did it in Devon. This is no different."

"But it is different." Eleanor paused as she tried to get her objections clear in her own head. "In Devon, we were searching into the past, getting information about Emily, who'd died, who was unaffected by our enquiries. Mrs Wilson is alive. If Julian discovered the truth of this matter, it could cause the ruin of Mrs Wilson and her children."

"Phish, Eleanor. If she's lied to my son, she deserves ruination," Lady Caroline interjected harshly, then added, "I know you pity her, but you and Julian shouldn't continue to suffer because of her perfidy. She acted in a wanton manner with Julian when she was already married, and if Robert hadn't meddled, it might have been Julian in that duel. And he would have been shot dead. No, that woman is not blameless, Eleanor, and both you and Julian deserve, and need, the truth."

"But what if we discover she is telling the truth? That these children are Julian's." Eleanor blinked as that thought settled.

"Then he can divorce you and remarry. He may even marry Mrs Wilson and adopt the children, make the eldest his heir." Lady Caroline could be refreshingly insensitive.

"That would be unacceptable, ma'am," Bertha cut in. "Children are illegitimate unless the parents were married at the time of birth and, as far as I know, illegitimate children cannot inherit an entailed title. It would also be intolerable in the eyes of society."

Lady Caroline glared at Bertha. "Then he must marry someone else and have children with them. I'm sorry, Eleanor. I've come like you, but the need for an heir must take precedence. And if Julian cannot have children, then Christopher must be prevailed upon to stop roaming around the world. He must settle and take a wife. He will be an acceptable heir, but we will have no more of this prevarication. The Heyer family needs an heir, and Julian is getting older."

Forthrightness, Eleanor thought, was much underrated. She almost laughed at the sheer audacity of her mother-in-law's stance. Lady Heyer represented the epitome of the aristocracy and a very determined champion of her family's needs, but she had little sympathy for anyone else.

"I'd still find it difficult to spy on Mrs Wilson. Julian will throw her out, and she and her children would be homeless if we discovered she had been duplicitous. She's no relatives from what we discovered in Devon. She might end up in the poor house," Eleanor argued.

"If she's lying, it's no more than she deserves. But if you worry about her, I'll provide for her needs. I'll make sure she has a position here and I'll put her boys through school. The Heyer family must take some responsibility for her, given Robert's reprehensible behaviour. Now, will that satisfy your missish sensibilities, Eleanor?"

"Yes, I suppose so, ma'am." Eleanor nodded, too tired to argue in the face of such maternal intransigence.

"Good." Lady Caroline appeared to be enjoying herself. "So, how do we go about this spying business? Any ideas, Miss Smith. You seem to be an intelligent sort of lady. Let's work out a plan."

Getting the address of Mrs Wilson's house in Richmond proved to be much easier than Eleanor had expected. On their return to London, Eleanor waited for an afternoon when Julian was out at his club. She had rummaged in the desk in his bedroom. There were several bills addressed to Swan Cottage, 12 River Lane, Richmond. Eleanor noted the address, and she and Bertha took a day trip to see Richmond Palace, strolled around Richmond Green and then explored the small laneways leading to the river.

Swan Cottage proved to be a modest two-storey building that fronted a narrow lane. It had a neatly tended side garden and looked well-appointed inside. It was tucked away from the grand houses and villas set around fashionable Richmond Green, but close enough to the park and river to provide plenty of space for young children to play.

The following week, Bertha took a room in a small guesthouse three doors down from Swan Cottage. Miss Smith was staying in the area to visit her elderly aunt, who had dropsy. Bertha selected a room on the first floor that conveniently overlooked River Lane. It afforded her a splendid view of the comings and goings on the cobbled street. It became apparent that Mrs Wilson and her boys were known to, and well regarded by, Mrs Logan, the proprietor of the guesthouse. "Oh, the Wilson boys." She smiled fondly when Bertha commented on the noise as the two boys' voices echoed loudly in the narrow laneway. "They can get unruly, but boys will be boys. They'd benefit from a bit more discipline from their mother, but she's a widow on her own, so it can't be easy. But the older boy turned out fine. He's in the Navy now and doing very well."

"It must indeed be hard for a widow alone with three boys to raise. Has she no help from anyone?" Bertha asked innocently.

Mrs Logan proved to be an attentive neighbour. "Oh, there is an uncle, ma'am, but he only visits occasionally. He might have a place in the country. He visits more in the spring, probably when he's up in London for the Season, but for the rest of the year you rarely see him. Mind, I've seen him take the boys and Mrs Wilson out on occasions. Takes them boating or up to the park in his fancy carriage, but he's not their papa, so I suppose he has no obligation, really."

Bertha learned little more about the Widow Wilson and her boys from Mrs Logan. She did note the comings and goings of Mrs Wilson's two servants, and was able to pass on to Eleanor, that the housekeeper regularly attended a small tavern at the end of River Lane.

Mary and Victor were requested to gain more information from the tavern owner. He sold beer, rum and gin, and was famous for his half-penny meat pies. Mary was proving to be adept at acting, and Victor was an astute man, and good conversationalist with an excellent memory. They reported back to Bertha and Eleanor on an afternoon when Julian was at his club.

"It was easy, ma'am." Victor shook his head in wonder. "I went there on Thursday evening and put it about that I was courting Mary, who was the maid, of a Miss Smith staying at the guesthouse in River Lane. I got to talking with the publican about women who drink too much, and he became most effusive about his regular customer, Mrs Molly Scales. He said she was a regular all week, but that every Friday, on her day off, she drank like a fish. Said he didn't know how she kept her position as housekeeper to the widow up the road. He didn't mince his words, ma'am, said she was a nasty piece of work."

Victor continued with a grin. "Well, on Friday night both me and Mary went in for a pie and an ale. It was getting late, and the housekeeper didn't show, so we were disappointed like, but then this older woman came in. The publican gave me a wink, so I gathered it was Mrs. Scales, and I pointed her out to Mary."

Mary interrupted. "Oh, ma'am, she was horrible. Had a red nose and veins all across her cheeks. Her clothes were dirty, her hair dirty, and she didn't look like a respectable person at all.

We wondered how we'd get her talking. She just sat at the bar in a corner. I thought she didn't look likely to enjoy a yarn. But Victor said he'd jostle her arm to spill her drink, then offer to buy her another. And he did, ma'am, and it worked a treat. So, we joined her at the counter. Victor brought her a big jug of gin, which was really clever, don't you think?"

Eleanor smiled. "Brilliant indeed."

Victor took up the story. "Mrs. Scales drank fast and deep, and it didn't take long for her to start moaning about her position. Claimed she used to be a cook in a grand house in London, but got told to come down here and look after the Lord's mistress and his by-blows."

"She was really nasty about Mrs Wilson and her sons," Mary cut in. "Called the boys 'little shits' — excuse the language, ma'am — and said Mrs Wilson was lazy and stupid, but took on all the airs of the gentry. She talked about how Mrs Wilson was married to a steward of a grand house in Devon and how her husband had been murdered by someone in the family. Said she now gets supported by the ones who murdered him. So, we knew we had the right person."

Victor resumed the narration. "I said, 'how awful for the poor woman', but Mrs Scales said adamantly, ma'am, that Mrs Wilson deserved no pity. She said that Mrs Wilson was cunning and made sure she got nicely set up. Said she'd been a widow for fifteen years and had another two sons and not a husband in sight. She reckons that Mrs Wilson has to pay for being 'supported by the family' and that just makes her a harlot. Got the impression that Mrs Scales really hates Mrs Wilson. She was right cruel in what she had to say about the two younger sons." Victor actually coloured at this recollection.

Mary, more aware of the reason for Eleanor's quest for information, spoke up. "Mrs Scales got nastier the more she drank. She said that Mrs Wilson got herself pregnant when the 'uncle' started to lose interest. Said that Mrs Wilson made sure she had a couple of by-blows to 'keep him strung along'. Hinted that there was a butler from one of the big houses on the green who called on Mrs Wilson regularly for a couple of years and that the children were probably his."

"Does she have any proof of what she said?" Bertha asked, thinking this information differed from Robert's implication that Mrs Wilson's manservant had fathered the children.

Mary nodded. "I asked, but Mrs Scales was well in her cups by then. She said the butler usually called when she had an afternoon off, and that Mrs Wilson would always send Jimmy, who was the manservant then, off on some errand, leaving her and the butler alone. She said she thought it was this butler who did the deed because he looked a bit like the uncle." Mary glanced towards Eleanor and flushed.

"Did she say anything about Mrs Wilson's benefactor?" Eleanor changed the difficult subject but hesitated to name her husband.

Mary blushed. "Mrs. Scales said that the 'uncle' was easily bamboozled and far too trusting. Said he just accepted that when the second son was born, it was his, even when Mrs Wilson claimed the babe arrived early by five weeks to fit with its conception. Mrs Styles said it was a big, healthy baby too, but he never suspected he may have been cuckolded. Mrs Scales said that he accepted a 'bag of moonshine' and took those boys on as his own with no questions asked."

Eleanor grimaced. She was asking her servants to undermine the very fabric of her husband's integrity and common sense. It was a horrible position to be in. She had contemplated not proceeding with her investigations. She had worried over it for hours, and it had taken considerable persuasion from Bertha to spur her forward. But her marriage was in jeopardy, and, as Bertha rightly pointed out, servants usually knew all about their employer's foibles and failings. Mary and Victor had helped before, understood her situation, and had proved loyal friends as well as discreet servants. Eleanor had acknowledged that truth, and the plan progressed. Yet, her spying had yielded little proof of Julian's ability to father children. She still had only speculation and the malicious opinions of a disaffected servant to guide the future of her marriage.

"Did you discover anything else?"

"No, ma'am." Mary sighed. "Mrs. Scales was truly drunk by then. She got sick, so me and Victor took her back to the cottage. The manservant there didn't act surprised. Gave the impression like this happened regularly. He spoke to Mrs Scales very roughly. He certainly doesn't like her, madam.

Eleanor nodded and found a smile for her enterprising servants. "Thank you, Mary, thank you, Victor. You have done well."

July 10th 1823

A week later, the Dowager Viscountess Heyer came to London for some shopping and a much-needed break from the duties of caring for her dying son. Eleanor had written a letter containing a brief summation of her investigation into Mrs

Wilson, but, of course, the Dowager Countess had to come, in person, to hear the full account. She had questioned Eleanor, Bertha, and even Mary for several hours. Once she had contemplated all the gathered intelligence, she insisted on having the final say in the matter.

"I refuse to accept that Julian would be so easily taken in by his mistress. He's a clever, sensible man in everything else, so why would he be so obtuse in this? Eleanor, I'll not be able to accept the matter unless I see those children for myself. I'll know my own grandchildren. We must visit Richmond and see them with our own eyes. I'll have the truth of it."

They planned the trip for a Saturday afternoon, reasoning that the children would not be in school and most likely be out and about. It proved easy enough to disguise themselves as a widow and daughter in full mourning with black bombazine dresses, gloves, and heavily veiled bonnets.

It was a warm day, so they conducted a stately stroll along the diagonal paths that traversed the wide expanse of Richmond Green. Eleanor became hot in the thick black dress, but Lady Caroline was not to be diverted from her quest. "Oh, stop complaining, Eleanor. It's the warmest I've been all year, and I'm quite enjoying the sensation. You can take a seat in the shade and then we'll walk over and get some tea and cake at the tea rooms on the other side. That will afford us a good view of the entrance to River Lane."

The tea house offered small tables under an awning. The attentive waitress gave special consideration to two ladies of the first order and efficiently supplied a large pot of tea and a selection of delicate cakes. As well as being overly warm, Eleanor found herself increasingly nervous about the prospect of seeing her husband's children and mistress. Her heart beat fast, her hands were clammy and her head ached.

She didn't expect to see Julian emerge from River Lane with an older, but still handsome, woman on his arm and two young boys running ahead, shouting with happiness at the prospect of flying the brightly coloured kites they held in their arms. The sight nearly made Eleanor drop her tea cup and produced an unexpected oath from her mother-in-law.

"God forbid, look at that, Eleanor."

Eleanor found she could do nothing but look. Mrs Wilson was smiling and appeared proud to be escorted by such a fine gentleman. She had a fuller figure, as was to be expected from the mother of three children, but she carried herself well. Her face was oval, with large dark eyes, and black hair that framed her face beneath a fine bonnet. Her dark-blue dress was modest and well cut and she wore cream gloves and black boots. They appeared like a married couple out for an afternoon's play with their family. It broke Eleanor's heart to see Julian look so happy.

"Well, she doesn't present like a trollop." Lady Caroline nodded in the direction of the passing couple. "But that's what she is, Eleanor, a common trollop."

"Mother, please." Eleanor hoped the couple at the next table hadn't overheard Lady Caroline's clearly spoken oath, and her assessment of Mrs Wilson.

"Hmph, but it's true Eleanor. She's nothing but a base-born mistress posing as a respectable woman," Lady Caroline said in a more acceptable mutter.

Julian walked Mrs Wilson to a bench in the shade and then proceeded with his sons to the middle of the green. And they could so easily have been his sons. They were dark-haired boys with knobbly knees and skinny elbows, their faces alight with carefree happiness as they ran around Julian, shouting instructions for him to hold the kite string. There was a small, errant breeze that made the kite-flying challenging and involved a lot of laughter, shouted instructions, and tossing the kites into the air. The whole exercise became quite pointless, as the kites would take to the sky for a few minutes, and then spiral into the grass. But Julian was patient and persistent, cajoling the boys to try again and again, laughing with them as the kites lost the breeze, and untangling the kite tails when they knotted. Eleanor had never seen her husband look so content.

After a half an hour, Mrs Wilson went over to the jovial group, nodded towards River Lane, and then, taking Julian's arm again, strolled towards the café. As they passed, Eleanor heard the youngest boy asking, "Can we take a punt out like last time, sir, and feed the swans?" And then they disappeared down the lane.

Eleanor's hands were shaking. She was light-headed and finding it difficult to breathe. Her heart raced, pounding in her ears.

Lady Caroline waved imperiously for the serving girl's attention. "More tea, immediately, please," she commanded, "and a glass of water straightaway. My daughter's feeling unwell."

Eleanor took a shaky breath and found that the pain in her chest eased. Another breath allowed her vision to return to normal, and she realised she had stared at her husband and his children for over half an hour, without wavering and hardly breathing. Lady Caroline and the rest of the world had disappeared, become totally inconsequential. It was a terrifying experience, and Eleanor was happy she was well hidden behind her black veil.

Another few breaths had Eleanor's roiling stomach settle. She shook her hands under the table and gasped with the pain as blood flowed into her clenched fingers. She searched in her reticule for a handkerchief and mopped her brow under the veil.

"Oh, my goodness." Eleanor took a sip of water and the liquid cooled her parched mouth and throat. "Oh goodness, Mother, I never expected that. I never truly accepted that he had children. But he has a family. Those boys are his family, no matter what their parentage. Those boys, to all intents and purposes, are his sons."

Lady Caroline's own hands were trembling, but her voice was firmer. "I tried to find fault with those children, but they looked just like Julian. Their colouring, their mannerisms, the way they laughed and spoke. They reminded me so much of him when he was their age, but he was never so carefree, always quiet and sad. I'm so unsure, Eleanor."

"Me too, Mother, but Julian looked so happy. They were all so happy. I always sensed he would make a wonderful papa, and he was so good with them. I can't accept they're not his children."

The arrival of the serving girl with a tray interrupted their discourse and allowed Eleanor to regain some equilibrium as Lady Caroline poured fresh tea. The hot beverage was sweet and welcome.

Putting the pot down, Lady Caroline huffed. "I thought to disclaim them, that it would be so easy. But those children could be my grandsons, Eleanor, and I find myself reluctant indeed to offer them, or poor Julian, further grief. Especially after learning of the character of Mrs Wilson's housekeeper. She's a confabulator. A drunken woman with no loyalty except to a bottle of gin."

Eleanor nodded agreement. "Yes, and I believe she is the source of Robert's nasty gossip."

Lady Caroline sniffed. "That woman needs to be dismissed, but I'm most angry at Robert. Even from his death bed, that boy can meddle and cause anguish."

The carriage ride back to Mayfair was blessedly silent, giving Eleanor time to reflect on what she had seen, while her mother-in-law shut her eyes and dozed.

Eleanor recalled her impressions of Mrs Wilson. She'd looked like a respectable widow, a widow who was highly regarded by her neighbour, Mrs. Logan. Her sons were carefree but polite, and this reflected well on their mother. The information that her eldest son had done well in the Navy was in her favour, too. Mrs. Anna Wilson appeared to be a pleasant middle-class lady. As she strolled with Julian and her sons in the park, it gave the impression of a contented family group.

Mrs Scales was a vindictive woman with a drinking problem who had a grudge against Mrs Wilson. She resented her situation as a housekeeper at Swan Cottage and had spread salacious gossip about her employer for little more than a few glasses of gin. Eleanor was sure that Robert had met Mrs Scales at some stage. She imagined the two of them concocting their lies and innuendos with just enough of the truth to make it feasible. Robert would probably have dropped in his own ideas about the parentage of the Wilson boys to Mrs. Scales. He was clever and convincing, and she would've been gullible and addled with drink, readily accepting Robert's version of the truth.

And Robert had proved he wasn't to be trusted and had reason to be vindictive towards Mrs Wilson. He would have no loyalty to a woman who had rightfully accused him of deception and rape, causing him to be exiled overseas. No, Robert wasn't beyond causing Mrs Wilson further harm from his deathbed.

Having seen Julian with the Wilson boys, Eleanor had no hesitation in believing that he accepted, even welcomed, them as his own. Robert may have implied that Julian was gullible, and delusional, but Eleanor understood that, unless he had firm evidence to the contrary, Julian would be proud of those boys, would enjoy them and even love them. To destroy that illusion would be extremely cruel and would likely shatter the lives of the hapless Mrs Wilson and her sons. And to what end? Eleanor still didn't have definitive proof Julian could not father children. It might still be her fault that she'd poisoned her chances of happiness by pursuing her passion for art.

And, in the end, Julian had been kind and responsible to a woman he'd romanced as a young man. He'd done the right thing when Robert had murdered her husband. He'd cared for her and had turned to her again when Emily became sickly and melancholic and failed to produce an heir. Who could blame him for his actions?

Eleanor discovered that she no longer held any ill feeling towards her husband. She better understood his actions and even forgave his deception towards her. As a gentleman, he had taken the decision of a husband to protect his wife from some unsavoury truths about his former wife and his mistress. It was wrong. It was demeaning, and caused her more pain than she needed, but he had done it for a reason.

Eleanor now knew that Julian, like many men in society, had a mistress and illegitimate children. A circumstance he would hardly disclose openly to his wife. She now had the truth, and the price of that truth was acceptance. Eleanor felt more at peace than she had for many years.

The noise level in the busy streets of London roused Lady Caroline from her slumber. She gave a little shake and stretched her neck, assuming the posture of an aristocrat with practised ease. "Oh, home already, I didn't realise I'd dozed for so long." She leaned forward and patted Eleanor's knee. "My dear girl, we both have a lot to ponder on. I suggest we gather in the parlour with Miss Smith after dinner, if you're up to it."

"I'm fine, Mother." And Eleanor comprehended she did feel fine. "After dinner will be good."

Julian didn't dine with them, but sent a note to say he would dine at his club and would be back late. Eleanor had little doubt that he'd tarried in Richmond with his mistress and her family. As she received the note graciously from the footman, Eleanor wondered just how many of the staff in London knew the Viscount had a mistress. The search for the truth had opened her eyes to the fact that the lives of the gentry provided rich fodder for speculation to those who worked for them. It was an edifying lesson to learn and would certainly make her much more discreet around servants in the future.

They brought Bertha up to date with the events of the afternoon, and she took some time to sort through the information with some pertinent questions.

"So, you suspect Robert has somehow engaged with Mrs Scales and concocted malicious lies about Julian and Mrs Wilson?" Bertha said.

"Yes. He was in London for several months after he left Spain. He would have acquainted himself with Mrs Scales before he removed to Surrey." Eleanor glanced at Lady Caroline, to see her reaction to the accusation against her son. She need not have worried.

"Most likely, Robert saw the opportunity to drop his poison into the mind of that horrible, stupid woman. He's a clever man, and manipulative."

"But what was his purpose?" Bertha continued.

Lady Caroline answered before Eleanor could make her own response. "Because he wanted to cause Julian grief, of course. Because he was determined to destroy his brother's happiness. He's always wanted to make trouble for Julian. I consider it stems from his poorly formed brain and jealousy, jealousy that he was born second."

Bertha took a moment to work through her reply. Eleanor realised she chose her words with precision and care. A technique to help arrive at a sound judgement. "I've not met Robert, but from his history and your experiences, Eleanor, do you think Robert could be so clever? It would appear that he has used you to cause your husband more grief."

Eleanor bit her lip as she reflected on the events of the past few weeks. She nodded as the realisation hit. "Yes, I suspect his plan was for me to confront Julian and plant doubts about the parentage of Mrs Wilson's sons, causing him grief. Robert probably thought I would then demand a divorce. It would have destroyed Julian's relationship with Mrs Wilson and the boys, and destroyed our marriage. Oh, yes, Robert is clever indeed, Bertha, and he would have extracted a great deal of pleasure from his meddling if I'd acted as he expected I would."

Lady Caroline sniffed. "But not clever enough, Eleanor. He didn't consider that I would become involved, that I would know my own grandchildren when I saw them. That I would put paid to his nasty schemes."

Bertha responded, "Ma'am, I don't think that it's possible to establish the parentage of children by observation alone, even if it is the astute observation of a grandmother."

"Rubbish. I know my own blood. How dare you imply otherwise, madam?"

"But do you, ma'am? Your description of today's events shows the Viscount accepts the Wilson boys are his. But there remain some questions. Emily didn't conceive for five years. Eleanor hasn't conceived for nearly six, and even Mrs Wilson's youngest son is about seven, so she's had no additional children either. Mrs Wilson's circumstances are such that she totally depends on the Viscount, and who'd blame her if she's had children and passed them off as her benefactor's? We cannot definitively rule out that the Viscount cannot father an heir, and that is what is important. To produce a legitimate heir."

Lady Caroline looked as if she would continue with her argument, but she was sharp and sometimes sensitive. She swallowed whatever severe words she had intended and glanced at Eleanor with a tight-lipped smile. "Yes, of course. Our beliefs about this matter are irrelevant, really. What is needed now is a plan for what we should do next."

Bertha responded with steel in her voice. "What Eleanor does next, ma'am, it is Eleanor's choice alone."

Eleanor wondered if another argument would occur, but Lady Caroline took a breath and seemed to deflate. Her sons had not given her joy, nor the grandchildren she desired, and that realization looked as though it struck with the force of a hammer. She nodded slowly and swallowed hard. "Yes, you're correct, as usual, Miss Smith. Eleanor is the Viscountess, the legal wife. She must decide how to proceed."

It was a cool evening, even in the middle of summer. Eleanor rose and stood before the small fire in the grate, enjoying the warmth on her chilly hands. Her own thoughts had coalesced into a determination. Yes, she wanted children to give Julian an heir, but she was not prepared to do anything that would destroy the lives of others. She regarded the Dowager Viscountess Heyer and her old governess and most stalwart friend. "I will do nothing."

"Nothing. What do you mean, nothing?" The Dowager Viscountess shook her head. "You can't mean it, Eleanor. You are the Viscountess. Surely you must do something. It's your duty to produce an heir."

"Yes, it is, but if I, or my husband, are incapable, then we may just have to accept that's our lot in life."

"But, but where does that leave my Julian? He deserves the chance to have a family, to have legitimate sons and daughters."

"Yes, of course he does." Eleanor kept her voice smoothly modulated.

"Then you must step down. He must remarry. You must ask for a divorce."

"No, ma'am." Eleanor looked her mother-in-law straight in the eye. "If Julian wants a divorce, I'll not stand in his way. But I believe that I can have children, as much as he believes he has produced children. I don't know if we will ever find out the truth of it, but I'll not take the blame anymore. I have allowed my life to become one of misery and despair by doing so, and it will not continue. Learning about my husband and his history in the past month has given me peace and understanding about him and his actions. But I don't condone his secretiveness and condemnation. If he wants a divorce, he must ask me and discuss our situation openly and honestly, including the reasons he deems he cannot be at fault."

Lady Caroline looked as if she had swallowed a bee. Her jaw dropped, and she went as red as a field poppy. She surged to her feet. "So, you want him to admit to having a mistress and children?"

"Yes."

"I know my son. He will not do it."

"Then we shall have a long and unproductive marriage. I will adhere to the vows I made during my marriage ceremony. I believe I can have children. I'll not relinquish my title and status to become a pariah in society without absolute proof of me being barren. Let Julian ask for a divorce and cite his infidelity as the reason. I have done nothing wrong and will not accept that blame as well."

"So, you will leave the Heyer family without an heir?"

"There's always Christopher."

Lady Caroline nodded, "Yes, there is always Christopher."

Chapter Nine

September 22nd 1823

Acceptance, Eleanor discovered, was nothing more than how one thought about a matter. Now that she knew the history of her husband, the sad truth about Emily, and had knowledge about, and, yes, even sympathy for Mrs Wilson and her sons, she discovered her own anguish faded. Her sleep improved. She enjoyed the flavours and textures of her food and drinks again. She saw the trees and flowers in the parks and garden, enjoyed the wind and sun on her face, and found peace.

It wasn't always easy. There were days when her thoughts churned and her mood was bleak. What if she had confronted Julian? If she'd asked for a divorce? If she had never taken up oil painting? But those thoughts were unhelpful. There were no answers to them. They made her head ache, her heart pound, and her sadness intensify to the extent that she would keep to her bed with the fear she would explode and shout out her anger and frustration, causing more misery.

Bertha proved astute at understanding her moods. She became even more of a tyrant, but always with the best of intentions. Making her dress, eat breakfast, and take a walk no matter what the weather. They played a game while out and about. Find the best-looking tree in the park, look for all the red flowers, name five different bird songs, and discover a scene you would like to sketch. At the end of their walks, Eleanor found it easier to talk, to open up about her doubts, and Bertha, with her carefully constructed questions, allowed her to understand that she had made the right choices.

Lady Caroline had left for Surrey several days after their visit to Richmond. Eleanor had worried that her mother-in-law would confront Julian, reveal that she knew all about his children, and insist that he ask for a divorce. But Lady Caroline surprised her, she had said nothing to her eldest son.

"She's probably delighted that Christopher will inherit." Bertha said.

"Yes, she seems inordinately fond of him, and I believe she would be most happy to have him as the next Viscount. And why not? He hasn't disappointed her, not like Robert and not like Julian and me."

Acceptance took time to work its magic, but by the end of summer, Eleanor had more energy and a new zest for life. She started sketching and using water colours, and found that her skills, while rusty, gave her immense pleasure. As she drew and painted, her whole being became engaged in the practice, and it led to a sense of tranquillity she'd not experienced for years. She wrote to her mama and sisters again, visited them when they were in town, had friends around for afternoon teas and then dinners, which she and Julian hosted and enjoyed.

Acceptance allowed Eleanor to listen to her husband, have small, inconsequential conversations with him, to smile at him and share some outings and entertainments. It was what was expected of a man and his wife, even if their relationship was shallow and based on lies. Julian responded with more consideration. He still expected Eleanor to uphold her marital duties, but he was more gentle, less driven, and he would not insist on sharing a bed with her every night of the week. It wasn't a passionate relationship, but it was tolerable.

Eleanor's thoughts about Julian were mixed. She would always be disappointed with his secretiveness and his cold blaming, but her antipathy was tempered when she considered his dreadful childhood and his awful grief at losing Emily in such tragic circumstances. He seemed weak to her but, like most men, he regarded the female sex as weaker than the male and kept his secrets to protect her from the truth. It was an erroneous belief and had caused most of the problems in her own marriage, and probably the marriages of many other women. And it was wrong.

Conversely, she was proud that Julian had supported Mrs Wilson. At the time of the murder, it would have been easy, and even acceptable, to discard Mrs Wilson, to denounce her as an adulteress and send her and her child to an unforgiving family or the poor house. Eleanor had little doubt such actions were common among the gentry, but Julian had taken responsibility. He had protected Mrs Wilson and her child, provided them with a good life and a home. She sometimes smiled at the thought that she knew of her husband's mistress and wished her well.

Bertha came up with a plan to deal with Mrs Scales by penning an anonymous note and having Victor post it in Richmond.

Dear Mrs Wilson,

I need to give you warning that your housekeeper, Mrs Scales, is not to be trusted. She drinks, and I have heard such dreadful reports

*about her utterances and slander about you and your sons when she
is in her cups in the tavern on River Road.*

You need to know, Mrs Wilson.
Yours truly,
A concerned neighbour

A week later, Bertha took a trip to Richmond and booked another night at Mrs Logan's guesthouse. Mrs Logan required little prompting to disclose that there had been quite a fuss in the street the previous week.

"Mrs Wilson was required to dismiss her housekeeper, and Mrs. Scales didn't take it well, Miss Smith. That woman shouted and swore outside number twelve for most of the morning. I thought they would have to call a constable, but she left in the end. Mr Higgins, who works at that tavern, said Mrs Scales likes her drink and can be nasty indeed when inebriated. He said it was 'good riddance to a bad lot' in his opinion."

Bertha's report lifted Eleanor's spirits, and she happily informed Mary that she and Victor's prying had had such a positive outcome.

Mary grinned. "She deserved it, my lady. She was disloyal, and no servant should be disloyal."

Eleanor nodded her thanks and requested Julian increase the pay of her lady's maid. "She's discrete, Julian, and always willing to do that bit more than her usual duties to see to my comfort. I don't know what I'd do without her.

In October, Julian received a black-bordered envelope. Lady Caroline had penned the brief letter herself.

19th October 1823

   My Dear Julian and Eleanor,

   It is my sad duty to inform you that Robert passed away peacefully last evening. He was attended by myself, Dr Wilson, Reverend Lackey, and Mr Perez.

   I would prefer that his interment be a small family gathering and have approached Mr Lackey to conduct the funeral service at St. Peter's in Ash on the 23rd of the month. Please confirm that these arrangements are suitable for you both.

   Please take care of the funeral notices in London and inform Mr Upton that he will be required to read Robert's will and settle any legal matters outstanding on the 24th October.

   Mr Perez has declined my offer of ongoing employment. He has stated a preference to return to Spain. Your brother, Christopher, is briefly in England and will delay his departure to America in order to attend the funeral. He will organise for a passage home for Mr Perez. I believe that some remuneration to this worthy gentleman is warranted and will leave it to you to provide a suitable amount.

   I will expect you on the 20th or 21st of the month, unless I receive your direction that these arrangements are unsuitable.

   Yours affectionately,

   Mother.

   Dowager Viscountess Heyer.

Julian read out the contents of the letter at breakfast. "Have you any plans for the week?"

"Nothing that can't be changed. I need to alter my black evening gown, so I'll attend the dressmaker and milliner today and discuss with Mary what other clothes will be suitable. I think half mourning may be acceptable, as Robert wasn't in society. It'll be a rushed, but I think I can organise everything."

"Good. I'll order the carriage and make arrangements to leave tomorrow."

And so, the passing of Robert Heyer became a matter of propriety and arrangements. It gave Eleanor a shiver of unease. Would this be her fate when she died? Would she be someone who had not loved or been loved? Someone who had no children to lament her wasted life? Oh, she had family and friends, but no family of her own. No joyous babies who would have every chance to grow into fortunate children. No grown adult children who would give her pride in their accomplishments, their character, and give her grandchildren whom she could spoil and cosset unreservedly. It presented a bleak future, and acceptance didn't always manage the grief. She could certainly understand Lady Caroline's disappointment and sorrow at her children's unhappy lives.

The afternoon was busy. Julian had to see his man of business and the family lawyer, organise the carriages and horses, roster servants, and provide for their transport to his mother's house.

Eleanor met with her housekeeper and had trunks packed with bedding, dinnerware, and cutlery. She asked the cook to pack a large hamper of food and arranged for a kitchen maid to travel to Ash and provide extra help. The funeral would be a private affair, but neighbours and friends of the Dowager

Viscountess Heyer would call to pay their respects, and they would need feeding. Eleanor also arranged for a housemaid as well as Mary to make the journey, feeling this would assist Lady Caroline's arrangements.

Mary proved to be invaluable in organising the modiste to alter the black evening dress to make it more acceptable for mourning. "You have the black bombazine day dress for the funeral, my lady, but you will need that black evening gown for dinner and another pair of mourning gloves. I'd suggest an Aigrette of black and grey egret feathers which can be attached to your black bonnet but also be pinned on a turban for the evening. I'll pack your lavender and grey dresses, too. They'll be suitable for the rest of the week."

Eleanor was surprised to learn that Lady Caroline had also written to Bertha and particularly requested her company for the week. Bertha showed her the letter, written as if to a close and trusted friend.

"Will you attend?" Eleanor asked.

"Yes, of course." Bertha had reached over and tapped Eleanor's hand. "It's still warm, Eleanor, and my knees will manage a brief journey, plus I'm curious to meet the impressive Captain Christopher Heyer. The way his mother talks, he is a fine but flighty bird who may not visit these shores again for many a year."

Eleanor grinned. "Oh yes, I'm looking forward to meeting Julian's brother. I just hope he can live up to Lady Caroline's glowing testimonials."

It was thirty miles to the village of Ash in Surrey from Mayfair, and the journey could be done in a day with good weather and dry roads. This required an early start and only one quick break for luncheon and a change of horses at the coaching house at Cobham.

Their coach pulled up in front of Ashfield Manor well after five. Bertha had not fared well despite her optimistic predictions. It took both Julian and a footman to help her down, and she limped alarmingly as she walked to Lady Caroline.

"My dear." The Dowager Viscountess stepped forward and pecked Bertha on the cheek. "Don't even try to curtsey, I'll not have it. Jenkins, get two bigger lads to take Miss Smith up in a chair."

They brought forward a large chair with a mesh seat and back and sturdy arms.

"Use it, Miss Smith. I have occasions to use it myself when the rheumatics are bad. I've arranged for a hot bath in your room."

"Thank you, ma'am." Bertha knew better than to argue when the arrangements were so beneficial to her comfort.

Eleanor smiled at her mother-in-law and managed a curtsey. "Mother, you're looking well. I'm so sorry for your loss."

"Yes, yes, I'm well." Lady Caroline waved away the condolences. "And Julian, thank you for coming so promptly. I'll leave you to settle in and change. It's such a long journey. I've arranged for dinner at nine, but will send up some tea and sandwiches to your rooms. Christopher is showing his friends the local area. I've asked them to meet us in the parlour at eight. I thought it best to do the introductions after you have refreshed. The evening will be interesting, to say the least."

As Eleanor entered the hall, the wonderful scent of roses assailed her. A long table set against the far wall was filled with a wide variety of beautifully painted pots of various shapes and sizes. Urns, bowls, and jars held white roses. It was a lovely tribute to Eleanor's mother that Lady Heyer had emulated her style in this arrangement. Eleanor could not help herself; she walked over and crouched down to examine the ceramic pots decorated with paintings of mountains, pagodas, and oddly shaped trees. In the centre of the table sat a small square pot, which contained what looked like a fully grown tree.

"It's magnificent, don't you think? Christopher brought it from China. It's called a Penjing, and they are exceptionally rare. It will normally be outside, but I couldn't resist showing it off to our visitors." Lady Caroline stepped up beside Eleanor. "He's the most generous son one could ever ask for, and so considerate."

Eleanor nodded and turned to catch Julian's eye roll. It would indeed prove to be an interesting evening.

"Brother, it's good to see you indeed."

Christopher proved to be a tall man, but he moved with grace and speed as he rushed to the door when Julian and Eleanor entered. He shook hands, and then grinned and gave his older brother a quick clinch, followed by a hearty thump on the back. He stepped back, looked Eleanor in the eye, grinned and bowed. "And this must be my new sister. It's wonderful to meet you at last. I have heard much of you from Mother."

Eleanor curtseyed and murmured, "Christopher."

Julian led her to a sofa near the fire, but a glance around the room made her stop in surprise. Lady Caroline and Bertha were seated on a sofa next to the fire, but the chairs opposite contained two strangers who could only be described as strange indeed. Lady Caroline looked highly amused as she watched for their reactions.

Christopher swiftly reacted to cover any initial awkwardness. "Julian, may I present my travelling companions. This gentleman is Captain Moses Black, my friend, and master of my barque, and this is Master Hu Shin, who is my man of business and interpreter in Canton."

As both men rose, Eleanor suppressed a giggle. Captain Black was the tallest man she had ever encountered and towered over his Chinese companion. The captain also lived up to his surname. He was the blackest man she had ever seen, his skin so dark as to be called ebony. His clothes were immaculate, white pantaloons, black jacket with white lace at his neck and wrists. He bowed low and smiled, which softened his severe, handsome face. Eleanor was intrigued, and her hand itched to grab a pencil and sketch this exotic man. She curtseyed and smiled, then looked at the shorter Chinese gentleman. He wore a white silk tunic over flowing trousers. His hair was pulled back severely into a long plait which reached down his back. He had an impassive face, his eyes half closed. "Captain Black, Master Shin, I'm delighted to make your acquaintance." Eleanor smiled at the two men.

Julian, to his credit, shook the hands of both his brother's companions and contained his surprise with a small shake of his head in his mother's direction. Lady Caroline smirked and nodded to Bertha. Eleanor had little doubt that their expected reactions had been a lively topic of conversation between the two ladies earlier in the evening.

Once everyone sat down, an uncertain silence was broken by Julian. "Christopher, it's been too long since we had the pleasure of your company. Will you be staying long in England?"

"I hope not. The trade winds in winter can be fierce and I wish to return to Shanghai with my new clipper while the weather is easy."

"A new clipper?"

"Yes." Christopher spoke with a touch of pride. "I've invested in a larger vessel for trading between China and England. My barque and junks are excellent vessels for the trade between Batavia and Shanghai, but I've always longed for a larger ship to sail around the Cape. It is a lucrative route, and the silk, tea, and artefacts from both China and Japan are most popular at the moment. And, of course, Moses here will manage the shorter journeys around the Eastern ports, so I'll have the pleasure of plying the wider oceans and bringing produce to England."

Julian nodded. "You'll be visiting more frequently. I think Mother will be pleased with that. It's been many years since you were last in England."

Christopher smiled at his mother. "I last came here six years ago, but I plan to do a voyage every year, at least for the next few years. I may then include the new continent of Australia in my schedules. That country is developing and there are many people emigrating. They will need produce from England, more than they need it in China and Java, and I'll start taking passengers."

"Australia, isn't that a penal colony?" Bertha leaned forward.

Christopher nodded. "It is, ma'am. But many people are now moving out to New South Wales as well as Van Diemen's Land. The land is plentiful and land grants are being offered to free men as well as prisoners of good moral character who have served their time. People see it as an opportunity to become a land holder and establish a home and income for their families. It provides a tempting prospect for people willing to do the hard work, and it is hard work. Settlers have to clear land, put up fences, establish roads and build their own homes. It is a hard life, and the climate is harsh, but the opportunities are boundless."

Christopher's enthusiasm and energy flowed, and while Eleanor listened to the conversation about foreign lands and trade, she took the time to study her brother-in-law's face. She wondered how she'd capture his passion and commitment in a portrait. Christopher looked much more like his mother than Julian. He had her wide brow, high cheek bones, and a narrow but strong chin. His skin was deeply tanned, but there were white crinkles around his hazel eyes. The nose seemed a little too long for his face and had a prominent arch. His hair was dark brown, like Julian's, but shot through with lighter, sun-bleached strands. Eleanor could picture him on the deck of a ship, his eyes on the horizon and a brisk breeze in his hair.

Captain Black smiled and nodded while listening to Julian and his brother converse. He had kind, intelligent black eyes set deep in his face. His hair was cut almost to the skull. All of his features were large and regular, and his teeth were blindingly white between warm, pink-tinged lips. His ebony skin picked up colours from his surrounds. One side of his face glowed gold from the firelight, while the features on his shadowed side were delineated by colours of navy blue and green melding into the black. He presented as a handsome man, and Eleanor thought she would paint him in partial silhouette facing a fire. She sensed both humour and sadness in him and wondered how she could capture those emotions.

Master Shin remained silent and barely moved. He had warm, honey tones to his skin, high cheek bones, and deep-set eyes which remained hooded all the time. His nose was small and wide, his face broad, and his lips full. With no facial hair he could have been aged anywhere between fifteen and forty. The expression was passive, an enigma, yet there seemed a coiled energy to him, a sense of pride and, yes, danger. He was intriguing, shut off, contained, and Eleanor realised she had no idea how she would paint the man. It was disconcerting indeed when he turned to regard her inspection with a haughty stare.

Eleanor blushed. She realised the room had gone quiet and everyone looked at her with curiosity, along with some amusement from Lady Caroline and a frown from Bertha.

"Oh, forgive me, Master Shin. I didn't mean to stare, but I find faces quite fascinating. I... I paint, and can get easily distracted when I encounter people. It's easy to get carried away with my perusal and, well, I meant no offence, sir."

"You are an artist, madam?" Master Shin's voice was heavily accented, soft, and a little amused.

"Yes, sir."

He nodded, and a small smile played around his mouth. "It is an impressive skill, madam. I am flattered by your attention."

Lady Caroline broke into the rather tense exchange. "Lady Heyer is a renowned artist. She used to have a studio in London and it was quite the thing to have a portrait painted by her. She has done a wonderful portrait of Julian for me. It hangs in the gallery upstairs. You must see it. I also have two lovely landscapes of the woods at the back of Ashfield. She really is remarkably talented."

Eleanor noticed Julian's sudden stillness and felt sick. She looked down at her hands and hoped that someone would change the subject. Her art and childlessness were intricately intertwined within her marriage and were awkward topics to continue with in this conversation.

"How have you found England, Master Shin?" Bertha came to the rescue.

"It is strange, and very cold and wet, Madam."

"But isn't it also cold in China? I have seen paintings of snow on mountains," Lady Heyer said.

Master Shin looked as if he could roll his eyes, but thought better of it. "China is a large country, Lady Heyer. It is cold in the north, but in Shanghai it is warm most of the year, although we can have low temperatures and sometimes snow in winter."

"And you, Captain Black. How do you find the weather in England?" Bertha took the conversation in a safer direction.

The conversation returned to less painful topics, and Eleanor relaxed as she just listened to the polite chatter. She kept her eyes lowered and was relieved when the footman arrived and announced that dinner was served.

Julian offered a prayer in remembrance of Robert and then made a salutation to acknowledge the passing of his brother before the food was consumed. Eleanor barely noticed what food she was eating and found that the wine gave her a headache. The men decided to take port in the library, and both she and Bertha welcomed Lady Caroline's suggestion that the ladies retire early.

Julian joined her in the early hours smelling of wood smoke and brandy and fell asleep as soon as he lay down. Eleanor guessed he had enjoyed the company of his brother and his unusual guests

Eleanor woke to the sound of birdsong and a thin sliver of light slipping through a chink in the bedroom curtain. Julian remained undisturbed by her waking, giving Eleanor a chance to study her husband. He looked younger when asleep, his lines of worry smoothed and his hair tangled over his brow. His mouth was relaxed, and that softened the lines of his jaw. He breathed deeply and turned. Eleanor smiled and got out of bed. She would leave him to sleep and would take a walk in the silvery sunlight.

She pulled on a dress and twisted her air into a messy bun. Mary had packed her stout walking boots and a warm pelisse, and she topped those with a hat that covered her ears and had a scarf attached to cover her neck. She finished with a light cloak, which she could easily discard as the exercise and sun warmed up the autumn morning. The gardens and woods around Ashfield Manor were a delight in the fall. Eleanor picked up her art bag with her sketchbook, pencils, and watercolour tablet, determined to capture the beauty before breakfast.

A brisk walk up to the woods behind the garden warmed Eleanor despite the chilly air. The sunlight was filtered by mist, and the reds and yellows of the horse chestnuts, elms, and birches emerged like spectral ghosts from the haze. It presented a magical view. Eleanor found a wooden bench and constructed her landscape.

She felt, rather than heard, that she was being observed. She turned to look behind her and saw the tall form of her brother-in-law leaning against a tree. A tremor of unease dissipated when Christopher smiled but stayed against the tree.

"Forgive me, Lady Heyer. I had no intention of disturbing your activity. I'll leave you in peace, you just have to say the word."

Eleanor thought about telling him to go, but she had nearly completed her sketch and she was getting hungry and chilled. It would be pleasant to walk back to the manor for breakfast and get to know Julian's brother on the way.

"No, sir, I've all but finished, and if you're returning to partake of breakfast, I'll gladly join you."

The tall man straightened and bowed, then walked over to the bench. He really was extremely handsome, Eleanor thought as he approached. She would like to do a portrait of him and capture that outgoing, adventurous spirit. He looked with interest at the sketch.

"You've captured the perspective well, but your drawing is not an accurate representation of the view. Those trees have been moved, and that log is in the wrong place," he noted with a smile.

"Yes, you've caught me out. But that's what an artist does, especially with a landscape. We move around features of the countryside to provide the essence of a scene but not overload it with extraneous details. Unfortunately, nature doesn't always provide us with the perfect composition. In Scotland, I've been known to move mountains to produce a better composition. It's called artistic licence."

Christopher chuckled. "I'd never realised the power of the artist. It makes you omniscient, being able to change around God's creations."

"Ah, but only on paper or canvas."

He helped Eleanor put on her cloak and looked at the view as she packed away her sketchbook and paints.

"Do you often get up at the crack of dawn to paint?"

"Not in London, but when we are at here or at Brampton Manor or up in Scotland, I'm out and about at dawn and dusk when the light is most favourable. I enjoy the outdoors and can always find something to paint or draw. I tend to be a dreadful walking companion, as I'll stop in the most unusual places to sketch, and my companions have to either walk on alone or sit and wait."

"So, you prefer to walk alone?"

"Yes, but what about you, sir? I left my husband snoring peacefully a full two hours ago, but you are up and exercising. Are you a crack-of-dawn person?"

He nodded. "I am indeed. I find it impossible to wake at any other time but sunrise. And no matter the lateness of my slumber, nor the fitness of my drink-addled brain, I need to rise and move. I find the prospect of lying-in bed when there is a new day to experience totally incomprehensible."

"Even when at sea?"

"Especially at sea. There are the waves to observe, the clouds to tell me the likelihood of a storm, or a new island or port to behold. The seas change constantly, the colours are magnificent, and the smell of the salt on the wind is fresh and exhilarating. I suppose I might stay abed more if my bed was not in a small and stuffy cabin, but I find I am still up with the birds when I am on land too, so I must confess to being a crack-of-dawn person as well."

Eleanor nodded in agreement. "You sound like you enjoy your occupation, sir, that the sea is your place of preference."

"It is indeed. I would hazard, my lady, that sailing to me is what your art is to you. That to be without it is to steal part of your soul, to deprive you of the greatest pleasure of your life."

Eleanor nodded again. It felt good to have this time with Christopher, to get to know the brother who'd lived his life so differently from Julian's. He proved to be perceptive and sensitive and had an openness and energy that made conversation easy and enjoyable. "You're right, sir, my life without painting is impossible."

"Julian showed me several of your paintings last night. He seems proud of you, but I sensed a reserve in his manner. He said that you used to paint more but had to give up oils on medical advice and now only paint smaller pieces in watercolours. That must've been difficult."

Eleanor hesitated, loath to go into her personal and painful history. She found a bright smile instead. "Oh, not really. I'm happy enough with watercolours. They're much easier to carry and far less smelly than oils. The medium is of less importance than the rendition of the subject."

Christopher proved to be perceptive to nuanced responses and turned the conversation to his mother's splendid garden as they walked through it to a well-deserved breakfast.

The rest of the day involved the immediate family getting dressed in full mourning and receiving visitors in the parlour. Eleanor found it a tedious way to pass the time, especially when she glanced out the window to see the sun shining. But the constraints of polite society enforced a semblance of grieving even when the departed was such a reprobate as Robert Heyer. Julian and his mother quelled the more enthusiastic visitors with a cool facade of genuine grief, but Eleanor had to work hard at keeping herself from laughing out loud at some comments about the "sad loss of such a young man". At one time, she caught the gaze of her brother-in-law, who rolled his eyes at one particular gentleman's gushing tribute to Robert, and realised he was having as much difficulty as she.

By the end of the afternoon, Eleanor was ready to burst with impatience and needed a brisk walk and fresh air. Julian had an appointment with his mother's steward, and Lady Caroline decided she needed a glass of Madeira and a lie down before dinner. Bertha was nowhere in sight, so Eleanor grabbed her warmest cloak and took to the garden to enjoy the last of the fading light.

It wasn't a surprise to find Christopher pacing the terrace as she emerged from the house. "Sister, will you join me for a walk? The light will fade soon and I needed some fresh air after that wearisome day."

"I'd be delighted, sir."

They walked in companionable silence through the beds of roses that were a favourite of the Dowager Viscountess. There were a few late blooms still on show, but the bushes looked tired and leafless.

"I thought it quite amusing how my brother Robert has achieved the respectability in death he never achieved in life. Some of Mother's callers obviously didn't know Robert, nor knew his reputation. One actually described him as a 'sadly missed family member.' I still have nightmares about the time he tried to kill me, and he certainly didn't improve after that incident."

Eleanor couldn't help herself; she actually laughed out loud, and in an unladylike manner. "Oh, sir, you are blunt indeed," she finally spluttered. "But it's a sad truth. He wasn't a good man."

"And did you not want to laugh when Lady Pritchard described his illness as a 'wasting disease'? The syphilis ate away his nose and left him in an appalling state. It's strange to me to see how English social rules can ignore the truth of a situation. Yet, Mother and Julian can conceal their emotions and act with a propriety that's astoundingly commendable."

Eleanor realised that Christopher, with humour and candour, was testing her out, finding her own limits of acceptability and honesty. She stopped and turned to look him in the eye. "Is it a commendable attribute to lie and deceive others, and even ourselves? I've found it discomforting to know the truth, but, in my experience, it's far better than being told falsehoods."

Christopher looked as though a weight had been lifted from his shoulders. He nodded and seemed to come to some sort of decision. "I saw Robert before he died, just one week ago, in fact. He proved to be horrid right to the end. He was the most evil man I've ever encountered. But he was so clever with it. He actually apologised for nor killing me in my cot, and we laughed about it, which was insanely bizarre but somehow healing. Robert also talked a great deal about Julian, blamed Julian for everything that's gone wrong in his life. He took absolutely no responsibility for anything. It was incredible."

"No, Robert had a unique view of the world," Eleanor started walking again.

Christopher continued more cautiously. "He quite gleefully boasted that Julian now suffers from not being able to produce an heir. Sees it as, I couldn't say divine retribution, but a just dessert for a brother whose major sin was to be born first."

Eleanor felt herself blush, glad of a cool breeze and the fading light. The light-hearted mood fled as she realised that Robert would have enjoyed recounting her investigations into her husband's infertility to Christopher. Her brother-in-law could now judge her actions, and that was uncomfortable to contemplate. "Yes, I can have little doubt that Robert would've enjoyed his last days, telling you all about the barren nature of our marriage. I'm sorry that you've learned of our problems from so biased and wicked a source. But I'm cold now and I wish to go inside. I bid you goodnight, sir." Eleanor couldn't wait to get out of the company of her husband's brother. She doubted she would ever be at ease in his presence again.

She was several steps towards the house when his words stopped her escape. "Eleanor." He spoke gently. "Robert thought highly of you, thought you had intelligence and courage. Said you reminded him of Mother, and I believe he admired Mother, at the end."

Dinner proved to be a subdued meal. It was as if everyone in the family were worn down by the display of feigned grief put on for appearances' sake during the day. Eleanor felt tired, and her thoughts churned with questions about just how much Robert had revealed to her new brother-in-law. Robert probably had portrayed her as a meddling, prying wife bent on fixing blame on her husband for being childless. She kept her eyes lowered, pushed the food around on her plate, and kept her comments perfunctory and neutral. There was a palpable awkwardness between herself and Christopher. Eleanor dearly hoped he would maintain his distance for the rest of the visit, and the tension between them wouldn't be noted by anyone else in the room.

Bertha broke the strained atmosphere with a question to Captain Black. "I'm curious, sir, how you met Captain Heyer?"

It was a question that should have been an acceptable topic. But the two captains looked at each other as if daring the other to expound, then both grinned.

"Captain Heyer won me in a game of cards, Miss Smith."

Bertha looked shattered and put down her knife and fork. "I'm so sorry. I didn't mean to pry."

Captain Blacks' voice slowed and became nuanced with the heat of the southern parts of America. "Miss Smith, I'm not sorry at all."

"You mean, you were a slave?" Lady Caroline sounded highly amused.

"I was, ma'am. Born and bred to it in South Georgia and got sold on many times. I was a young man with a yearning for freedom, and that didn't make me a good slave. My last owner ended up in Plymouth, of all places. They chained me to the mast of a Dutch East India ship that was going out to the West Coast of Africa to pick up some poor souls from the jungles. I objected strongly about being on a slave ship and got a whipping for my ethics. Your son saw me and decided that he needed me, so he followed the Dutch captain to a local inn, flashed a bit of money, and pretended to be drunk. Then he got himself into a game of Faro. The Dutchman proved a slow devil and didn't realise he was being gulled by an expert, and an hour later I had a new owner."

"Good God." Julian actually swore. "I didn't think that was done in England."

"It isn't anymore, thankfully," Christopher answered, "but this happened nine years ago, brother. The Abolition Bill came into force in Britain in 1807, but the Dutch could still come into English ports with slaves until 1814. I won Captain Black in 1812 in an unfair game of cards, but I'd never regarded slavery as fair, so had no scruples in cheating."

Julian laughed loud and long. "Well, brother, I would say well met indeed. And, Captain Black, how did you end up a captain? That must've been a rapid rise in your standing."

"Aye, sir, it was rapid. That night, I was handed over in chains to your brother. He sensibly came along with several fellow officers and a couple of burly sailors. The Dutch captain grumbled a lot but was persuaded to provide the paperwork. On the wharf, I got set free from the chains, handed the paperwork, and offered a paid position as a general sailor. I picked up that offer straightaway, learned myself to read and write and talk like a gentleman, and took every opportunity to learn about seafaring. When your brother got his first ship in Java, he offered me the position of first mate. His second ship got me promoted to captain, and I've aspirations of making it to admiral in the longer term."

Everyone laughed. It made such a rollicking story, and with such a good outcome. Eleanor had little doubt that Captain Black had suffered far more than his good-humoured account allowed. She looked at Christopher with fresh eyes. He was a good man, a man brave enough to set himself against injustice and discrimination. It occurred to her that maybe he wouldn't have been easily swayed by Robert, that his negative judgement of her was more in her own mind. It was her own fear and her shame which she had assigned to Christopher, and he did not deserve her condemnation. She determined she would do better, that she would give her new brother a chance. He deserved to have her friendship.

Chapter Ten

October 21ˢᵗ 1823

Julian came to their bed early that night. He smelt of brandy but did not fall immediately to sleep. She heard his breath in the darkness and then felt his soft lips on her cheeks and eventually her mouth. Eleanor responded, not with fervour but with warmth. They made love, and it was comforting, but sad when it finished. They had drifted too far apart emotionally to reignite the lust of their honeymoon year, and there wasn't any joyful anticipation of a child to ignite their passion now, only the sad surety of failure.

Julian must have sensed it, too. He spoke in the darkness. "I'm glad for this time to get to know Christopher. I saw him infrequently when we were children and hardly at all after he got commissioned into the Navy. We worked it out tonight that we've not met for the past ten years. I've been remiss. When he's returned to England, I haven't tried to meet with him. That must change. I've only one brother now, and I've come to respect and admire him. He'll make a good Viscount. He's a good man, I'm glad that he's now my heir."

"He'll make a splendid Viscount, but I'm not sure he will be happy to give up seafaring and with God's blessing, he may not have to. We can still have children, Julian. I'm only twenty-four. We mustn't give up hope," Eleanor gently chided.

"Eleanor, I'd do anything to have our own children." He sighed in the darkness. "I pray every night and every day to be blessed with a child, but I've lost faith that God hears my prayers anymore. But if we're to remain childless, I'm at ease that Christopher is there to take on the responsibility. Or perhaps it will be his son in the future. I will say that Robert's passing has relieved my mind immeasurably. I dreaded the idea that he'd succeed me. Eleanor, I hated him all my life." Julian finished emphatically.

"Yes, I can understand that. Still, we must mourn him for the week even though he'll not be missed. But I'll never forget him. He was a most unhappy and unpleasant man."

"Mother said that you'd braved the sick room and spent some time with him before you went to Bath. It shocked me, Eleanor, that you wanted to meet him. I did caution you about his nature."

Eleanor realised she approached dangerous territory. She feigned a yawn. "Curiosity, Julian. I was curious to meet my brother-in-law. And I am the Viscountess. It is the expected thing to visit the sick and dying."

Julian's words had haunted her throughout the night and she had long periods of sleeplessness as she pondered their fate. He so rarely shared his frustration and sadness with her. His acceptance that Christopher would be his heir had a terrible finality about their childless marriage. Her husband had given up.

There was no more hope, no more plans for their future. Eleanor imagined them slipping into old age, a sad and lonely couple who had to endure the pity of their family and friends. It seemed so unfair. They were not bad people. They didn't deserve this deprivation. She reflected on the boundless fecundity of her own family, her mother's last letter proudly announcing that her brother, Bevan, and his wife, Angela, were having their third child, and that Isabel was expecting her sixth child at six and thirty. Mama had known better than to wax too lyrically about the "happy events" and had added, 'But, Eleanor, I'm sure your time will come, and you and Julian can add to the family soon'.

It had tempted Eleanor to write to her mama and tell her that her prediction had no foundation. That they'd been trying for six whole years, had seen so many doctors, taken cures, had marital relations most nights and prayed and prayed. They'd done everything they could, but it was impossible. The family news seemed nothing but cruelty. She didn't, of course, reply in this manner, but it had taken several days of writing and rewriting her response before she was satisfied that her jealousy and resentment were under control and she was able to send heartfelt congratulations.

As the morning light stole through the chink in the curtain, Eleanor realised she was tired and out of sorts from a lack of sleep. Tossing and turning had made her tense, angry — angry at the world and her fate.

Robert and his malicious meddling increased her anguish. Even though he was dead, he still disturbed her peace of mind. Yesterday, she had run away from Christopher, not ready to discuss her situation. She had said that truth and openness were important, then she'd been a coward and coldly shut down their conversation. Much of her sleepless night had been spent wondering just what Robert had told his youngest brother. Had he informed him of her trip to Devon, her investigation into Mrs Wilson? She wouldn't put it past Robert to have been most forthcoming with the truth. He'd have found it entertaining recounting her exploits and wouldn't have resisted the urge to meddle even from his death bed. Oh, yes, she was curious indeed. She decided she needed a stroll and hoped Christopher would find her so they might talk.

Christopher was waiting for her on the terrace and nodded as she approached. "Good morning, sister. I'm in need of some exercise and fresh air before having to endure another tedious day of pretending to be bereft at the loss of my mad, bad brother. Would you like to accompany me?"

Eleanor smiled. "I would, sir. I'd like that very much."

They walked through the garden with no conversation. The sky looked grey and a light drizzle misted the air around the autumn-coloured trees on the hill. Eleanor had to rush to keep up as Christopher, being tall, marched with long strides. He showed no signs of breathlessness by the time they crested the hill, while her own lungs struggled.

Eleanor stopped at the bench where she had sketched the previous day. As her breathing slowed, she realised she needed to start the conversation. Christopher seemed an astute man who would take the direction of their discourse from her. She had closed him down yesterday. Now she needed the courage to open up and be honest.

"I owe you an apology, sir. I find it difficult to discuss the problems in my marriage but I also, as I said yesterday, appreciate honesty." She stopped and took a deep breath. "Julian and I are childless. I'm uncertain if it's my fault or that of my husband. But I realise it doesn't matter where the blame lies. Robert, of course, took a great deal of pleasure in Julian's discomfort and encouraged me to seek answers. He urged me to go to Devon to learn the truth about Lady Emily's death and his own history of murder. He also sent me to Richmond to spy on Julian's mistress and her sons. I imagine Robert wanted me to fight with Julian, to confront him and cause him distress. I assume his goal was to bring about a divorce and cause a scandal for the family. Thankfully, I came to see that Robert uses people to provide for his twisted entertainment and I chose not to fall in with his wicked plans. But I can honestly say I'm glad he's dead."

Christopher laughed and nodded. "Robert was an evil bastard. Excuse my language, but there's no better description that fits. He told me he'd sent you to Devon and then to confront Mrs Wilson in Richmond. He said initially he assumed you were 'naïve and pliable' and that he'd hoped you would confront Julian with whatever truth you found, causing you both unhappiness. I agree with you that his ultimate aim was to prompt a divorce and bring your difficulties to the attention of all society. He wanted it known that Julian was incapable of producing an heir. I think he viewed it as his ultimate revenge, but you saw through his scheme and thwarted his plans. You didn't confront Julian, did you?"

"No, I discovered instead that I admired my husband, that he'd acted honourably and with compassion regarding Mrs Wilson. I'm uncertain if her sons are Julian's, but I know he loves them as his own. I also learned the attending physician in Devon told him his first wife had been bearing his child when she died, so he had good reason to believe he could father a child.

Robert's accusations proved to be vicious assumptions." Eleanor reflected on her sad conversation the night before. "I've come to love Julian again. I didn't wish to cause him any more grief. Both of us desire to have children more than anything in this world. We cannot and I accept that is the way of it."

"So, it left Robert to gnash the few teeth he had left and complain to me."

"Serves him right." Eleanor chuckled.

They took the path leading into the woods. There was no breeze, and the day had become overcast. It was dark beneath the trees and where the light seeped in, it delineated the tall trunks and merged the ferns beneath into a soft expanse of green and gold. The path twisted like a pale snake through the gloom. Birds called to each other, and a blackbird trilled its sweet song in the still air.

Christopher broke the comfortable silence. "Is there no chance that you'll have children, Eleanor?"

Eleanor noted he had called her by name for the first time. It seemed appropriate, given the personal nature of their conversation. She sighed. "I'm not sure, Christopher." She used his Christian name, sensing the distance between them diminish. "Some days I'm hopeful, but most days I suspect it's a lost cause. I don't know."

"Well, from a purely selfish position, I sincerely hope that you and my brother succeed." He spoke brusquely.

Eleanor looked up. Christopher's lips had tightened into a grimace of discontent. She was correct in thinking he wouldn't take to becoming a Viscount happily. "I take it, sir, that you don't relish the prospect of inheriting?"

He laughed to ease the tension. "No, not at all. It may sound strange and certainly Mother cannot understand, but I've no desire to become a Viscount. I never expected it would be my fate and have made my own way. My life is exciting and free of all responsibilities and constraints except those that I've chosen for myself. And now I have to contend with Mother's expectations that I'll return to England, buy a house and land, find a wife and produce heirs for the Heyer family. And my mother can be very insistent."

Eleanor nodded. "Oh, I understand her expectations are difficult to withstand. Mama can be adamant indeed, but I think it's more than that. She sincerely wants our happiness. She has never said as much, but I sense she regrets the way Robert's madness split the family apart. I believe that if we produced some grandchildren, she would have another chance at creating a loving family. It would give her great joy."

"It would give everyone great joy, Eleanor." Christopher said.

They continued on in silence until Eleanor felt the need to offer some solace to her new friend. "I don't suppose that we'll need to worry for many years to come. Julian is robust and I'm young and healthy. You may never have to return to England to inherit."

"You are an optimist, sister. I'm thirty-one and if I'm to be the heir, I'll need to marry, settle and produce some children for the family reasonably soon. No, Robert's death has placed pressure on us all. I cannot procrastinate. Changes will have to be made. No, Eleanor, I need to accept that I'll probably lose the life that I had planned."

"It seems so unfair."

"Life is unfair, my dear sister, but it seems more so when all it would take is one little baby to solve all our unhappiness."

"Oh Christopher, to hold a baby in my arms, I can't imagine any greater pleasure." Eleanor stopped, aware of the tears cold on her cheek. Christopher handed her a kerchief, but said nothing.

Eleanor wiped her face and anger bubbled up in sadness' wake. "Robert must've found our family predicament amusing in his last days. He enjoyed discomforting people. He certainly discomforted me. Was he aware that you'd also be affected? Did he take pleasure in seeing that, in our childlessness, your life would change and that you would join in the family's unhappiness?"

Christopher chuckled. "I wish it otherwise, but Robert's mind remained keen even as his body disintegrated. I don't comprehend how he bore the pain and humiliations of his sickness, but talking about our family's history and its future, at least gave him some solace. He was unbearably smug and gleeful about my likely future course in life."

"Oh, why am I not surprised?" Eleanor realised her anger showed, so she softened her voice. "One can only wish that his suffering had made him reflect on his life, made him atone for his evil ways. Did he not look for any forgiveness? Didn't he want to confess his sins and die in grace?"

"No, he remained true to his nature, right to the end. Mother stayed by his bedside for weeks hoping he would relent, that he'd allow her to summon Reverend Lackey to prepare his soul for the hereafter. Robert just laughed at her."

"Poor Mama. It must've been horrible."

"Yes, but at one point, I thought Robert had become more reflective. On his last day, early in the morning, he drifted in and out of consciousness. Our mother had gone to get some rest so I took a turn at the bedside. He woke and told me to appreciate Mother, that she was strong and intelligent. He spoke about you as well. Said 'Eleanor is more like Mother than she knows'. And then, just when I considered he might have some semblance of humanity, he made a disgusting suggestion and sniggered, then coughed and coughed until he couldn't breathe anymore and fell into unconsciousness. He died later in the evening without waking again. It was a blessing that Mother didn't witness his last words. And it was good for her that Robert slipped out of this life in a semblance of peaceful sleep."

Eleanor realised they had travelled a long way from Ashfield Manor and had come to the end of the woods. The ground fell into a small valley of fields where a herd of cows munched on the lush green grass. It seemed a good place to turn around. They ambled back through the woods in silence. Eleanor appreciated that her brother-in-law was comfortable with silence, didn't consider the need to interrupt her whirling thoughts and newfound knowledge about Robert's demise.

When they became enclosed by the darker woods, shaded by the green and gold canopy, Eleanor voiced the one notion that wouldn't go away. "Christopher, what were Robert's last words? What did he say that would have upset Mama?"

Christopher said nothing for several strides, then muttered. "Sister, he spoke nonsense. Just Robert's final sinful offering. I believe that if he'd recovered from that last coughing fit, I would've been tempted to kill him myself. As I said, he was an evil bastard. You don't want to hear his last suggestion."

Eleanor took her time to reflect on Christopher's response. She understood herself too well, needing to know even as she realised Christopher seemed reluctant to disclose his secret. Eleanor also assumed he wouldn't have told her about Robert's deathbed curse unless he was of the opinion she needed to know. Was it Christopher's way of offering her the choice? She suspected Robert's last words were about herself.

"Christopher, I need to hear the truth. It concerned me, didn't it? His last words were about me? I might pretend that it wasn't the case, but I'm insufferably curious and I will ponder and ponder and waste much of my time and energy in suppositions and conjecture. You've let the cat out of the bag, so I beg you to tell me the truth of it. I promise that not knowing will be more distressful than knowing."

"Are you sure, Eleanor?"

"Yes, perfectly sure. Please do not spare me. It may be hurtful, but I'm a person who doesn't cope well with falsehoods and secrecy."

They stopped on the narrow path. He looked down at her from his superior height, his face a mask, but his eyes glinting in the dull light. He nodded. "Robert suggested that all our family's problems would be solved if I took Julian's place in your bed and we produced an heir between us."

"He really said that?"

"Well, not in those words, of course. His proposition was far more offensively stated, but his intention was clear. It was a good thing he never regained consciousness or I... I would've murdered him."

"Oh, if I'd been there, I would've helped." Eleanor found herself torn between horrified amusement and disgust. Quite flabbergasted, she wasn't sure how to voice her thoughts. She eventually managed an appropriate angry response, albeit delivered with inappropriate humour in her voice. "Oh, that's so, so typical. An abhorrent suggestion delivered by such an odious man. You must've been shocked, Christopher, to hear such plans from your brother in his dying moments."

"I was speechless, ma'am."

Eleanor resumed moving, looking at the leaf-strewn path. She pictured Robert's face, or what remained of it, heard his muttered, malevolent words. There was little doubt that he had intended offence and outrage and had enjoyed the outcome in his last conscious moments.

"I'm glad he's dead, Christopher. I'm sorry to say it to anyone, but I am glad he's dead. But pray, don't trouble yourself that Robert's vile proposition will upset me. He was vile to the very end. I won't give him any further attention. He doesn't deserve it. Today we must again endure the charade of mourning for him, but tomorrow we can bury him. And I, for one, will be happy to do so.

But it proved less easy than expected. Despite taking a hearty breakfast and determining that Robert's suggestion was ridiculous, the idea would not leave her at peace. The thought wormed through her head. Robert's words whispered in her mind. She deemed herself a lady, and ladies had little knowledge of slang and cursing, but her brain was creative and came up with so many horrible ways for Robert to offer his immoral recommendation. And what did Christopher really think of the suggestion? Her thoughts made her blush.

It didn't help that for most of the morning she had to sit in an overly warm, darkened room and endure a steady stream of estate workers, neighbours and local tradespeople who wanted to pay their respects to the Heyer family. They particularly wanted to express their condolences to Lady Caroline, who, as the local noblewoman and a large employer of the parishioners, was someone to whom you showed homage.

While Lady Caroline epitomised the grace of stately mourning and murmured appropriate acknowledgements to the insincere commiserations of her servile sycophants, Eleanor experienced an almost uncontainable desire to shout out, "We aren't sorry at all. We're glad he's dead".

It was a blessing that Christopher stood behind her chair and she didn't catch his eye. By luncheon Eleanor was ready to explode and was exceedingly grateful that the afternoon would be free of visitors. Julian and Christopher went out riding with Captain Black and Master Shin, to take in the splendid views from the local ridge called the Hog's Back. Julian had suggested she accompany them, but Eleanor declined, knowing a brisk walk would clear her mind of its pernicious notions. She also declined to join Lady Heyer and Bertha in the parlour, where they would probably enjoy some reflective time for sewing, reading, chatting and napping. Eleanor found it heart-warming that Lady Heyer and Bertha had formed an alliance. It was sorely tempting to join the older ladies just for the pleasure of watching the budding friendship, but the thought of sitting still seemed impossible to bear.

Eleanor decided she would go to St Peters, the lovely Norman church serving the small village of Ash. The place where Robert would be interred. In London, a lady of quality would never take a walk without a maid, but in the country, it was more commonplace. Eleanor declined Mary's offer of accompaniment. She needed to be alone with her wayward thoughts.

St Peters was set on a small rise at the end of the village, accessed through lanes without passing the popular Greyhound Inn, with its leering drinkers. Eleanor enjoyed the walk, despite the blustery, chilly wind. She marched along the path and warmed up quickly, but all the while, her thoughts turned back to Robert's proposition.

It was an appalling idea but it also provided an elegant solution to all the family's woes. Julian would have his heir. Christopher wouldn't have to give up his life on the sea. She would have a longed-for child and her mother-in-law would have a grandchild to spoil. Most important of all, the Heyer family bloodline would remain true and secure.

Robert would have reasoned his way through all the ramifications of his plan. He would've enjoyed that it presented her and Christopher with an awful dilemma. A solution that would curse them with secrecy and betrayal. It would mean doing all the wrong things for all the right reasons. It was a torment to offer such an answer to all their prayers. The remedy would place her in a position of such sin it would be unendurable. Or would it?

"God curse you, Robert. You're a clever bastard indeed," Eleanor shouted into the wind and felt better for her damnation.

St Peters was cold and empty. Thick white pillars supported a soaring wooden roof and small stained-glass windows let in a little of the autumn light. Eleanor slipped into the pew nearest the door and fell to her knees. Prayer, usually an unthinking practice, seemed impossible today. Eleanor had never been sure praying did any good. She had prayed fervently as a child, but her belief in prayer as a solution to life's woes had been tested in recent years. It had become another expected ritual, a necessity in life, but had she ever prayed with all her heart and soul, with surety and belief? Today she would pray and do it properly. She recited the Lord's Prayer and, for once, concentrated on the words. "Forgive us our trespasses as we forgive those that trespass against us." Was deliberately planned adultery forgivable? It seemed to be trounced by "Lead us not into temptation and deliver us from evil". Could you commit a sin and receive forgiveness even if the outcome came to provide for the greater good? There seemed to be no straightforward answer in the Lord's Prayer.

Eleanor murmured the beautiful twenty-third Psalm in remembrance of Robert, but found no answers there either. She reverted to personal prayer, asking for relief from the burden of barrenness, but her thoughts remained in turmoil. With her knees getting sore and her shoulders stiff in this cold house of God, she rose to her feet, preparing to walk back to Ashfield Manor. Recalling previous sermons in her life, Eleanor was unable to recall anything in the Bible that would provide her with solace for committing adultery. Christianity meant telling the truth, no matter what. She returned to Ashfield Manor with a headache. God might forgive her, but would she ever forgive herself if she followed through with Robert's sinful suggestion?

The morning of the funeral dawned clear with bright sunshine. They had planned the service and interment for eleven and the family decided they would follow Robert's hearse to St. Peter's on foot. Lady Caroline and Bertha would follow the small procession in the Heyer coach.

Eleanor took her place at the head of the line with Julian. As the Viscount and Viscountess, they had to take the lead. Christopher followed with Mr Perez. The housekeeper and butler and five senior servants made up the rear. A few men stood at the side of the road and doffed their hats, while the women and girls curtseyed as they passed. Eleanor was glad she had worn full mourning, with a heavy black veil shielding her pale face and hiding the dark circles under her eyes. She hadn't slept at all during the night, Robert's last words destroying her rest.

The Honourable Reverend Lackey presented as a man with absolute commitment to his faith but little imagination. His intonation of the expected prayers and readings was soporific, while the lack of music and hymns did nothing to break up the tediousness of the service. The emphasis of the sermon focused on forgiveness, with Psalm 107 read out in full. Eleanor got the impression the clergyman clearly understood the nature of the departed.

Eleanor tried valiantly to concentrate, but her thoughts slipped away to contemplate the true nature of the deceased. Robert Heyer was the worst sinner she had ever encountered and she didn't think he'd be redeemed by her prayers. He didn't deserve them, anyway. He had left her with the dilemma of sinning for her heart's desire or leading a life of, if not misery, at least dissatisfaction. She discovered she loathed Robert Heyer during his funeral more than she had when he'd been alive.

When Reverend Lackey launched into "May God, the Father, forgive us our sins and bring us to the eternal joy of his Kingdom, where dust and ashes have no dominion", Eleanor grimaced as she imagined Robert leering at her from the red-hot depths of Hell. *Damn him, damn him and his malevolent interference.*

Psalm 23 calmed her shocking thoughts a little and the service concluded with brief prayers for the mourners which provided some comfort. Bertha took her hand and gave it a squeeze as they followed the coffin out to the graveyard.

Relatively new to the area, there was no family plot. The coffin was lowered into a lonely section at the rear of the church. Eleanor took delight in throwing her handful of earth into the grave. No-one cried, no-one mourned, no-one prayed. Robert Heyer was dead and buried in all but his final cursed suggestion. Even Mr Perez looked rested and at peace as they trooped back to Ashfield Manor. He would leave after the reading of the will on the morrow, returning to Spain in Christopher's new clipper. Eleanor envied him his escape to his beloved, warm Spain, with a generous pension for the rest of his life. He certainly deserved every penny.

Luncheon, as expected, was a subdued affair. Afterwards, the men rode out for exercise and fresh air. Christopher had persuaded Mr Perez to accompany them, a further example of his kindness and consideration.

"Well," Lady Caroline stated as they watched the men clatter out of the yard, "I believe I'll enjoy a turn around the garden. Will you join me, Miss Smith, Eleanor?"

Bertha's knees slowed the pace, but it provided comradeship and a chance to offer condolences and support to a mother.

Eleanor sighed as she struggled to find words of comfort. The service had been tedious and done little to assuage grief. Lady Caroline remained stoic and unreachable behind her facade of mourning and it proved impossible to glimpse what emotions she experienced at the death of her middle son.

But Lady Caroline proved again she had a sturdy disposition. She raised her face to the sun and smiled. "You know, Eleanor, I'm glad Robert has passed. He led a dissolute life and his suffering at the end proved terrible indeed. But Christopher has been a great comfort, telling me all about the religions of the Orient. In Eastern religions, they do not condemn sinners for eternity to purgatory, but souls can work their way out of Hell by doing good deeds. It was all quite complicated, but I must say, the idea gave me some comfort."

"Is that the Buddhist religion?" Bertha asked.

"Yes, I believe it is. Christopher has made quite a study of Eastern religions. He said that the Buddhists, and the Hindus too, consider that after we die, we don't always go to Heaven or Hell but may be reborn. In their belief, it is possible to redeem our sins and attain a better life next time. Christopher said that Robert's dreadful physical suffering would counteract some of the sins he committed in his earlier years and that he might be, the word is reincarnated. Given another chance at life to improve his character."

Eleanor doubted that Robert's sins could be redeemed in twenty lifetimes, but she was glad these foreign ideas gave Lady Caroline some comfort. "That's a pleasant belief indeed, Mother."

"Yes, I find such ideas much more tolerable than imagining my poor son burning in Dante's Hell forever. But enough about Robert. What are your plans for the winter, Eleanor? Will you be going to Scotland for Christmas?"

"I'm not sure, Julian hasn't decided, but I'm hoping we'll have Christmas in Derbyshire this year." Eleanor said, glad that the conversation had turned to lighter topics.

The stroll wearied both older ladies and they returned to the parlour for another glass of Madeira before taking an afternoon nap. Despite being tired, Eleanor took a longer walk alone. She hoped it would help clear her head of the barrage of opposing thoughts. She yearned to talk everything through with Bertha but something held her back. Maybe it was the shame of what she contemplated, but she believed she already knew what Bertha would say. It would be an admonition that she would have to live with her sin for the rest of her life, and she already realised that. No, it was not something she would share with anyone, even her best friend. If she sinned, it would be her sin alone. She would not compromise her friend's conscience with the burden of it. Eleanor realised that, for the first time in her life, she was truly alone in this dilemma. She realised this choice required her to take her destiny into her own hands, to act alone, to be completely an adult.

As she went through the dark woodlands, Eleanor's thoughts turned to the lessons she had learned from Bertha, from her mama, from Julian and from her mother-in-law. Bertha would advise that intractable problems were best solved by breaking them into the positive and negative potential outcomes. So, as she strolled through the trees, Eleanor constructed a list.

On the positive side, she might conceive a beautiful baby, providing an heir for the Heyer family, a much-loved son or daughter for Julian and a grandchild for her mother-in-law. Christopher wouldn't have to give up his seafaring life. And the child would be of the Heyer line.

The negative outcomes made for a much longer list. She would be an adulteress; she would live a lie and be living in sin. It was highly probable that Christopher would be horrified and refuse to comply. He might inform Julian of her intended infidelity. He was his brother, after all. She could commit the sin and then be discovered. She could commit the sin and still not get with child, then have to live with the sin with no benefit to counter it.

Her Mama would certainly counsel against the sin of committing adultery. She would be horrified that her youngest daughter had even contemplated it.

Julian wouldn't forgive infidelity, even though he'd committed that sin himself. It didn't seem fair that, in society, a man might remain respectable and have a mistress while they would condemn a woman for taking a lover, even if it was with the best of intentions. No, Julian had been secretive and dishonest. Then had no qualms in justifying his lies on the basis of protecting her from the harsh realities of life. Julian didn't deserve her consideration for this. She deemed he'd sinned too much himself.

Lady Caroline? Eleanor realised she did not know how her mother-in-law would react. She would probably be as torn as Eleanor. Lady Caroline was a pragmatist and had gone to extreme lengths to assist her in her finding out about the family history. She'd counsel that getting an heir had to be Eleanor's primary duty. But she'd also be happy for Christopher to be the heir. Her favourite son would eventually do his duty by marrying and producing an heir, even if such a course in life wasn't agreeable to him. No, Lady Caroline would win no matter what Eleanor decided.

Society would certainly condemn her if her infidelity was discovered. Men, particularly married men, held all the power. Wives and daughters were the property of their husbands and fathers, with no rights to income or influence. A wife's adultery prior to the producing of a legal heir would be regarded as the worst of sins. The bloodlines had to be pure. The man had to be certain his heir flowered from his own seed. Julian would divorce her and the rest of society would shun her if what she contemplated was ever revealed. Unfaithfulness remained an anathema, particularly in the higher echelons of society.

By the time she emerged from the woods, Eleanor had another headache and her shoulders were stiff with tension, but she'd come to a resolution. She would resist temptation, refuse to heed Robert's last words and continue to pray that her marriage would bear fruit. It would be God's will. The devil and Robert be damned.

The evening meal proved a lively affair, despite the funeral earlier in the day. Christopher and Captain Black entertained the family with outrageous tales of storms and thwarted pirates, new lands discovered and the strange animals and birds that inhabited the countries to the east. Even Master Shin was prevailed upon to explain the history of his ancient homeland and describe the lives of the Mandarins as they vied for the favours of the emperor and his court.

"It sounds so exciting, Captain Heyer. It makes me want to travel and explore. And the heat sounds like a blessing for older bones," Bertha commented towards the end of the meal.

"It is indeed, ma'am. But the heat can be uncomfortable too. It's unbearable just before the monsoons, when the air is heavy and there's no breeze to dry the perspiration from your brow. The nights are hot and sleep impossible to find. Then the skies open, lightning and thunder shake the ground and the rain is a torrent. The children all go out and play in the flooded streets and everyone smiles again."

"I consider, sir, that the East is where your heart lives," Bertha said.

Eleanor looked up and noted the sadness in her brother-in-law's face. "No, ma'am, the sea is where my heart resides. Ports and towns are welcome breaks, but then I get restless for the sea. I've spent too long at sea, it's in my blood. It's all I know."

"Oh, phish, Christopher," Lady Caroline snapped. "You must settle eventually. You can find an estate near the sea, if you cannot manage without it. Maybe we should open up Heyer House in Devon for you. It's close to Lynmouth and you can keep a boat there, if you needed to."

"Mother, I don't think a fishing village and a small boat would satisfy Christopher," Julian interjected on his brother's behalf.

"Well, Lynmouth is close to Plymouth. He could have a ship there if he absolutely needed one. Eleanor, your brother and his wife live near Plymouth. They've an estate there. Is he still sailing with the Navy?"

Eleanor blushed at her mother-in-law's temerity. "He's finished with the Navy, Mother."

"But does he have ships, Eleanor? In Plymouth?"

"He does, Mama," Eleanor said reluctantly.

"There, you see, Christopher. You can have ships and an estate too. You could still sail to the Americas and the colonies in Newfoundland. It would be just as diverting, I'm sure."

Eleanor blushed to see Christopher's grimace as his mother's plans for his future were so neatly mapped out. Lady Caroline appeared as formidable as a monsoon storm and just as destructive for a pleasant family meal.

Julian caught her eye and smiled with a shake of his head. "It's time, gentlemen, for a cigar and port in the library. Mother, Eleanor, Miss Smith, we'll bid you goodnight."

As the door closed behind Julian, Lady Heyer sighed. "I wish it was otherwise, but Christopher must accept his responsibilities. He needs to find a suitable bride and settle down. Don't get me wrong, Eleanor, I realise you're still young enough to have children and I pray every day for a joyous event. But Christopher is the heir now that Robert has passed away. He needs to settle. Now, please ring for some tea. It has been a long and difficult day and I'll retire early."

Eleanor wished she might drink and smoke with the men. Maybe imbibing strong liqueurs and smoking cigars, like them, would mollify the unhappy lives they all had to contemplate.

Eleanor fell asleep quickly, exhausted with worry and the effects of the past few nights of broken slumber. She blew out the candle and fell into a deep sleep as soon as her head hit the pillow. It must have been several hours later when Julian disturbed her. Her bed dipped as he entered. She smelt again cigar smoke and brandy.

"What time is it?"

"After one."

She half expected that Julian would take her in his arms, but he just pecked her cheek and settled to sleep. Within minutes, she heard the regular rhythm of his breathing. She rolled over and hoped she would fall asleep again, but it proved a hopeless cause.

The conversation over dinner played through her mind. When Christopher and his friends recounted their adventures, it had energised the room. It was like a light shone and the air was full of banter and fun. And then it had all changed. "No, ma'am, the sea is where my heart resides." Eleanor remembered how Christopher's sadness had been palpable. His face had fallen, sadness had suffused his eyes. The light had gone out in the room.

"Damn it."

There were no arguments left. She wanted a child. Julian wanted a child and Christopher wanted his life at sea. Infidelity might give them what everyone wanted: an heir. Procrastination was a curse and she would have no more of it. Sometimes you just had to take a risk. She waited until Julian had turned and breathed more deeply and slowly. He was a good sleeper, rarely roused even on a stormy night, or by the loud noises that beset London's streets at all hours. Anyway, she could say she couldn't sleep and had gone to the kitchen for some milk or taken a book into the parlour to while away the night hours.

Eleanor slid out of bed, gathered a shawl around her shoulders and tiptoed to the door. She paused. There were no sounds, no light slipping beneath the door. It was the country, with country hours. Everyone would be abed.

Her stomach fluttered with nerves as she crept along the night-black hallway. *Good God, don't let me trip and fall and rouse the house*, she prayed to a hopefully forgiving deity.

Christopher's room was in the opposite wing of the house. Thankfully Ashfield Manor only had six bedrooms. She knew Bertha's room and her mother's suite were at the front of the house. They would lodge Captain Black and Master Shin in the smaller guest rooms overlooking the stables. Christopher should be at the back with a view of the garden and woods.

She stopped outside the two guest bedrooms but heard no sounds to indicate their occupants remained awake, although a light showed beneath Captain Black's door. Eleanor listened carefully, but there were no voices, so she tiptoed past, seeking the door at the end of the passageway.

Eleanor took a deep breath. Should she just open the door or knock and open the door? But a knock might alert someone to her nefarious intent. Dear Lord, why wasn't there etiquette for scandalous liaisons, rules for how to seduce a member of your husband's family? She giggled at the notion and realised her nerves had lightened her mood.

Eleanor didn't knock, just turned the handle and tiptoed into a completely dark space. It was impossible to see anything. She realised she didn't know where the bed was, who was in the bed, or what kind of reception she would receive. If the worse came to the worst, she would say she'd been sleepwalking. Her breath sounded so loud she was certain she would wake the household or at least whoever was in the bed, wherever it was. Taking large, slow breaths helped. As her own breathing slowed, she noticed someone else breathing softly in the room.

"Christopher."

No response.

Taking a small step forward helped, and as her eyes became accustomed to the darkness, she could make out the closest post of the bed, a darker line in the dark. With arms outstretched, she moved forward and, using the bed edge as a guide, made her way along its side. As far as she saw, the person's head on the pillow had a fair complexion and the length of the body showed it was a tall man. She exhaled; reasonably certain it was Christopher.

She moved forward and bent to whisper in his ear. "Christopher."

Nothing.

She leaned closer and spoke a little louder. "Christopher."

The breathing stopped, but then resumed in a steady pattern.

Eleanor huffed. Here she was trying to seduce her brother-in-law and she couldn't even wake him. She poked him forcefully in the shoulder. That roused him to a semblance of wakefulness. "Damn it, Christopher, wake up. It's me, Eleanor," She hissed.

"Eh what. Who's there?" he spluttered.

"Shush. It's Eleanor. We need to talk."

"Eleanor?"

"Yes."

"What's wrong? Is something happening? Is the house on fire?"

"No, of course not. I just wanted to talk."

"Oh." The penny seemed to drop. The shape in the bed changed as he sat up. "Good Lord, Eleanor, I wondered if you might come, but I didn't really expect it. Does Julian know you're here?"

"Of course, he doesn't." Eleanor smelt brandy fumes and wondered if her brother-in-law was sober.

"Oh, I see." Eleanor sensed, rather than saw, that his head was shaking. "Is this about what Robert suggested?"

"Yes. I couldn't sleep worrying about it. I've tried and tried to put it out of my mind, but I'm desperate to have a baby and nothing has happened for years and years and I... I considered Robert's suggestion was so horrible, but I can't stop thinking about it. I needed to talk to you. You're going away tomorrow and I may never have another chance. I just don't know what to do."

"Eleanor, you do understand what Robert suggested, don't you?"

"Yes. He said we should make a baby, because Julian can't."

"What do you think about that idea?"

Eleanor realised this possibly presented the last chance she would ever have of having a child. She would not enter into this lightly, or naively, or without complete commitment. She raised her head and spoke with gravity. "I want to have a child. Julian wants a child. And the family need an heir. I realise what I'm asking is a grievous sin, but it's a sin I can, and will, live with. But it's your decision too."

His spoke tenderly. "Eleanor, are you sure this is what you want?"

"Yes. What about you?"

He ignored her question and added, "It may not happen, Eleanor. It might not be your fault, but you may not get with child from just one encounter. Can you live with that? We may need to repeat tonight. Are you prepared for that?"

"Do you have natural children?"

"Yes, a boy and a girl."

"Good. Then I can live with this decision. It's possibly the only chance I'll have. Please don't deny me."

Eleanor shivered. It was freezing, and she had no slippers on her feet and only a light shawl to cover her night-robe. Goodness, she hoped he'd decide before she froze to death.

"Eleanor, I comprehend this is wrong in so many ways, but I'm a selfish man and I don't want to give up my life. If this produces an heir, I'll be happy indeed. It's not the most romantic way of securing the lineage, but if I can contribute," — the last was said with a chuckle — "then I'll happily take you to bed."

"Thank you." Eleanor dived to get under the covers to warm her freezing feet.

It seemed the same, but also so, so different. Their lovemaking was tentative and tender and at times funny, which seemed peculiar, but it wasn't about them. It had a purpose, a means to an end. There was no passion or excitement, but no embarrassment or pain either. It reminded Eleanor of the medical examinations she had endured. And she prayed all the time for forgiveness and that she'd produce a child out of this sin.

Afterwards, they lay in the bed like two old friends. They talked about his planned travels and how to get in touch secretly upon his return. She felt happy that he was willing to meet again, to provide her with other opportunities to conceive a child. Both swore to maintain absolute secrecy. It was imperative that no-one must know, or suspect.

"It's our secret, Eleanor. But, if I could, I'd sing your praises from the rooftops. I'm honoured at your trust, in awe of what you are prepared to do for my brother. I rarely pray, but I'll pray for you and Julian, and maybe for myself too," he finished with a quiet chuckle.

Eleanor smiled in the darkness. "And pray for Robert too. It's his suggestion. In fact, all of his machinations have had the opposite effect to what he intended. He so wanted to cause trouble between myself and Julian, to force a divorce, but following his directions has strengthened my marriage and my resolve to give Julian happiness, to give us all happiness."

"So, you'll not come to regret tonight?"

"No, I don't suppose I will. I've done the wrong thing for all the right reasons. If I must face the consequences with my Maker when the time comes so be it, but, right or wrong, successful or not, I'll not regret my choices in life."

"Eleanor, I believe Robert expected you to lack courage. To not follow through with his evil plan. But I predict that if we're successful, he'll roll around in his grave, gnashing his teeth."

"We can but hope, Christopher, we can but hope."

Epilogue

July 16th 1829

The carriage turned into the long drive of Ashton Manor and Eleanor sighed a heartfelt sigh of relief. Even when stopping at Cobham overnight, the journey from London was difficult with children. Jenny, her angel of a nurse, nodded in sympathy. Alexandra had been good during the morning, but cried for most of the afternoon. Of course, she'd slept soundly for the past half an hour in her cradle on the floor, just in time to be disturbed by a doting grandmother and aunt.

"Mama, Mama. Will Grandmother be in the bath?"

Eleanor gave Adam a quick hug. At three, her son struggled to comprehend that Bath was a town that had become a regular attraction for his grandmother and Aunt Bertha. "No, Adam, Grandmother and Aunt Bertha are at home today to meet Alexandra. They came home especially early to see us all."

"Will she have presents for me?"

"I'm sure she'll have presents. She usually does."

"Will there be gifts from Uncle Christopher?"

"Yes, there might be some." Eleanor thought of the exotic toys and amusements that regularly arrived from faraway ports for the children. She was sure Christopher spent most of his days ashore seeking playthings and curios for her boys. She knew he sent them to his mother, so she got the joy of distributing the gifts on his behalf.

"I can see her. I can see her. And Aunt Bertha too." Adam stuck his head out the window and waved exuberantly. It relieved Eleanor when Jenny reached across and took hold of her son's jacket.

Ahead, Eleanor could see Julian lowering their eldest son, James, down from his saddle into the waiting arms of a groom. It was lovely to watch James run over to his grandmother, bow, and then hurtle into her arms. She couldn't hear his greetings, but the smile on her mother-in-law's face was priceless.

The carriage rounded at the top of the driveway and Eleanor's tiredness evaporated. Ashton Manor had a special place in her heart. They often stopped here on their way down to Heyer House. The Devon estate was their country seat now, where they spent their summers when the Season in London ended in July. It was their place for holidays and fun. Adam's birth had finally persuaded Julian to reopen the estate in Devon and they'd closed the house in Scotland. The long journey north was just too difficult with a young family. She missed the beautiful mountains of the highlands, but Devon, with its warmer weather and sandy beaches, was a lovely alternative. They spent most summers and autumns there before returning to Derbyshire for Christmas.

"Grandma, Grandma." Adam scrabbled down from his seat and jumped out of the door almost before the carriage had stopped. Victor caught the little bundle of energy and set him on the ground. Adam wriggled out of Victor's arms, ran and nearly bowled over his grandmother.

Eleanor thought Alexandra would wake with the cessation of the rocking carriage and the noise of her brothers, but the baby remained asleep in her cradle on the floor.

"I think, ma'am, that she's exhausted herself crying after luncheon. She'll probably sleep now until she's hungry," Jenny said. "Do you want me to take her out of her crib?"

Eleanor felt the stiffness of her body and shook her head. "No, leave her be until we can get her inside. Lady Heyer will need to be seated when she holds Alexandra. It's better to leave her sleeping in the cradle."

Eleanor sat and watched as Victor and Jenny manoeuvred the travelling cradle out of the carriage. She looked around the interior to see if Adam had left any toys or pieces of clothing behind, then gratefully accepted Julian's helping hand to step down from the carriage.

Julian was beaming and pointed to where Victor was holding the cradle up so Lady Caroline and Bertha could get their first view of the new Heyer baby. "I didn't think it was possible after James was born, but mother seems to get more excited with every addition to the family."

"She never considered it would happen and being a grandmother was so important to her. And now she has a granddaughter. I'm glad we've made her happy."

A small fire warmed the parlour, despite it being mid-July. Eleanor managed to have some tea and cakes before Alexandra roused and demanded a feed. The warmth of the room was comforting as she unbuttoned her gown to satisfy her daughter's hunger. Eleanor had decided not to use a wet nurse for her children, but she would normally have gone up to her room or the nursery to feed the baby. Today she found she was still too stiff and weary to be bothered to climb the stairs. Julian nodded and took the two boys outside to play a vigorous game, which involved much running around and screams of excitement.

Julian had proved to be the wonderful father she had expected him to be. He played with the boys constantly, patiently explaining how things worked, reading storybooks last thing at night. His latest joy was teaching James how to ride his new pony. In Devon, both boys had dogs and a long-eared donkey that pulled a little cart. Julian loved to explore the area with his sons, walking and guiding the donkey cart around on most fine afternoons. He'd spend hours making castles and forts in the sand, paddling and splashing in the sea. It was as if he wanted nothing more than to make up for his own sad childhood, to provide his boys with a better life.

Yes, Julian thrived on fatherhood. His hair was a little greyer, but otherwise he kept himself fit and trim at every opportunity, walking, boxing and riding as often as he could. He hardly drank at all. Merriment and contentment had replaced the haunting sadness in his eyes. He was funny and generous and extremely pleased with himself and with the wife who had provided his children.

Alexandra finally finished feeding. She was the largest of the babies and perhaps the most challenging. She still woke every three to four hours, insisting she was starving and she was strident in her demands. Eleanor was exceedingly grateful to have Jenny and Mary to share the burden of caring for the infant. Even Julian sometimes took his turn at night. He'd become competent at jiggling Alexandra back to sleep. Eleanor found it exhausting with a baby and two robust sons. It made her wonder how mothers without a nanny and maid managed. Bertha said poorer parents would depend on grandmothers and older children to manage a new feeding baby. It was a sobering thought.

"Mother, would you like to hold Alexandra now? She's full and will be most happy to be introduced to her grandmother."

Lady Caroline settled herself more comfortably in her chair and held out her arms as if expecting a benediction. Eleanor stood with the baby and placed her gently into the arms of her grandmother, touched to see the older woman's eyes were moist.

"Oh, Eleanor, she's so beautiful. Look, Bertha, she has the prettiest blue eyes. And I swear she has my chin and nose. What do you think?"

Bertha, who had never been fond of babies, preferring older children she could teach, dutifully limped over and peered at the bundle in Lady Caroline's arms. "She is beautiful, but those blue eyes will probably turn brown soon."

"Oh, phish, Bertha," Lady Caroline snapped, then laughed. "She's adorable. Look, she's smiling at me. Oh, she is, look she's smiling."

"It's probably wind, my dear."

"Bertha, you are just too much. But you must admit she is beautiful and perfect in every way."

Eleanor had to laugh. The two ladies had become firm friends and often had good-natured disagreements. The relationship had firmed when Bertha had persuaded Lady Heyer to visit Bath for the curative hot pools and mineral water.

Lady Heyer had been delighted with the elegant spa and enjoyed immensely the genteel older company and the proffered entertainments. She'd finally been persuaded to bathe in the heated Queen's pool and had sworn it had rejuvenated her joints and improved her digestion. The two friends now visited Bath several times a year and Lady Heyer had bought a small terrace house which allowed the ladies to walk easily to the Upper Assembly Rooms and the Pump Room, avoiding the worst of the steep inclines of Bath's streets.

Alexandra must have decided it was wind and that she would not be perfect in every way as she gave a loud wail and became inconsolable despite the valiant attempts of her doting grandmother to get her to burp.

Eleanor decided, rather mischievously, to allow her mother-in-law a few minutes to settle the baby before ringing for Jenny. "She probably needs to be changed, Mother. Jenny will see to her needs and bring her back for more attention when she's comfortable."

"Yes, of course." Lady Caroline passed the noisy bundle to the nurse with a small sigh. "One forgets they can be a little trying. Is she a good sleeper?"

"Not at all. She enjoys waking me regularly throughout the night, but I'm blessed to have Jenny and Mary to help. And even Julian takes a turn, settling her in the middle of the night. He is the most assiduous of fathers."

More shouts and squeals were heard from the garden. Lady Caroline glanced out the window with a smile. "He's happy at last. He has what he's always wanted."

The Dowager Viscountess rang for tea. The room was quiet while a footman carried in the tray. She waved away his offer to pour with an imperious hand. Bertha got up, filled each cup and handed around another slice of cake.

Lady Caroline nodded at Eleanor. "I was rather pleased when Julian wrote and said you'd been blessed with a daughter.

I always thought that a third boy could be a bit of a problem. The youngest son, through no fault of his own, must find his own way in life. The first son gets the title, and the entailed estates, the second son may inherit his mother's property but the third son is at a definite disadvantage. No, a daughter is most satisfactory."

Eleanor frowned, "But, Mother, without younger sons our armies and navies would be unmanned and we wouldn't have men taking on trades or the professions. Why, even our churches would be deprived. Without additional sons, who would ensure our lives are morally correct and our souls secured for the afterlife?"

"Hmm." Lady Caroline didn't appear to concur.

Eleanor bit into her cake, hoping the conversation would veer away from third sons. It was always awkward to discuss Christopher with his family.

"But, of course, you're right," Lady Caroline amended. "It's those third sons who keep this country improving, who go out into the world, make a life out of nothing but good breeding and a sound education. I must say that Christopher is a wonderful example of a third son. Done so well for himself. He has another clipper now and regularly sails to Australia from London, as well as sailing to the middle east. Bought warehouses and offices in the East End. He informed me on his last visit that he's very rich indeed."

"He's done exceedingly well, Mother."

"Yes, that's all very well, but I'd hoped he'd be settled by now. He's nearly thirty-seven. He should marry and have children of his own. But he just laughs, says that he has nephews now and he's happy with that. He plans to leave much of his wealth to your children, you know. He's inordinately proud of them. I'd hoped it would spur him on to marry and have children of his own, but he says he's content with being an uncle and won't be swayed."

Eleanor just nodded and took another bite of cake.

Lady Caroline continued looking directly at Eleanor. The scrutiny was uncomfortable, the eyes of her mother-in-law a little too keen. "But maybe it's for the best. Christopher always was so very different from his brothers. There was such a long gap between their births. It was a blessing to have another son, but in so many ways, I wish he'd been a girl. Still, he's been a godsend to me, to the family. I'll not regret his making and I'm happy if he has happiness. And I now have the granddaughter I've always craved and I'm content. I'm so, so grateful, Eleanor, for what you've done in giving us these children."

Eleanor contemplated her mother-in-law's words. Wondered, did this astute lady guess at the truth? She had sometimes wondered about Christopher's parentage herself. The gap between the twins and the youngest son. Did that explain Christopher's fertility compared to his brothers? Was she alone in her sin? Did she really want to know? No.

Eleanor remembered the last time she'd seen Christopher a year ago. He had been so proud of his nephews, so pleased for Julian and herself and delighted that he was free to roam the seas. No, Christopher would never settle down, was more than happy to produce an heir rather than be one himself. He was as happy with his lot, as she was delighted with hers. No, she had no regrets.

"I'm also grateful for my family Mama, and exceedingly content."

Luckily, Jenny came in before the conversation could go further. She handed the baby into the welcoming arms of her grandmother. Alexandra was full, dry and ready to capture hearts again.

Eleanor leaned back in her chair and contemplated her blessings.

The End

About Elsie King

I was born in England and always loved its history and the beautiful countryside. Moving to Adelaide, South Australia as a teenager, I grew to love the desert landscape and the magnificent wildflowers. Painting has been a lifelong passion.

My career as a Social Worker and Behavioural Therapist allowed me the privilege of meeting people with all sorts of problems. Listening, empathy and problem solving were well-honed skills underpinned by the principles of social justice, equal opportunity and feminism.

Combining my love of history with the observations of an artist and my insights into how people tick led to my writing career. As a devotee of Jane Austen and Georgette Heyer, I was inspired to write my novels in the Regency Era. A time of transformation for many women in society, but also a time of high principles and heady romance.

I am a member of the Romance Writers of Australia, Create/ Write a critique group and Indie Scriptorium, a self-publishing collective.

I have written two novels, A Suitable Heir and A Suitable Bride (to be released later in 2023). Both were shortlisted in the Romance Writers of Australia Emerald Competition for emerging writers. A short story, The Houdini Lollipop is also to be published in the RWA Sweet Treats anthology in August this year.

Please visit my website: www.elsiekingauthorartist.com[1] for information about releases of my books.

---

1. http://www.elsiekingauthorartist.com

Don't miss out!

Visit the website below and you can sign up to receive emails whenever Elsie King publishes a new book. There's no charge and no obligation.

https://books2read.com/r/B-A-ZKZY-QJBLC

BOOKS 2 READ

Connecting independent readers to independent writers.